# THE DEATH
_and_ LIFE _of_
# GABRIEL
# PHILLIPS

# THE DEATH and LIFE of GABRIEL PHILLIPS

## STEPHEN BALDWIN
### and MARK TABB

*Faith Words*

NEW YORK   BOSTON   NASHVILLE

Copyright © 2008 by Stephen Baldwin
(The author is represented by Ambassador Literary Agency.)

FaithWords
Hachette Book Group
237 Park Avenue
New York, NY 10017

Visit our Web site at www.faithwords.com.

Printed in the United States of America

First Edition: November 2008

10  9  8  7  6  5  4  3  2  1

FaithWords is a division of Hachette Book Group, Inc. The FaithWords name and logo are trademarks of Hachette Book Group, Inc.

Library of Congress Cataloging-in-Publication Data

Baldwin, Stephen, 1966–
The death and life of Gabriel Phillips / Stephen Baldwin and Mark Tabb. — 1st ed.
p. cm.
Summary: "With all the drama of one of his blockbuster movies, Stephen Baldwin shares a stirring tale of a father's loss and a community's struggle to comprehend his peace that surpasses all understanding"—Provided by publisher.
ISBN-13: 978-0-446-19699-4
ISBN-10: 0-446-19699-1
I. Tabb, Mark A.  II. Title.
PS3602.A59542D43 2008
813'.6—dc22
2008016198

*This book is dedicated to my earthly father,*
*Alexander Rae Baldwin, III, and my mother, Carol M. Baldwin,*
*who imparted to me the understanding that it was possible*
*to achieve any goal.*

# ACKNOWLEDGMENTS

The authors would like to thank Clark Mercer, retired Indiana State Trooper and former police chief of Greenfield, Indiana, for his technical assistance in writing this book. We would also like to thank Wes Yoder and the Ambassador Agency family; Michelle Rapkin; Cara Highsmith; Harry Helm; and all our friends at the Hachette Book Group; along with Rolf Zettersten and our FaithWords family. We would also like to express a special word of thanks to Gary Terashita for his friendship, vision, and perseverance. This book could not have been written without you. (Mark especially appreciates your tireless efforts to get Stephen on the phone while he was apprenticing with a certain billionaire.) Above all, we give all glory and honor to our Father in heaven, our Lord Jesus Christ, and the precious Holy Spirit.

Stephen would like to thank his heavenly Father; his three earthly angels: Kennya, Alaia, and Haley; as well as his brothers and sisters. He would also like to thank his ministry family: Daniel Southern, Nicholas Riccio, Daniel Gonzalez, Mario D'Ortenzio, Derek Vaksdal, and everyone at the Global Breakthrough Ministry (www.globalbtm.com).

Mark would like to thank Valerie, Bethany, Hannah and Sarah for your patience through the insanity of my writing two books simultaneously. I will never do that to you again (until the next time I have overlapping book deadlines).

# THE DEATH
### *and* LIFE *of*
# GABRIEL
# PHILLIPS

# CHAPTER

*1*

ANDY MYERS DIDN'T want children. That was one of his conditions when he married my mom. No kids. Period. Case closed. You would think someone so adamant about not reproducing would have gone out and had a vasectomy, but Andy didn't think that way. He didn't want kids; keeping that from happening was my mother's responsibility. When she failed, he immediately made an appointment for her at an abortion clinic in Indianapolis. He didn't ask. He just assumed she would terminate my life before my feet ever hit the ground. She refused. He walked out. And I didn't hear from him until I was thirteen. I think he sent money to my mother every month, at least while he was able. I'm pretty sure he did. The courts probably made him, and a cop like my dad wouldn't risk going to jail, at least not over something as insignificant as money.

I guess that explains why I always hated my old man. Despising him was imprinted on my DNA just as surely as my dark brown hair and blue eyes. The girls always loved my blue eyes. More than one lost her moral resolve when I put those baby blues to work. I got my eyes from Andy. I think they may have been part of the hook he used on my mom. I'm not sure. My mom never talked about him that way. For that matter, she hardly talked about anything that happened before she and I moved to St. Louis from her hometown in Indiana when I was really little. I didn't even know I had my dad's eyes until I looked into them for the first time ten years ago. There was no mistaking the eyes, even with that thick sheet of glass between us.

I think of that hatred in a different way, now that I am on the other side of the equation, with a son of my own. And I think about Andy Myers a little different as well. You know, life is funny. If my life had gone the way it was supposed to, I wouldn't be sitting here with you right now. I would be somewhere, assuming I survived as long as I have, but I wouldn't be sitting on the beach of Lake Michigan, watching my wife and son play in the water and talking to you. When I stand back and look at my family in this place, we look like the happy ending of one of those Hallmark Hall of Fame movies my wife loves to cry through. My life shouldn't have turned out this way, not that I'm complaining. But it strikes me as sort of hilarious to think that if my father hadn't walked out on me, none of this would have happened. I hated him for what he did. Who would have ever thought it would have led to this?

It all goes back to when I was about the same age as my little boy. Back then my dad worked as a cop in Trask, Indiana. Believe it or not, my wife and I live there now. We moved there a few years ago, but that's another story in itself. As for my dad, everyone in town knew him when he lived there.

That doesn't mean they liked him, but they knew him. He grew up just outside of town, and made a name for himself as the star athlete in the local high school. In a school as small as Trask High, it doesn't take a lot of talent to stand out from the pack. After high school, my old man got it in his head that a career in sports was in his future. He tried walking onto the Ball State football team, but didn't make it past the first few days of practice. After Ball State, he tried a few of the local small colleges, without success. Eventually he quit college altogether and joined the navy before the army could draft him. Vietnam was still going on, so my old man figured spending a couple of years on a boat beat getting shot at in a jungle. My dad wasn't a violent man, but he never lost that star athlete swagger he carried around the high school campus.

I'm not sure why he moved back to his hometown after the navy. I guess there are worse places to live. He met my mother soon after, but that didn't turn out so well. Around the time the two of them got married, he joined the local police force. No one ever told me why my dad became a cop. I don't know if a career in law enforcement was his lifelong goal, or if he just sort of fell into it. At this point, I guess it doesn't matter. All these years later I occasionally hear stories about him, but I think that has more to do with the way his career ended than anything else. No one ever signed off from police work quite like my old man.

I came along less than two years after my parents got married. By then my mother was a single mom. My dad walked out on her when he found out she was pregnant. Now I could understand him leaving if she'd been out whoring around, but my mother wasn't like that. No, my dad walked out because my mother made the mistake of giving birth to *his* child. Like I said, Andy Myers didn't want children, and my arrival did nothing to change his mind. He was gone by the time I was born, and my mom moved the two of us to St. Louis not long after.

Like I said, when I was about the same age as my son, Andy Myers (and if it is all the same to you, I would prefer calling him by his given name. I've already called him "dad" more in the last few minutes than I have in my entire life) worked as a cop in our beloved metropolis of Trask. I don't know if living alone was making him have second thoughts, but he started seeing another woman. He'd been with other women before Loraine Phillips, if you know what I mean, but those relationships were all very short-lived. Loraine was different. His time with her could actually be measured in months, not hours. The way he tells it, they weren't so much dating as using one another to cure one another's loneliness. That sounds like a load of bull to me, but, hey, it's his life. He can tell himself whatever lies he wants. The two of them met in a bar, and they ended up in bed back at his apartment the same night. Again, that wasn't exactly a remarkable event for Andy Myers. He thought of himself as six feet one inch, 205 pounds of sex appeal. And he had those killer blue eyes. Throw the whole package together, and look out. At least that's what he says. He seems to think he was really something back in the day. But I don't think getting Loraine into bed had as much to do with my old man's charms as it did with her sexual appetite.

After that first encounter, he tried to play the gentleman and begin a real dating relationship with her. But the first time he went by her place to pick her up, she met him at the door wearing nothing but a twelve-pack of Bud and a see-through gown from Frederick's of Hollywood and started clawing at his clothes. I'm thirty-two, and it still creeps me out to think my own father told me this stuff, but he did. I guess he needed to. My story doesn't really make sense without it.

That night pretty much set the tone for the rest of their relationship. They never went out on actual dates. For that matter, they never really had an in-depth conversation, either live or over the phone. They would go as long as two or three weeks without talking, but then she would call and ask my dad if he had time to drop by. He knew what that meant. And he never said no. At times he felt a little guilty about the whole thing, but the sex was good and Loraine never seemed to want much more than a purely physical relationship. Besides, with a body like hers, few men would have complained. Andy's friends thought he'd fallen into every man's fantasy: a hot woman, wild sex, and no strings attached. What could be better? He knew the answer even then, although he couldn't admit it to himself.

Andy didn't know Loraine had a kid until he'd been with her for several months. The boy was never around when Loraine called, and she kept any signs of him out of view when Andy came by. Her system worked pretty well until the kid walked into the kitchen one Saturday morning. Andy was sitting there, eating a bowl of cereal in his underwear, when the boy came up, stuck out his hand, and said, "Hi, I'm Gabriel. Gabriel Phillips. What's your name?" Finding a strange man sitting in his underwear in my kitchen when I was Gabe's age would have sent me running down the hall screaming for my mother, but the sight of Andy didn't seem to faze Gabe. He sounded like he was running for mayor at eight years of age. I bet my old man nearly crapped his pants at the sight of him. Then the kid said, "You like Cap'n Crunch, too? It's my favorite, but my mom hardly ever buys it. Says too much sugar is bad for me. But it sure does taste good." Andy fumbled over his words and said, "Yeah, they're real good," or something like that. He always was a great conversationalist.

I don't know which is weirder: the fact that Gabe wasn't scared by a strange man in his kitchen, or that Andy wasn't scared off by discovering the woman he was seeing had a kid. Neither one makes much sense to me. I guess I should be jealous of Gabriel Phillips since he was the only exception to the "no kids allowed" rule my dad ever made. I should, but I'm not. Not anymore. Andy told me there was a quirky, awkward charm about Gabe that drew people to him. He was a little guy, really small for his age, which he came by naturally—the kid's dad wasn't exactly Shaquille O'Neal. Once you got to know Gabe he didn't seem so small; he almost seemed like an adult. Keep in mind, I got all of my information secondhand several years later, and time has a way of glossing over any faults and amplifying people's good qualities. Be that as it may, Gabriel Phillips, I am told, genuinely cared about people, especially people others overlooked. People were just drawn to him. Maybe it was something supernatural. I'm not sure. But it sure cast a spell over my old man.

Meeting Gabe didn't make Andy run away. If anything, it made him more of a "boyfriend" than he'd ever been before. He started going by Loraine's house on a more regular basis. And not just for sex. He tried taking both mother and son

out on something like dates. When Loraine feigned head-
aches, Andy still took Gabe. They went to ball games, or to
the local hamburger stand, or wherever. Andy often said, "I'd
never met another child quite like him." And the first time
he said it to me, I walked out on him. The last time they were
together, Andy drove Gabe down to Cincinnati for a Reds
game. Loraine was supposed to go, too, but she didn't. I doubt
if she ever said why. Maybe she didn't want to be stuck in a
car with the two of them for two hours each way. Or maybe,
like me, she thought it a little strange that my dad took such
an interest in the kid. Andy wasn't trying to replace the boy's
father. Gabe already had one of those. I like to think maybe
Andy saw in Gabe a little of what he could have had with me,
but that's more wishful thinking than anything else. And
wishful thinking only makes things worse, not better.

About a week after the Reds game, Andy was fighting to
stay awake while working the graveyard shift. The Trask
police force was always woefully understaffed, then and
now, which meant Andy had to pull all-nighters at least one
week out of the month. On this particular night he couldn't
shake the cobwebs out of his head. It wasn't just because of
the late hour. He'd been over at Loraine's house right before
reporting for duty, and was still in the fog that sleep usually takes care of after such activity. He was so out of it that
the police dispatcher didn't get a response from him until
she radioed a second time. "Trask 52-2," the dispatcher said,
"we have a 10-16 at 873 East Madison, apartment 323. That's
a report of a domestic disturbance at eight-seven-three East
Madison, number three-two-three." He switched on the car
dome light and fumbled for a pen and paper to write down

the apartment number. They didn't have fancy in-car computers back then.

Andy suppressed a yawn, picked up his mic, and radioed back, "10-4, dispatch. Trask 52-2 is 10-8." 10-8 means "in service."

"10-4, 52-2 at two-oh-six. By the way, Andy, we've had three calls from the same location. You want me to get the sheriff's department headed that way to back you up?"

"Naaaahhhh," Andy yawned and said. "Let me check it out first. Probably nothing. No sense dragging anyone else out at this godforsaken hour if we don't have to." The mic hung in his hand as he stared at the apartment address he'd written down. He cursed under his breath, then said to no one, "Good old Madison Park Apartments. What would an overnight shift be without at least one call from there?" He let out another yawn, arched his back in an attempt to stretch the fatigue out of his body, then started his patrol car.

Andy and every other Trask police officer could make the drive to the Madison Park Apartments from anywhere in town in their sleep. Late-night calls came from there at least once or twice a week. The walls were so thin that when someone coughed in one apartment, the people next door shouted, "Shut the hell up." Most of the emergencies turned out to be nothing more than blaring televisions or couples arguing a little louder than they should. Andy figured this call would be more of the same.

A handful of people milled around under the only working streetlight in the complex parking lot when Andy pulled in. A woman wearing an oversized T-shirt came running over as soon as he stepped out of his car. Immediately she started chewing on his ear. "What took you so long?! I called half an hour ago." Andy recognized the woman everyone in town called "Crazy Cathy," although she didn't recognize him. At least not right off. About a month earlier he'd arrested her for public intoxication. One day around noon she'd gone for a walk down Main Street, bombed out of her mind, screaming obscenities at the lunchtime crowd going into the diner. She was notorious for that kind of stunt, which is why everyone called her Crazy Cathy, although Cathy wasn't her real name. Even when she wasn't drunk, she would walk around town, acting all nuts. All the kids in town thought she was hilarious, especially when she'd been drinking. They would yell things at her to try to get her riled up. She died a few years before I moved to town. The way I hear it, she wandered out into the street while drunk and was hit by a truck. That's not much of a way to die, even for Crazy Cathy.

But she was cold sober the night she got my old man out in the middle of the night. At least she appeared to be. She kept yelling at Andy, "I know no one gives a damn about what happens out here. You think we're all just a pain in the ass." Her call to the police couldn't have been much more than ten minutes earlier, but time slows to a crawl when you are waiting for a cop to show up. Andy didn't try to defend himself. He just kept walking across the parking lot, growing more coherent with each step. There's something about the gravelly sound of a chain-smoking woman's voice that yanks you back to reality. "I'm sorry, ma'am. It's been one of those nights" was all he could say.

"Like hell it has," she yelled back. "You think your night's been bad? You should have to listen to that kid carry on. He was screaming so loud it sounded like he was right there in my apartment with me. Sounded like something out of that damned *Exorcist* movie. Kid couldn't have screamed any louder even if his head had been spinning around. Made my skin crawl. And it wasn't the first time I heard that damn kid yelling. It gets worse every time he's here. I called you people about him before. Called last week. But nobody did nothing."

She didn't stop yelling until Andy got to the stairway leading up the outside of building three. He did his best to ignore her. "I'm sorry, ma'am, but you're going to have to stay down here," he said to her as he reached the stairs. "Don't get too far away because I will need a full statement from you as soon as I check everything out."

Andy went about the business at hand. He went up the stairs of building three in search of apartment 323. Another neighbor waited for him at the top of the stairs. "Oh, Officer, I'm glad you're here," the woman said. To Andy, she looked like she may have been maybe twenty. As it turns out, she was a twenty-four-year-old single mother. Seems like half the population at Madison Park has always been made up of single moms. "My son came running into my room scared and crying, which is why I called," she continued. "I started to go over and knock on the door myself, but I was a little nervous about doing it. I've met the guy a few times. Our boys play together when his son stays with him, but I don't know him well enough to knock on his door in the middle of the night, especially after what my son heard."

"That's probably wise, ma'am," Andy said. He felt a little funny about calling someone "ma'am" who looked like she had just graduated from high school. "You said your son heard something that shook him up?"

"Yes, sir. My son, he's eight. He came running into my room. He was shaking, he was so scared."

"I'll check it out. You should go back to your apartment, miss. I'm sure everything is fine. There's probably nothing here for your son to be afraid of, but if there is, I will take care of it. Which apartment are you in, just in case I need to get a statement from you?"

"I'm right next door in 325."

With that, the woman went back into her apartment. Andy heard the dead bolt turn and the slide of the chain into the extra lock. "These people sure are jittery," Andy said with a sigh. He'd never seen so many people get so shook up over a blaring television. Calls like this at this hour always turned out to be someone asleep in front of a blaring television stuck on the late, late show. Even before twenty-four-hour cable networks, local stations broadcast late into the night, usually filling the dead air with old movies. Andy walked over to apartment 323 and listened at the door. He didn't hear anything. No yelling. No banging. Nothing. He looked at his watch: 2:17 a.m. All the local stations would have switched from movies to test patterns by now. No wonder it was quiet. "Police department," he called out as he knocked on the door. No response. He could see a light shining through the peephole. He knocked again, with more authority this time, and called out even louder to wake up the sleeper in front of the television, "Police. I need you to open the door, please." As he waited for a response, he heard the muffled sound of a man's voice on the other side.

Andy reached up to bang on the door again, when it opened. A man in his mid-thirties motioned him inside as he continued talking on the phone. "Yes. Yes," the man said, "thank you, Father." The man turned his back and continued talking on the phone as though no one else was in the room. Andy took a quick glance around. A brown couch with oversized cushions, along with a ratty recliner, were the only furniture in the room. Andy also noticed the living room didn't have a television. He looked closely at the man on the phone. He was wearing a faded polo-type shirt and a pair of Levi 501's, but no shoes or socks. He was walking around barefoot on the linoleum tile of his apartment.

"Sir," Andy said, "I need you to get off the phone."

"Amen. Thanks, Eli. Hey, I gotta go. The police are here now. Thanks for praying. Keep it up." The man spun around to untangle himself from the extra long cord, then hung up the phone. "I'm sorry, Officer. I was just about to call. You were next on my list. He's back here." The man turned down the narrow hall toward the smaller of the two bedrooms. "It happened so fast," he said with a matter-of-fact tone, "there just wasn't any time. I ran in there as fast as I could, but by the time I got to him, it was already too late. I just had time to tell him good-bye and then he was gone." Andy felt like he'd walked into the middle of a conversation. The guy's words didn't make any sense and his demeanor just didn't seem right. At least that's how Andy remembered it when he told me about that night. He had trouble reading the guy, which set Andy's nerves on edge. As a policeman, he prided himself on his ability to figure people out in an instant. I never thought he was as good at it as he did. "He's in here," the man said as he motioned into a small bedroom. Andy thought it odd that the man wouldn't move past the doorway.

When Andy looked into the room, the entire floor appeared to be painted red. The room was pretty small, maybe seven feet by nine feet, and most of that was filled with furniture and toys, which made the scene look bloodier than it really was. The remains of a shattered goldfish bowl lay near the dresser, the bottom drawer of which stood open. A small boy, maybe eight years of age, was on the bottom bunk. His skin had a bluish gray tint to it. Even before he got to him, Andy knew the boy was dead. Blood soaked the pillow under the child's head, with a smear running along the side of the mattress up from the floor. Andy's feet slipped as he hurried across the room, his adrenaline kicking into high gear. Instinctively, he knelt down beside the child and felt for a pulse in his neck. Nothing. Then he laid his head on the boy's chest and listened for sounds of breath, but didn't hear a thing. "How long has he been out?" Andy shouted toward the boy's father.

"Ten...maybe fifteen minutes. I...I'm not sure," the man replied. "I don't know how to do mouth-to-mouth, but I didn't think it would do any good. I knew he was gone right after I got to him." The man's voice cracked just a little as he spoke. He swallowed hard and said, "I just knew he had already gone home."

Andy shook his head and muttered something under his breath that questioned the man's emotional stability. He reached under the boy's body to lift him off the bed and start CPR. As he raised him up, the boy's limbs hung limp and lifeless. Most of the bleeding had stopped, although a few drips fell from the back of the boy's head. The pillow was soaked crimson and the boy's hair and shirt were wet. "My God," Andy said as he looked for a place to lay the boy on the floor. About the only time my old man ever mentioned God or Jesus was when he was really upset. Even then, they were nothing but words, not divine beings. "Holy, holy Christ," he said as he laid the boy on the floor and squared himself around to try to revive him. He reached under the boy's neck to raise his head up for the three quick breaths he had only performed on Resusci Anne, the CPR dummy, up until that day.

Only then did Andy take a close look at the boy. He looked him right in the face and it hit him. "Wait a minute. No…Gabe?" he said. Suddenly adrenaline gave way to nausea. A lump of bile hit him in the back of the throat as Andy fought to keep his composure. "Gabe?" he repeated.

"You knew my son?" Gabe's father asked. "How?"

Andy kept staring into the boy's face. "I'm a friend of his mother," he replied but didn't elaborate. "How did…" Andy cleared his throat and tried to speak again. I guess in all the excitement he forgot about trying CPR, not that it would have done any good. The kid's lips had already turned blue and his body was slightly cool to the touch. "How did this happen?"

"I—I…I'm not exactly sure," the boy's father replied. "It all happened so fast. My boy had night terrors, and he would wake up screaming all the time. I guess you sort of get used to things like that after a while. They got even worse after his mother and I split up a while ago. I heard him screaming, but I thought I was the one having the bad dream. I woke up just in time to hear him fall. I ran in here, but I couldn't do anything. I tried. Really, I tried, but I could feel his life slipping out of him, felt his spirit leaving. All I could do was kiss him good-bye and promise I would see him soon. Then he went home." The boy's father paused, then said, "Do you know what my son's name means, Officer?"

That last question really got to my pop. He didn't know what the meaning of a kid's name had to do with anything, especially with the man's kid lying dead on a cold, bloody linoleum floor. My old man also found the dad's lack of emotion rather odd. This was far from the first time Andy had dealt with a family member after a death, but this was the first time he'd seen a parent show so few signs of grief. A couple of years earlier he'd had to break the news to a couple closing in on retirement age that their thirty-seven-year-old son had died in a car crash. A doctor had to come to the house to sedate them both. But this guy was calmer than a televangelist during a tax audit. Maybe he was in shock. Everyone responds to death in different ways, that's what I think. My old man, he wasn't so sure.

"God is my strength," the father went on. "Gabriel means 'God is my strength.' His mother wanted to name him Keith, after Keith Moon, the drummer from the Who. She's a big fan of the Who. The name just didn't seem to fit. I took one look at him and knew I had to name him Gabriel. It took me a few years, but I finally figured out why. God had talked to me through my son, Officer. Didn't know it at the time. God was telling me to make Him my strength. Right now I don't know what I would do if I hadn't listened."

Andy made a mental note of how the father seemed to keep his distance from the boy. He never moved from the doorway as he spoke, while Andy stayed on his knees next to the body, his pants legs soaking up the liquid on the floor. As Andy looked down, Gabe seemed much younger to him than eight—younger and smaller. The boy's mother had once said something about how the other kids picked on him because of his size. Now he seemed smaller still. Andy knew the boy was dead, but he felt a strong urge to reach out and protect him. He grabbed his radio with his left hand, the hand that was covered with blood from the back of the boy's neck. "Trask dispatch, 52-2. I have a 10-100. Request you get the coroner and Harris County started out here right away." 10-100 means a "dead body."

"10-4, 52-2," the radio crackled back. "Are you sure you want to make the call on the body, Andy? I can have a paramedic and ambulance to you in no time."

Andy paused for a moment. I don't know what he hoped to accomplish, but he told the dispatcher, "Okay. Do that. I guess it couldn't hurt." Maybe he wanted the kid to still have a chance. More than likely, he just didn't want to be haunted by the "what-if" questions that follow emergency responders even when they do everything they possibly can. "What-ifs" are about as useful as wishful thinking, but they can sure be hard to shake in the middle of the night. Andy reached over and lightly stroked the boy's head with his right hand, then stood to his feet. I think it was his way of telling Gabe good-bye. Once the paramedics and sheriff's deputies showed up, he wouldn't have another moment alone with the boy. Well, almost alone. The dad was still standing in the bedroom doorway.

"Did you know my son long, Officer?" the father asked.

"No, not too long," Andy replied as he let out a long sigh. Turning from the boy, he scanned the bedroom. Toys were scattered across the floor, along with a variety of clothes. Typical kid's room. The sheets and blankets of both bunk beds were strewn about, which seemed odd if Gabe slept in the room by himself. "Did you stay in this room with your son, sir?"

"No, he's a big boy. He's able to sleep in his room all by himself," the dad smiled and said.

If my old man wasn't already about to pop, that smile put him over the edge. He couldn't figure out how any father worth a dime could carry on a normal conversation right after his son died in his arms. "Which bed was your son sleeping in?" Andy asked. He also wondered why such a small room had bunk beds if Gabe was the only child in the house.

"I tucked him into the bottom bunk, but I guess he climbed up on top sometime during the night. You know how kids are." That's just it. Andy didn't know how kids were, but he nodded his head as if he did and kept studying the father. About that time he heard the dispatcher notifying the local ambulance service, which back then was run by the volunteer fire department.

"I'm sorry, sir, I didn't catch your name," Andy said.

"John, John Phillips. And you?" he replied with a smile as he stuck out his hand. Andy refused it, using the blood on his hand as a convenient excuse. *Funny. I've never known anyone who shakes with his left hand.*

"Officer Andrew Myers," he replied.

"Are you the same Andy Myers who took my boy to a ball game a few weeks ago?" Andy nodded. "Oh, I have to tell you, my son never stopped talking about that game. He had the time of his life. Thank you for taking him."

Andy didn't reply. The ball game felt like a lifetime ago. I guess in a way it was, because nothing was ever the same after my dad walked into that apartment. Nothing.

# CHAPTER

## 2

A LOT OF YEARS went by before my old man told me about that night. Called it the longest night of his life, when he did talk about it. He arrived at the apartment complex somewhere around two in the morning, and didn't get back to his apartment until nearly noon. He tried to wash away the night with a thirty-minute shower, and when that didn't do the trick, he tried to wash it away with a couple of bottles of Jack Daniel's. That was his third time to fall off the wagon, but who's counting? Jack didn't help, which made the longest night of Andy's life stretch out over a couple of days. He was pretty much sober by the time he reported to work the next evening at eleven, but I'm getting ahead of myself.

You'd think that finding the dead body of a little boy my dad was growing to love was what haunted him. That's true, but that was only part of it. A small part of it. Finding the body was only the beginning of his problems that night.

The first cop to arrive on a crime scene cannot leave until dismissed by a superior officer, who then assumes control of the situation. In the middle of the night in Trask, the superior officer usually meant someone from the sheriff's department, at least in a case like this with a dead body and more blood than any one child should have been able to produce. As it turns out, there wasn't nearly as much blood as it appeared. The water from the broken goldfish bowl made the scene look a lot worse. None of the first responders made the connection—not my dad, and not the volunteer firemen who came in with the paramedics. Those guys, God bless them, only made matters worse. The first two in the room immediately recognized Gabe. Apparently, he played on the same Little League baseball team as their sons. As soon as they made the connection, they lost it. Add vomit to the blood and you have a real mess on your hands. They also tracked blood all over the apartment. That caused a lot of confusion later on when the district attorney got involved. Andy could not remember seeing bloody footprints leading out of the room when he first arrived, although investigators found some bloody house shoes and pajamas in the bathroom, both of which belonged to the father. The first responders also shoved the small chest of drawers next to the bed out of their way when they started working on the body. Like I said, the bedroom was really small.

The room was small, and bloody. Very bloody. But, as I already mentioned, the water from the shattered fishbowl made it worse. No one caught that little detail until Dr. Daniel Warner, the county coroner, showed up. Warner was a royal pain in the butt, but he knew his stuff. He was already in a bad mood when he arrived. "Christ," he said as he walked into the apartment, "I think the whole town turned out for this little party. It looks like a freaking carnival out there. I nearly ran over a couple of little kids chasing each other around the freakin' parking lot. And did we really have to call in every emergency vehicle in the entire county for a dead kid? Holy crap."

Before he could take another step, a young rookie sheriff's deputy with a clipboard stopped him. Unfortunately for her, she was both a rookie and a woman, a bad combination when it came to Warner. "I'm sorry, sir," she said. "Authorized personnel only in this area. I'm afraid you cannot come in here."

"What the hell is this, amateur hour?" he growled. "Do you think I would venture into this little slice of heaven if I didn't have to be here, sweetheart?" Then he looked over toward Andy, who was sitting on the couch next to John Phillips. "Hey, Barney Fife, you running this show? You wanna tell Farrah Fawcett here who I am?"

Before Andy could respond, the lead detective for Harris County stepped out from the hallway. "Sorry, Dan," Deputy Ted Jackson said. "It's okay," he said to the rookie with the clipboard, "he's the coroner." Jackson then took Warner by the arm and said, "Good to see you. Sorry to have to get you out in the middle of the night." Jackson was a twelve-year veteran of the sheriff's department and had been a detective for the past two.

"Whatever," Warner replied. "What have we got?"

"Eight-year-old boy, dead. Father claims it was an accident. Says the kid fell out of bed and hit his head."

"It's always an accident, isn't it?" Warner said. "Pronounced a woman dead once, bullet hole right in the middle of her forehead, back half of her skull blown off completely. Husband claimed it was an accident. Said he only wanted to scare her by popping a couple of rounds over her head, but his aim was low. True story. Accident. Hell, no one ever does anything on purpose. It's always an accident. Like that dead baby last week up in Middletown. Mom had shaken the crap out of the kid, turned its brains into scrambled eggs. By the time I got there, the woman's crying like there's no tomorrow. Can't believe her baby is dead. All an accident, she said. Says she was just trying to get the kid to stop crying. Yeah, she stopped it, all right. Friggin' idiot. Some accident. Just once I'd like to meet someone who'd say, 'Yeah, I killed the bastard. What of it?' But, no, it's always an accident. No one ever means to do nothing. So where's this accident?" Andy told me that Warner's rant was the only thing that made him smile all night.

"Up here," Jackson replied without commenting on anything Warner had said. Like I said, Warner was a royal pain, but he knew his stuff. Most people said it was a good thing he spent the majority of his time around dead people, because they were the only ones who could stand to be in a room with him.

Jackson started to lead Warner back to the bedroom when Warner stopped, pointed toward Andy and John, and asked, "So what's the story with these two and what are they doing in the middle of my crime scene?"

"That's Andy Myers," Jackson replied. "He found the kid's body. The other man is the boy's father, John Phillips." Andy stood, but Warner ignored him. Phillips continued sitting with his head down and eyes closed. "I asked Andy to stick around to answer any questions you may have. We've established that the accident was confined to the bedroom, not the whole apartment, which is why I let them stay in the living room," Jackson said. "As you've already seen, it's sort of a circus outside."

"So that's the boy's father. What happened to the mother? Don't tell me she's in the back, holding the dead kid or something?"

"The parents no longer live together," Jackson said. "The mother lives in Adamsburg, and I've already arranged for another officer and the department chaplain to break the news to her. Don't worry. She won't come here. I told them to not allow her to come here and to take her to department headquarters. She's probably already there by now."

"Good," Warner said, "that's all we need is a hysterical mother running around here." Then he looked over at John. "So what's the deal with the dad. He stoned or something?"

"I think he's praying," Andy replied.

"Praying? Really. Huh. No kidding? Well, if this thing wasn't an accident, then he's going to need it. So where's the kid?" Warner said.

Andy didn't *think* John was praying, he knew it. If he didn't know it then, he knew it later. At the time Andy assumed the guy was asking God to forgive him for what he had done. Already parts of John's story didn't add up. For one thing, he wondered how falling out of bed could kill a child. If every kid who ever fell out of bed died, they'd have to start shutting down grade schools all over the country. And then there was all the blood. The image of so much blood pooled across the bedroom's tile floor made Andy shudder. And the damp feeling of the blood of the only child he ever cared for soaked into his slacks and sloshing in his shoes made him want to run out, screaming, into the night. But he couldn't run away. He had to sit there next to the one person who really knew what happened in that room, while the blood slowly dried into his uniform trousers. He kept asking himself how he got there, and it wouldn't be the last time he had that thought.

Andy settled down onto the sofa and waited for the coroner to do his work. In those odd moments when he could shove the image of Gabriel Phillips's dead body out of his head, he immediately would think of Loraine. He beat himself up for a long while because he wasn't the one to tell her that her only son was dead. But he couldn't leave, not until the coroner let him go.

Even if he'd been able to pull away long enough to break the news to her, Andy didn't know what he would have said. They were lovers, but they didn't feel like friends. The more he thought about the past several months, the more Andy realized he didn't even know Loraine. He wondered if his presence would comfort her, or make matters worse. As it turns out, he had good reason to wonder. Except for the one morning when Gabe happened into the kitchen, Loraine always made sure the boy was gone when Andy slept over. There really wasn't any regular pattern to when she would call, which made Andy think that she didn't schedule her romps in the hay with him around the boy's regular visitation time with his father. If the boy even had regularly scheduled visits. The father talked like he and his wife hadn't been separated for long, but Andy had been seeing Loraine for quite a while. He let out a long sigh, and stopped running down that line of thought. Deep down he knew where it could lead, and he didn't want to go there, at least while he had a choice.

\*          \*          \*

Ted Jackson led the coroner to the back bedroom, where Gabriel Phillips lay dead on the floor. No one had lifted him back onto the bottom bunk after Andy's and the paramedics' failed attempts to revive him. Bright flashes from the back of the apartment lit up the hallway every few seconds. Matt Rivers, who took the phrase "boys from the lab" to a whole new level, was busy snapping pictures of everything, and everybody, in the bedroom. When he first arrived, Andy thought the kid was all of fifteen. He looked more like a reporter from the local high school paper than a part of the county investigative team. Rivers had taken pictures of Andy's bloody hand and pants legs, then snapped several shots of John, especially his hands. Only then was Andy allowed to wash. Once he was finished with the two of them, Rivers went down the hallway, snapping pictures every foot or so, carefully placing numbered placards into each shot. For the past half hour he'd been in the tiny bedroom.

Although the apartment was small, Andy could only make out bits and pieces of the conversation between Dan Warner and the detectives in the bedroom. There was no missing Warner's shout of profanity when Rivers made him wait before entering the room. Andy also heard Warner say with a loud, clear voice, "Yeah, hard call on this one. The kid's dead." Andy wouldn't learn all that Warner discovered in Gabe's bedroom until several days later. Yet, he was already growing suspicious that everything was not as it appeared. A few minutes after the coroner started his work, Ted Jackson walked out and said, "Andy, would you do me a favor and take Mr. Phillips over to the sheriff's department? We need to get a full statement from him." Jackson hadn't said much, but what he did say spoke volumes to Andy. It wasn't so much Jackson's words in that moment that grabbed Andy's attention, but the look the two exchanged. Andy and Ted went way back. They'd worked together on the Trask Police Department before Ted moved on to bigger and better things with the sheriff's department. The two had even been drinking buddies before Andy's first stroll through the twelve steps. Then Jackson said, "Ask Duncan to handle it for me. He's on duty tonight. You might also make sure he asks the standard questions and follows Miranda." The Supreme Court Miranda decision made sure all suspects were read their rights. Andy read this as Jackson saying, *This is important. We don't want to screw it up.*

Andy smiled and replied, "Yes, sir. I will be happy to do it." Now that was a bunch of crap, because in that moment Andy wasn't happy to do anything but go home and try to scrub this night off himself.

"What about my son?" John asked without looking up. It was the first thing he'd said to anyone but God in nearly an hour. "Who's going to take care of him if I leave?" Andy found his question to be pretty ridiculous, since the boy had died while in John's care.

Ted Jackson played it cool. "I understand your concern, Mr. Phillips," he said. "We'll take good care of him. The coroner isn't quite finished. Once he is, we will release your son's body to you. For now, the best thing you can do for him is to go with Officer Myers so that we can clear this whole thing up as quickly as possible." When John hesitated, Jackson tried to reassure him. "This is all standard procedure with accidents like this. Thank you for being understanding. And again, I'm very sorry for your loss."

"But it's not a loss," John said as he rose from his chair. Those words really stuck with my pop. "It's not a loss," John said, "because to be absent from the body is to be at home with God in heaven, the final resting place. That's what the Bible says. How can I call that a loss?" he said with a smile. Yeah, with *a smile*. Andy thought that to be the single most absurd moment he'd experienced in his whole, entire life. The man's kid is lying in a pool of his own blood, dead and cold, and the guy can smile about it. My dad looked at his friend Ted Jackson, and Jackson looked at him. Neither needed to say a word, because they both knew what the other was thinking.

"Come on, John, this won't take long," Andy finally said after a few moments of awkward silence. The two of them walked out of the apartment and down the stairs toward Andy's patrol car. It was a little before four in the morning. The carnival at the Madison Park Apartments was starting to wind down.

.  .  .

ANDY'S NIGHT STILL wasn't over. A wave of fatigue washed over him as he climbed into his patrol car. Every time he closed his eyes, he found himself staring into Gabe's lifeless face. He wanted to scream and yell and pound the steering wheel, but he had to keep his composure, since the boy's father was sitting in the passenger seat next to him. Andy glanced over at John as he put the car into gear. Maybe by that point Andy had already spent more time on the case than he should have, because his nerves were frayed in a way that usually didn't hit him for months, if at all. He kept staring at John Phillips, wondering how someone who had known this child for such a short time could be more upset by his death than the boy's own father. John noticed Andy's staring at him. It was a little hard to miss, since Andy wouldn't let up on the brake and pull the car out of the parking lot. I imagine he looked like he was in some kind of a trance.

"Would you like me to pray for you?" John asked.

"What?" Andy replied. The absurdity of the question broke the trance.

"Would you like me to pray for you?" John replied. "It looks like this night is tearing you up inside, Officer Myers. You don't have much of a poker face."

"No thank you," Andy replied without a hint of emotion in his voice. He'd pulled himself back into full cop mode. Cool on the outside, even as his anger raged inside him. "That won't be necessary," he said as he pulled out onto the street. The drive to the county seat of Adamsburg would take less than twenty minutes. Andy figured he could keep it together until then. And he might have, if John had kept quiet. But since this was the longest night of Andy's life, you know John kept talking. And talking.

"Really, Officer," John said, "it's no trouble at all. I know the sight of my son lying there had to be hard on you, since you knew him and all. And again, I can't thank you enough for the kindness you showed my little boy. He loved baseball. After that Reds game, he became the biggest Johnny Bench fan in all of Indiana. I bought him a team poster, but he hung it up in his room at his mother's house, since he spends more time there than with me."

Andy really didn't need to be reminded of the boy's mother. In his mind he pictured her when the chaplain knocked on her door. "Christ," he muttered under his breath.

"Excuse me, Officer, did you say something?"

"Listen, Mr. Phillips, would you do me a favor and just shut the hell up?" Andy's wall of control started to crumble.

"I understand you are upset. Please, Officer, let me pray for you."

The wall started to fall faster. "You know, you're right," Andy snapped back. "I am upset. I can't get over the sight of seeing that little boy lying there. And here's the hell of it, Mr. Phillips, here's what really has me messed up inside. I hardly knew your boy, and yet it appears I am more upset over his death than you are."

"You are," John replied.

Andy knew he should cut off the conversation right there. He knew he needed to let the cop in him take over, but he didn't. Not yet. "You are one smug son of a bitch, aren't you, John? I—" Andy stopped himself before he said anything else.

"That's not it at all, Officer."

"Then what the hell is the matter with you? Your son is dead. Doesn't that bother you at all?"

"Of course it bothers me." Although the words should have been full of emotion, John spoke them with an easy calm. "It bothers me more than you can understand," he said. "Gabe was my son, my only son. It wasn't easy for me to let him go, but I have a hope that's bigger than grief."

Andy didn't buy any of it. "Whatever."

John tried to reply, but Andy cut him off. Slowly the cop in him took control. "You need to be very careful about what you say, sir. Your son's death is being actively investigated. Anything you say to me or to any other police officer will be considered evidence in this case. I'm sorry I blew up at you. That was very unprofessional of me. It's been a long night." Andy paused for a moment and said, "I thought a lot of that little guy."

"Thank you," John replied. With that, the conversation ended until they arrived at the sheriff's office.

Andy pulled his Trask patrol car around to the side entrance of the sheriff's department building and led John inside. Deputy Michael Duncan, a department detective, was waiting for them near the entrance, along with a younger man Andy had never met. "Hey, Andy, I've been waiting for you," he said. "Tough night. Sorry." He then turned to John and said, "Mr. Phillips, I need you to go with Donny Phelps here. He's one of our techs. He just needs to take a few pictures and get a few samples from you. Nothing to worry about, just standard shhh...er...stuff in an investigation like this."

"But one of the officers on the scene already took several pictures of me, at least of my hands," John replied.

"I realize that, sir, and I know this must be very difficult for you, but if you would just bear with me a little while longer, we can have this wrapped up in a short time. Now if you would just go with Donny."

John turned to Andy and said, "So what am I, Officer, a suspect or some kind of witness?" Andy knew John had been right about one thing that night. He didn't have much of a poker face. My old man started having doubts about the kid's father from the word "go." Before anyone could answer John's question, Donny Phelps put his hand on John's shoulder, reassured him, and led him down a long hall to a room on the left.

As soon as John and the tech were out of earshot, Duncan said to Andy, "Man, I thought you'd never get here. The mother showed up over an hour ago, and, my God, you will not believe what she had to say. I've got her in an interrogation room, kept her around so you could hear this for yourself."

Andy groaned. "I don't think I can do that, at least not in an official capacity," he said.

"What the hell are you talking about?" Duncan asked.

"I've got a—how do I put this delicately—a bit of a personal connection to the case. Loraine and I have been seeing each other for a while."

"Holy crap. Is she the nymphomaniac you've been nailing? Lucky stiff—"

"Hey, Mike," Andy cut him off, "show a little restraint. She just lost her son."

"Settle down, cowboy. I wouldn't say this in front of her. You know me better than that. I'm a pro. But I still think you need to talk to her. First words out of her mouth when she walked in here are 'I can't believe that bastard actually did it. I can't believe he really killed my little boy.'"

"She what?" Andy asked.

"Yeah, said she wasn't surprised. Said that's why she didn't want to let the boy go over to the guy's apartment, but her lawyer wouldn't listen to her. And did you know her ex has a record?" A little smile broke out on Duncan's face as he said this.

"No. Wow. That surprises me. On the way over, he offered to pray for me."

Duncan laughed. "Well, from what the mother told me, the guy better start praying overtime. He did time for assault. Mother said he beat up a guy in a bar not long after the kid was born. She claims this whole God and Jesus act was something he cooked up in the pen to help make parole. Like I said, Andy, you gotta talk to the woman yourself."

"Yeah, okay," Andy said. He wanted nothing more than for that night to end, but it wouldn't, not for a few more days. "Which room is she in?" he asked.

Duncan pointed down the right-hand hallway. "Room two."

Andy let out a long sigh, hesitated, then started walking slowly down the hall toward interrogation room two. It was, he later said, the longest walk he ever made. I guess that only fits, since it was part of the longest night of his life. He tends to overuse his metaphors. When he got to the door, he heard Loraine's voice echoing on the other side. Andy could hear a mixture of sobs and shouts of profanity. Although he wasn't a religious man, he muttered, "God help me," before turning the knob and stepping through the door.

"What have we done?" Loraine said as Andy walked into interrogation room two. Her back to the door, she didn't turn to see who had entered. She seemed instinctively to know it was Andy. "You know why he did it, don't you? He knew about us. He knew I kicked him out because of you." Slowly she turned and looked Andy in the eye. He hardly recognized her in this state. "He always told me that he would make me wish I were dead if I ever left him. Well, he was right. I wish I was dead right now." Her voice broke as the words spilled out, tears began flowing from her swollen eyes. "Oh, God, what have we done?" She bent over, sobbing, then sunk to her knees, her shoulders heaving.

Andy hesitated. His first instinct was to cross the room, put his arm around her, and comfort her. But stabs of guilt froze him in his steps. *We?* he thought. *We?* His mind went into quick rewind. He thought back to the efforts he'd made to get to know Gabe. At the time it felt like the right thing to do. Loraine seemed like a struggling single mother, and boys in that kind of household need a man who will take an active interest in their lives. Even though Gabe talked about his father, Andy wondered what kind of relationship the two of them really had. Maybe guilt was driving him. The amateur psychologist in me wants to say he transferred his relationship with me onto Gabe. Since my old man had abandoned me, he must have figured Gabe's dad had done the same. This was his chance to play the hero, by filling the void in a poor child's heart left there by a heartless father. That's what I would like to think was going on. The truth is probably less noble. My pop probably figured the best way to stay in the mom's pants was to act like he cared for her kid. Women just love a sensitive, caring man.

Now Andy wasn't so sure about anything he'd done over the past six months. His no-strings-attached, purely physical relationship suddenly had strings, and he felt those tightening around his neck. He knew he should have walked away from this relationship, right from the very beginning. It didn't take the death of Gabriel Phillips to make Andy realize he had been using the boy's mother. He'd known it all along. From their first night together he knew he never intended to build any kind of long-term relationship with her. The only reason they'd lasted this long was because she initiated the contact when she wanted him. He'd phoned her once, maybe twice, in their entire time together. That is, until he got to know her son, but even then he wasn't pursuing her. He felt more like a Big Brother volunteer with fringe benefits than a serious boyfriend. Some benefits. The boy was dead, and Andy felt responsible.

I don't know how long Andy stood there watching his woman break down on the floor. A little internal battle broke out between his internal cop and boyfriend. Getting involved in the case in more than a professional manner could bring down everything for which he'd worked over the past ten years. But Loraine cried harder, and Andy finally decided, *Screw it,* and walked across the room. He knelt down beside her and pulled her close to him. She didn't fight him, but she didn't melt into his arms, either. Like everything else about their relationship, she reacted with warm restraint, if that makes any sense. They stayed like that for what Andy said felt like an eternity. Finally Loraine looked up at him and said, "You aren't going to let him get away with it, are you?"

"Don't worry," Andy said in a near whisper. "I'll personally look into this. If he had anything to do with Gabe's death, I'll take care of him. I guarantee, I will take care of him."

After the trial, Loraine would no longer call to ask Andy if he had time to drop by. They talked from time to time after Gabe's funeral, but, with time, Andy never heard from her again.

# CHAPTER

3

ANDY HATED FUNERALS. He used to say that staring at a corpse in a box while some moron drones on and on about what a saint they were (even when they weren't) wasn't his idea of a good time. My mom says it went back to Andy's dad's funeral. The way I hear it, my "grandfather" (and boy, oh boy, being a crappy father sure runs in my family) was a drunk who would disappear from the family for weeks at a time. Andy said he was more of a sperm donor than anything approaching a father, which is pretty much how I described Andy for most of my life. Andy's mother never divorced his father. She was too good a Catholic for that. And besides, people didn't get divorces back then. They just put up with the other person's crap and prayed the "death do us part" part of their wedding vows would come sooner rather than later. Her prayers were answered soon enough. Andy's father literally drank himself into the grave when he died in the midst of a bender. Even so, at his funeral the priest made him out to be a cross between Mother Teresa and Albert Schweitzer. After that, Andy never really cared for funerals.

But he went to Gabe's. He didn't want to, but he felt like he had to. He wrestled with the decision for two days. Guilt makes a mother of a wrestling opponent. But he finally convinced himself he wasn't responsible for Gabe's death in any way. If his involvement with Loraine had pushed John over the edge, that wasn't his fault. He hadn't done anything wrong, and besides, he needed to go. Loraine needed him, at least that's what he told himself while driving to the funeral home. She didn't, and she let him know that in a very firm but polite way not long after he arrived at the funeral home. Deep down he knew that's what he should have expected. Loraine had never really needed him. By this point it was finally dawning on Andy that she'd been using him just as much as he'd used her. For what, he wasn't quite sure. Not yet, at least.

No, the real reason he had to go to Gabe's funeral is Andy had to tell the little guy good-bye. Andy Myers, the man who never liked children in the least, had actually grown to love Gabriel Phillips. He realized the depth of his feelings for the boy as he was paraded past the open casket with the rest of the mourners at the close of the service. Most people hustled by, hardly even looking down at the body. Not Andy. He stopped and looked Gabe in the face. He stood there so long that it created an awkward moment for the people in line behind him. Tears rolled down his cheeks, and he didn't fight them. If Andy had stood there much longer, he would have had a full-scale emotional breakdown. As he reached down to touch the boy, he felt a hand on his shoulder. It was John. Apparently, John had watched how upset my dad had become, and walked over to comfort him. Talk about bad timing. Don't get me wrong. Andy didn't create an ugly scene. He was too good of a cop for that. But inside, his blood started boiling.

Immediately Andy pulled his hand back from the casket, wiped his eyes, and headed toward the door. He never even acknowledged John's presence. He couldn't, without blowing up. Andy already held John responsible for the boy's death. Gabe died on John's watch. It was as simple as that. Even if it was an accident, John could have kept it from happening. After all, what kind of idiot puts bunk beds in the room of a boy who suffers from dreams so horrific that they make him thrash around at night. In Andy's mind, anyone should have known that was a recipe for disaster. The more he thought about it, the more Andy thought that might just be the point. Either John Phillips was very stupid, or very clever.

♦ ♦ ♦

ANDY WENT STRAIGHT HOME after the funeral and nearly wore a hole in the carpet from pacing around his house. He wanted a drink, but he had to report for duty at three, which was just over an hour away. That gave him plenty of time to get smashed, but no time to get over it. He may have been an on-again, off-again drunk, but he at least had enough integrity about him not to show up at the police station gassed. Since Jim Beam wasn't an option, he tried to work off his nervous energy by pacing and talking to himself. The image of Gabe lying in the casket kept flashing in his mind; that was better than the image of Gabe lying in a pool of his own blood, which had haunted him for the past few days. "I gotta do something," he said to no one. "I have *got* to do something. Anything."

He paced around for a while longer, his mind racing. When he couldn't take it any longer, he grabbed a Big Chief pad, sat down at the kitchen table, and started writing. (If you don't remember them, a Big Chief pad was sort of like a yellow legal pad except the pages were white and there was a picture of an Indian chief on the red cover. The pages on the one my dad used are yellow now, but the words are still legible. Andy gave it to me a few years ago. I still have it.) At the top of the first page of the pad, he wrote in large, bold letters: **TRUTH OR PROOF?** Then he quickly turned the page and wrote at the top of the next one: **WHO?** Turning the page again, he wrote: **HOW?** Finally he turned the page one last time and wrote: **WHY?**

Then he started pacing again.

He walked out of the kitchen and into the living room, the pad in one hand, a pen in the other. Flopping down on the couch, he went back to the first page and started writing. Beneath his original question he asked another: "Can I remain objective while investigating this case?" He drummed the page with the pen for a few moments, let out a deep sigh, then made two columns on the page, one he labeled "yes," the other "no." Under "yes" he wrote a series of words, including "professionalism" and "duty" and "self-control." Then he scribbled a sentence so quickly that you can hardly make it out. I think it says, "I'm a cop, dammit, of course I can remain objective."

In the "no" column he wrote a single word: "Loraine." In his mind, she was the only emotional attachment that would keep him from being completely objective. He paused a little longer and stared at her name. Over the past few days he'd tried contacting her, with no luck. Then there was the cold shoulder she'd given him at the funeral home. Part of him wondered if, in some way, she blamed him for her son's death. She claimed John killed the boy because of her relationship with Andy. If Andy had stuck to his usual MO, John wouldn't have had a beef with him because Andy would have dropped Loraine the second he met her kid. Now he wondered if perhaps that was part of her reason for allowing the chance meeting in the kitchen that morning. That thought pushed him up from the couch and made him walk around his house until he came to his bedroom. Sitting on his bed, he made one final note on the first page of his Big Chief pad, then turned the page.

He sat and stared at the word at the top of the second page without writing anything new. He sat there so long that he was nearly late for work. "Who are you, John Phillips?" he said to himself. Andy thought he should already know the answer. "I should have been paying attention," he kept telling himself. "I let myself get distracted and I didn't pay close enough attention. The moment was there and I blew it. 'You knew my son,' the guy says to me. Think, man. Think. 'You knew my son? How?' he said to me. So how did he say it? Crap, I can't remember. Dammit, Andy. Listen closer. How did he say it? What kind of inflection was in his voice? Did you hear fear?" Andy got up and punched the air. "Stop staring at the boy. Listen. What did he say about himself? What did he give away?" He let out a long sigh. "I don't remember. DAMMIT!"

This little conversation doesn't make a lot of sense to me, but then again, I'm not a cop. Andy had this theory that you can learn more about a person at the scene of the crime in the moments right after the deed is done than you can any other time. That's when you get the raw emotion, the real person, before they've had a chance to put up a wall to hide behind. And, in Andy's mind, the moment he recognized Gabe and said his name was the key to reading John Phillips. But he let himself get distracted, and he would never get that moment back. He needed to knock that wall down one more time. Outside of the wall, John Phillips didn't match anything Andy knew about him. Mike Duncan said the guy had spent time in prison for assault; but at five-eight, maybe 150 pounds, John Phillips didn't look like the assaulting type. Of course, looks can be deceiving. Bad guys rarely, if ever, look as bad as they do in *Walker, Texas Ranger* reruns. "So who are you, John Phillips?" Andy said as he got up to get dressed for work.

*   *   *

BEFORE LEAVING for the station, Andy phoned Ted Jackson to call in a favor. Ted personally delivered his response an hour into Andy's shift. "Trask, 52-2," the dispatcher called Andy and said, "please return to the station. A priority package has just arrived." Andy knew this call was coming, which was why he'd parked his patrol car conspicuously on Main Street a few blocks from the station. Just the sight of a police car on a busy street makes every car slow down, even those that aren't speeding. Not that it mattered. Andy wasn't in the mood for pulling over speeders. He had a bigger fish in mind.

"10-4, dispatch. I will be right there."

A couple of minutes later, Andy walked into the back room of the police station, where Ted sat waiting for him.

"You know I wouldn't do this for just anyone," Ted said as he stood and handed Andy a file folder.

"But I'm not just anyone, Jax," Andy laughed and said. "I'm part of the investigative team, right?"

Ted sort of rolled his eyes. "Yeah, sure. Whatever you want, *Detective* Myers. Whatever you want."

"Screw you," Andy said with a smile. He sat down at his desk, opened the folder, and asked, "So whadda we know about this guy?"

"Interesting fellow, this John Phillips. Doesn't look like much of a menace. Little guys who like to fight as much as Phillips apparently does usually carry their emotions on their sleeves. One look and you know they think they are the baddest sons of bitches on the block and you better not cross them. You've met the guy. That ain't Phillips."

"So what's his story?" Andy asked. "I was told he did time."

"Damn straight," Jackson replied. "He beat a guy nearly to death outside a bar up in Fishers eight years ago. Said the guy was coming on to his wife, and he didn't like it. Guy he kicked the crap out of was nearly twice his size, but the big guy never saw it coming. Apparently, our Mr. Phillips is a bit of a rageaholic. He looks all nice and calm and easygoing; then something snaps and he goes nuts. A real Bruce Banner type, except he doesn't turn green. In his trial Phillips claimed he couldn't even remember beating the guy up. He said he simply asked the man to kindly leave his wife alone. That wasn't his first arrest, but it was the first time he did any real time."

"How much time?" Andy asked.

"Three years at Pendleton."

"Any problems there?"

"At first, yeah. Apparently, with his size and body type, he figured someone would try to turn him into their bitch, so he started acting all badass the moment he first went in," Jackson said. "Quite a few write-ups in this first few months. Then, after about six months, he became a regular at chapel. Started right after some church group did one of their 'ministry' weekends."

"His ex-wife told me he found God in prison," Andy said. "She said it was all just an act to make parole."

"Yeah. Maybe," Jackson replied. "Me, I figure to each his own. I don't try to overanalyze that kind of stuff."

"So the guy finds Jesus, keeps his nose clean, and makes parole. Any trouble since he got out?" Andy asked.

"Weeellllll, he didn't keep his nose completely clean," Jackson said. "There's one last incident report from Pendleton on the guy, and this one doesn't make a lot of sense. Happened toward the end of his first year in the joint. Phillips got into a fight in the yard. Says it wasn't his fault. Claims the other guy attacked him with a knife. Seems there was some bad blood between these two that went back to when Phillips was first locked up. So Phillips says the guy came at him from behind and he defended himself. By the time the guards got there, the other guy was on the ground and Phillips was on top of him. The guy on the ground had a crushed windpipe. Like I said, when he snaps, Phillips can do some damage. Before the guards could get him off, Phillips had cut a hole in the guy's throat with the guy's own shiv."

"Holy crap. So how'd he ever make parole after that? I'm surprised they didn't ship him up north and put him into maximum."

Jackson smiled and said, "Like I said, this doesn't make a lot of sense. Phillips wasn't slitting the guy's throat. He did a tracheotomy. Cut a hole in his throat and shoved a tube made out of a Bic pen in there so the guy could breathe. Turns out, he saved the guy's life."

"What?!" Andy asked. "You telling me he nearly kills the guy, then turns around and saves his life?"

"That's what the incident report says."

"So how'd he know how to do that?" Andy asked.

Jackson shrugged his shoulders. "Who the hell knows? Get this. The report goes on to say the two guys became inseparable after that. Both were regulars at the chapel until they got out. Weird, huh?"

Andy shook his head, then turned his attention to John's file. He didn't do more than thumb through it. Later that night he read the entire file for the first time. In the months that followed, he studied that file like it held the secret to life itself. I don't want to say Andy became obsessed with this guy, but his actions speak for themselves. That day in the station he only gave it a quick glance, then tossed it onto his desk and asked his friend, "So, Jax. What does your gut say about this guy? Think he's capable of killing his own kid?"

"I'd say we're a long way from jumping to that kind of conclusion. The guy says the boy had a bad dream, fell out of bed, and hit his head on the bottom drawer of a dresser. The only thing that definitely says different right now is a bitter ex-wife."

Andy paused and looked back down at the file. "Mind if I go talk to the guy, myself?" he asked. "Nothing too formal. Just a little fact finding on my own."

Ted shook his head. "What? You want to blow this case, if

it even is a case, before we even get to dig down and do our job? If you interrogate him without his lawyer present, the D.A. will shut this whole thing down so fast, it will make your head spin. Is that what you want?"

"I don't intend to ask him about the case," Andy said. "I just want to get a read on him. That's all. Trust me. If he hurt the boy, I want to make sure he gets what's coming to him. I would never do anything to get in the way of that."

"Just watch yourself, Andy. Believe me, when you're dealing with the death of a child, it's easy to get sucked in emotionally. We just want to uncover the truth of what happened in that room. We're not doing any kind of witch hunt here. Who knows? The guy's story could well be completely true. Stranger things have happened."

Andy nodded his head in agreement. "I know, I know. Don't worry."

Ted got up to leave. "Oh, I almost forgot, I have another little gift for you." He reached into his pocket and pulled out a cassette tape. "I got a full statement from the kid's mother yesterday. Thought you might want to hear what she had to say."

"Yeah, thanks," Andy said as he took the tape. His voice cracked just a little. Or at least he thought it did. A shot of fear went down his spine. It surprised him. Suddenly he realized that Loraine might not only throw the entire investigation for a loop if she got too specific about him, but that she could also cost him his job if she made it look like he'd crossed a line. "Want to give me the *Reader's Digest* version?" he asked.

"I think you will really want to hear it in her own words," Ted replied. "Anyway, I gotta go. I was supposed to be off duty an hour ago. My kid's got a ball game tonight. I can't miss another one or my wife will kill me." With that, he walked toward the door to leave. "If you do go see John Phillips, be careful. Don't let yourself get too wrapped up in the emotions of all this, Andy, or it might come around and bite you in the ass."

"Got it. Enjoy the game. Tell Janey I said hello," Andy said.

◢   ◢   ◢

AS SOON AS the door closed behind Ted Jackson, Andy locked the file and the tape in his locker. He went back to the Madison Park Apartments to try to find John Phillips, but John wasn't there. The police tape designating the Phillips apartment as a crime scene had been removed the day after Gabe's death. Detectives come in and get their work done quickly so people can get their lives back into gear. They only mark off crime scenes for weeks at a time in the movies. Andy banged on the door several times without an answer. Under normal circumstances Andy would have walked away and come back at a later time. But normalcy had long since disappeared when it came to this case. When John wouldn't answer his door, Andy went to the complex office, where he found Jeanine Martin, the fifty-something, heavyset, very matronly-looking apartment manager. For a place like Madison Park, she was the perfect fit. She came across as a very caring, very compassionate grandmother type, but she wasn't afraid to boot people out of their apartments when they became delinquent on their rent (which happened all the time). All Andy had to say was "Gabriel Phillips," while wearing his police uniform, and Martin did anything he asked.

She grabbed her master key and led Andy back to John's apartment. The entire time she talked about what a sweet little boy little Gabriel was and how tragic the accident was and how much poor John Phillips must be hurting. Andy didn't say much in response. When they reached John's apartment, she turned the key in the lock, pushed the door open, then said, "Oh, my." The apartment was empty. What little furniture had been there the night of Gabe's death was now gone. "But he still had three months left on his lease," she said. "Looks like he won't be getting his deposit back."

"You mean you didn't know he'd moved out?" Andy asked.

"Heavens no. Not until right now," she said.

Andy muttered some profanities under his breath.

"Listen, would you do me a favor?" Andy reached into his uniform shirt pocket. "Here's my card. If you hear from John Phillips, or anyone connected to him who might come by, would you give me a call. I'll put my home number on the back in case he comes in while I'm off duty."

Jeanine Martin looked at the card, turned it over a couple of times, and gripped it tight with her right hand. "Of course. Whatever you need."

Andy asked if he could look around for a few minutes. "Stay as long as you need to," the manager said, and left.

As he walked around the apartment, Andy tried to replay the night of Gabe's death in his head. Without the furniture, the entire place seemed much smaller than it did on that night. He walked down the hallway, which now turned out to be little more than three or four steps long. The two bedrooms were barely offset from each other on opposite sides of the hall. Four nights earlier, the distance appeared to be much greater. Andy paused at the doorway of Gabe's bedroom, standing in the same place where John stood that night. He looked down. The floor, no longer red, now glistened. The white linoleum tiles with brown and black streaks looked as if they had been waxed. Both the bunk beds and the dresser were gone, as were the piles of clothes and toys that had been scattered across the floor. The room seemed very bright. The sun shone in the room's western window. Andy hadn't noticed the window that night.

There were a lot of things he hadn't noticed, including the closet on the wall perpendicular to the window. He opened it and looked around. It was empty. That is, almost empty. Andy noticed something atop the closet's wooden shelf, a photograph lying facedown. The developer's date stamp on the back read, "August 17, 1977," which made the picture just over a year old. Flipping it over, Andy saw Gabe sitting on his mother's lap, her arms wrapped around him, a huge smile on his face. Loraine's slight smile appeared forced, at least it looked forced to Andy. He recognized the background as the front gate of Kings Island amusement park. Andy stood and stared at the picture for a long time before placing it in his pocket and walking out of the apartment. "Where is that son of a bitch?" he said as he returned to his patrol car.

Andy didn't get the opportunity to go looking for him. The moment he put his car into reverse to back out of the parking lot, the dispatcher called. "Trask, 52-2, we have a 10-16 at 117 South Adams. That's one-one-seven South Adams, report of a 10-16. Time out, 18:02."

"10-4 dispatch. Trask 52-2 is 10-8," Andy radioed back.

"Not another one," he groaned to himself as he placed the mic back in its holder. The last 10-16 he'd responded to left him trying to revive Gabe Phillips's dead body. He flipped on the lights and sirens and flew out of the Madison Park Apartments. Adams was on the opposite side of town, a little less than ten minutes away, depending on the stoplights; even less when you don't have to bother with such things. Turning right on State Street, he shot through four lights to Main, hung a left, and proceeded to Adams, on the far eastern end of town. A couple of neighbors stood on their porch across the street as he pulled up in front of the house with the reported domestic disturbance. Walking up to the door, he could hear the domestics in full disturbance mode. If the couple inside wanted to keep this private, they should have closed the windows and doors. Andy banged on the screen door and identified himself.

"I told you someone would call the police!" came the shout of a woman's voice from inside. "Now you're going to get yours, you sorry bastard."

The man in the house yelled something back, like, "shut your f-ing piehole," along with another long string of profanity. All in all, it was a great way for a husband and wife to communicate. When the guy pushed the screen open, he pulled a Jekyll and Hyde. "Yes, may I help you, Officer?" He sounded like Eddie Haskell charming Mrs. Cleaver right out of her pearls.

"Is everything all right in there, sir?" Andy asked.

"Sure. Everything is under control. I'm sorry you—"

"Like hell it is," the woman's yell interrupted. The shriek of the woman's voice made the guy forget there was a cop at his door. He turned around and started yelling at the woman, who sat in an oversized chair with her legs pulled up to her body. The argument took off again. The louder they shouted, the closer the man moved to the woman until he was in her face. Andy pushed his way into the room and tried raising his voice to get their attention, not that it did any good. Neither seemed to notice anyone else was in their living room. Finally he stuck his index fingers in the sides of his mouth and whistled so loud, it was surprising he didn't shatter a mirror. Both people's heads snapped around and looked at him.

"Enough," he shouted. "Sir, I need you to step over to the opposite side of the room." The man moved toward the far side of the living room. Andy then turned to the woman, who, he now saw, had a butter knife in her right hand. "Ma'am, has he physically harmed or threatened you?"

"I didn't do nothing to that fat bitch!" the man yelled, and took two or three steps toward her.

"Sir, I told you to stay on the other side of the room. I suggest you comply," Andy said.

The man walked closer to the woman. "Don't listen to anything she tells you. She's a lying bitch. Ain't that right, YOU BITCH!" he yelled. The whole time the guy's yelling at his wife, she's yelling back at him using every bit of profanity in the book.

"Sir, I am not going to tell you again. Move to the other side of the room. Now," Andy said with a firm, loud voice.

"Why don't you shut up!" the woman yelled back at the man.

"Like hell I will," the man screamed back. Once again he moved toward the woman, screaming at the top of his lungs, completely oblivious to Andy's presence.

"Sir," Andy said. He took two steps toward the man, and

in one motion, he swept his right leg under the man's legs, sending the guy sprawling up in the air, then flat on his back. "Comply," Andy said as he sprang onto the man, spinning him over onto his stomach and planting his knee into the middle of the man's back. Andy then yanked the man's left arm behind his back with such force that it nearly pulled the guy's elbow out of joint. "I told you to step away from your wife," he said as he pulled the man's right arm behind him and handcuffed them together. "I've had just about all of your crap that I intend to put up with." As Andy said this, he grabbed the man's head with his right hand and planted the guy's face into the carpet. The man let out a gurgled yelp as he bit down hard on his tongue. Blood began flowing out of the man's mouth and onto the carpet. I have to say, my old man was not a violent person, but he could be if someone pushed him hard enough. And on that day, all of the frustration that had been building for four days exploded. But even though the man had his face planted in the carpet, Andy's problems still weren't over.

"Get the hell off my husband!" the woman shrieked. "What are you doing to him?" she yelled as she started toward Andy, the butter knife in hand.

"Ma'am, I suggest you drop your weapon and sit back down," he said. She took another step toward Andy, until she saw him reach for his gun. Immediately she plopped back into the chair.

"We didn't do nothing," she yelled.

About that time Andy noticed a girl that had to be all of three years old moving slowly from the hallway. He could barely see her because the chair in which the woman sat obstructed the view of the hall from the living room. Tears streaked down the little girl's face and she trembled as she walked. Once she moved past the chair, her head turned first toward her mother, then her father. Her presence drained all the hostility out of the room, at least from the girl's parents. Andy walked over and scooped the girl up in his arms. "It's okay, sweetie, no one can hurt you now," he said to her. I can't even describe how weird that motion was. Like I've said about a thousand times, Andy Myers did not like kids. At all. Period. And here he was playing Captain America, rescuing a three-year-old damsel in distress. He grabbed his radio from his belt and said, "Trask dispatch, 52-2."

"52-2, go ahead."

"I'm going to need some backup. I have two prisoners to transport and I don't want to transport them together. I also need someone from child protective services to meet me at this location."

"But—but—but, Officer, we didn't do nothing," the woman protested. She tossed the butter knife on the floor. "The knife, it's not what you think. I was just making him a sandwich, that's all. He's says I used mayonnaise, and he hates mayonnaise, but I said it was Miracle Whip. We have little arguments like this all the time. They don't mean nothing. We'll stop fighting now. I promise." The man chimed in from on the floor and tried to talk Andy out of hauling them in. I think it's hilarious how quickly people in these situations go from enemies to allies.

Andy just looked at them with disgust and said, "Save it for the judge." He pulled the little girl tighter in his arms. She'd buried her face in his shoulder and continued crying. "That's all right, sweetheart. Everything will be all right." I jokingly refer to this as Andy's superhero phase. Superman was out to save the world. Batman was there to protect Gotham City. And Andy Myers was going to save all the hurting children of Trask. You know, *No one else is going to die on my watch!* That sort of thing. It was like he now saw Gabe in the face of every at-risk child in the entire town. He never told me this, but I imagine there was a part of him that said, *I'm doing this for you, Gabe,* when he lifted that girl up to protect her from her angry parents. He started doing a lot of things for Gabe after that, which is weird since Gabe was dead and Andy hadn't done that much for Gabe before, except hang out with him and treat him like a human being should treat a child. But for Andy, that was a pretty big step. After all, we're talking about a guy who walked out on his wife because she was pregnant with his own child; a guy who, up until this point, had pretended he didn't have a son. It was quite a step.

Hauling in the domestic disturbancers gave Andy the opportunity to check on the investigation into Gabe's death. He walked into Mike Duncan's office. "So, do you live at this place, or what?" Andy asked.

Mike looked up. "It feels like it. Let me tell you, it feels like it. So whadda you doing down here?"

"Had to bring in a couple I'd arrested and thought, since I was here, I would check in to see what's happening in the Gabe Phillips case."

"Well, I can tell you what killed him. It was the drawer. The dad was telling the truth. Autopsy shows the cause of death to be a blunt-force trauma to the back of the head. The cracks in the kid's skull match the corner of the drawer exactly," Duncan said.

Andy shook his head. "I still have trouble believing that falling out of bed can kill a kid."

"We're working on that. Want to have a look at what we've come up with so far?" Duncan asked.

"Hell yes," Andy replied.

Duncan led Andy into the lab, where several items from John Phillips's now-empty apartment sat on metal tables that were very much like those you find in a high school chemistry classroom. (You have to keep in mind that the lab wasn't quite as sophisticated back then as it is today. They didn't have DNA sequencers, computers, or other high-tech gadgets. Forensic science has come a long way in nearly thirty years.) Andy recognized a few of the items, others he did not. "So here's what we know so far," Duncan said. "The drawer over here, it delivered the fatal blow. There's no doubt about it." Pulling a pen out of his pocket, he pointed to the front corner that had been closest to Gabe's bed in his room. "This part is pretty beat-up, and you can see hair and blood inside the grooves of the broken wood. The pattern here lines up exactly with the back of the kid's skull. Here, check it out for yourself." Duncan pulled an autopsy photograph of the back of Gabe's head over from another table and held it up next to the drawer. The indentions in the photograph formed a perfect right angle. Andy was more than a little nervous about looking at the photograph. However, the image pulled so tight to the skull that nothing in it looked like Gabe, giving it all of the emotional impact of a photograph from a criminal pathology textbook.

"How can falling out of bed produce enough force to do that kind of damage?" Andy asked.

"From the top bunk, it's possible. At least I think it is possible. To say for sure, I probably need to drop some weighted dummies onto empty wooden drawers."

"When you gonna do that?" Andy asked.

"Later this evening," Duncan said.

"Don't you ever go home?" Andy questioned.

"What the hell for? There's nothing there," Duncan replied. Shifting the conversation back to the evidence in the room, he said, "Another thing about this drawer. It was empty when we pulled it out of the apartment."

"So?" Andy replied.

"So the dad said that this drawer doubled as his kid's toy box."

"Yeah?"

"Where were the toys?" Duncan asked.

"Scattered across the floor. When I walked into the room, there were clothes and toys all over the room. I don't have a lot of experience with kids," Andy said in a classic under-statement, "but that seems pretty normal to me."

"Could be. Probably is," Duncan said. "But in his state-ment the other night, the dad said the boy had to pick up all his toys and put them away before he went to bed."

"From what I recall, it didn't look like much of anything was put away in the room that night."

Duncan nodded his head. "Yeah, I've seen the pictures. The room was a mess. Do you remember whether or not the toys were all close together or if they were spread out when you walked in?"

Andy shrugged his shoulders. "When there's a bleeding child lying on the bed, who notices anything else? Why do you ask?"

"If everything was in one place, then that could mean the

drawer was dumped out all at once. If they were spread out across the floor, then that would indicate the boy took them out a few at a time as he played with them," Duncan said.

"Does that matter?" Andy asked.

"Maybe," Duncan said. "Take a look at the back of the drawer." Mike Duncan slipped a pair of gloves on his hands and spun the drawer around, where Andy could see the part of the drawer that was stuck inside the chest. The dovetail joint had clearly been repaired. "This thing's been busted and glued back together very recently. The glue is still soft in places. John Phillips even admits that. He says these draw-ers were constantly breaking and he had to glue them back together. He claims he fixed it the day before the accident. His prints are in the glue."

"So he fixed a busted drawer?"

"We didn't pick this up until the next day. It was so late the night of the accident that we walked out and forgot it. That means we have no way of knowing when he fixed it," Duncan said. "But his prints aren't just in the glue. We lifted handprints off both sides toward the back."

"Meaning?"

"Meaning he picked it up like this"—Mike Duncan turned the drawer upside down and grabbed it on the sides. His fingers curled around on the inside of the drawer, while his palms pressed hard on the outside—"and when he did, he gripped it pretty tight. We pulled nice wide prints off this part of the drawer, the kind that comes when someone applies a great deal of pressure."

"I'm missing something here," Andy said.

"The drawer killed the kid, just like the dad said. It's pos-sible that it could have happened more than one way. The boy may well have fallen out of bed and landed on the corner of the drawer, which is the father's explanation. Or, the drawer may have fallen onto the child's head, with added force, if you know what I mean," Duncan said. "It's all in the way you look at the evidence. Of course, you would think if he'd slammed it down hard enough to crack the kid's skull, the whole damn drawer would have busted apart."

"What?! Are you telling me that John Phillips pulled this drawer out and used it to crack open his son's skull?" A rush of anger swept over Andy.

"I'm just saying it's possible. That's all," Duncan replied. "Don't go jumping to any conclusions. We've got to keep a clear head and go where the evidence takes us, not force it in a direction it doesn't want to go. Bottom line here, Andy: the mother said the guy killed the boy. The evidence says the drawer delivered the fatal blow, which makes the dad's story a very plausible explanation. All I'm trying to do is figure out if there is any way the woman's charges could be true. And with the way the fingerprints line up on the back of the drawer, I would have to say, yes, it is possible that our guy used a dresser drawer to kill the boy. If it weren't, this whole investigation would now be over and the cause of death would most definitely be accidental. That doesn't mean the dad killed the boy. I'm only saying it's an interesting coincidence that the drawer with the dad's fingerprints all over it is the same drawer that cracked this kid's head open.

"And then there's this," Mike Duncan said as he pulled out another set of photographs. These were of Gabe's abdomen and back. "A few were snapped at the scene before the body was moved." Duncan slid three others closer to Andy. "These with the rulers in the shot, Warner took them during the autopsy. The bruises on his abdomen and chest appear to be several days old. The ones on his back," he said as he fished out a couple of other photographs, "are from the night the boy died. They may have been made by the fall out of bed, if that's how he died."

"And if not?" Andy asked.

"Then someone had been beating the crap out of this little guy on a regular basis," Duncan said. "We also found some fresh scratches on the backs of his hands, like he'd put up a fight against something." Mike Duncan must have seen Andy's face flush red, like he was about to pop his cork, because he immediately said, "Now settle down. That doesn't mean the dad was the one abusing the boy."

"Like hell it doesn't."

"Think about it, Andy," Duncan said. "The kid was on the top bunk. The ceilings are pretty low in that dump of an apartment complex and they all have that blown-on, popcorn-looking texturing. You ever hit your hand against that crap? It can do some damage. And what do kids do when they have a bad dream? They roll around and fight the demons attacking them in the night. There's a pretty good chance the kid scratched his hands on the ceiling."

"If he fell out of bed while having a nightmare," Andy said.

"Exactly."

"And if he didn't?"

"You tell me," Duncan replied.

Andy paused and let that soak in for a moment. Duncan started putting the photographs away when Andy said, "You know the guy has already cleaned out the apartment, don't you? Scrubbed it clean from top to bottom and moved out."

"What?!" Duncan shook his head. "Holy crap. And right about the time I'm ready to give this guy the benefit of the doubt...Man, that's quick. The kid's been dead, what, three whole days?"

"Four," Andy said.

"You clean out a place that fast, it sure looks like you have something to hide."

"Tell me something I don't know," Andy said.

The rest of Andy's shift went by without any major incidents. He made a few traffic stops, and was called out to a possible fire. The fire turned out to be nothing more than smoke wafting through a window from a neighbor burning trash. He cited the neighbor for burning after dark, and watched as the fire department dumped a few gallons of water into the trash barrel to douse the flames. Throughout his shift Andy kept an eye out for John Phillips, but he couldn't go off searching for him. For that matter, he didn't even know where to start looking. At 11:00 p.m., he dropped back by the station to clock out and brief the poor sap pulling the graveyard shift. Andy had to go back into the station a second time to retrieve the folder and cassette tape from his locker. Flipping the tape around in his right hand, he said, "God, I hope she didn't talk too much."

# CHAPTER

4

"I'VE ALWAYS HEARD that prison changes a man, but I never knew how true that really is. John changed while he was in the joint. By the time he got out, he wasn't the man I married. Funny, I never really heard of people changing like he did. He came out sooooooo religious, it was nauseating. Don't get me wrong, I liked some parts of the new John. He stopped drinking, which was good because he usually got violent when he got too drunk. But I didn't think that meant I had to stop drinking. I wasn't the one with the problem, so why should I quit? I've got to be honest. I missed hitting the bars together. Yeah, he got mean when he got drunk, but he was also fun. And funny. I know Jesus can change people. I just never knew God wanted 'em so dull."

Fast-forward. It was Andy's third time to listen to the tape. He wanted to hit the highlights one more time while it was all fresh in his mind. As he listened, he made notes in his Big Chief pad.

"...could take the personal changes. I could live with going to church on Sundays and not getting stoned at the occasional concert. You know, Gabe was getting old enough that we didn't have any business doing that stuff anyways. And he really liked going to Sunday school. Gabe loved Sunday school. I think it was the favorite part of his week. I kept taking him even after his father and I split up. Gabe really loved Sunday school."

Fast-forward.

"...so I don't know a lot about God and Jesus. I mean, I went to church when I was a kid. My mother made me and my sister go to nearly every Vacation Bible School in town in the summers when we were kids. We had fun, and for her it was a week of free child care each time. So I know some things about God, not a lot, but enough to know that John wasn't normal. Like I said, I didn't have a problem with him cleaning up his act. He landed in prison, for Christ's sake, he needed a little cleaning up. It's when he started giving things away and bringing people home, that's when the problems started."

Fast-forward.

"...things like food, clothes, even money. It wasn't like we had an overabundance. I'll never forget the time he gave a hundred dollars to some person he hardly knew. I didn't know them at all. Our rent was due in a few days, and he gave a huge chunk of it away. When I asked him what the hell he thought he was doing, he told me to 'trust God.' He said God wouldn't let us down when we obey Him. Okay, I'm all for helping people out when they need it, but John's helping others made us candidates for charity ourselves. I managed to juggle around some of our other bills to make rent, but it put a lot of stress on me. John took the fact that we didn't lose our home as proof that God had come through. I didn't see it that way."

Fast-forward.

"...different people. Never anyone we knew. Sometimes they were homeless. I pleaded with him to stop. I told him that bringing strange people into our home put both me and Gabe in danger. John would just quote some Bible verse about 'the least of these' and tell me not to worry. I do not know or care what the least of these are. All I know is bringing a stranger into your home when you have a wife and small child is not safe. Period. He never understood why I would worry. Trust God, he would say. Trust God. Trust God. Just trust God. He said it so much that I thought it was just some cliché he hid behind when he didn't want to take responsibility for what was going on."

Fast-forward.

"...the prostitute was the last straw."

Rewind.

"...but the prostitute was the last straw."

Rewind.

"The down-and-out bums were bad enough, but the prostitute was the last straw. Yeah. He brought a prostitute into our home. Even introduced her to Gabe. Like all the other people he let sleep on our couch, John said she didn't have anywhere else to stay. Said she'd just given her life to Jesus and she needed a safe place where her pimp wouldn't find her. I shudder to think what might have happened if he had. I was furious. I threw out the sheets she slept on. I can only imagine what we might have caught from them. She stayed with us for three days until John found somewhere else that would take her. Three days. He even went out and bought her some new clothes. Like we could afford to buy some whore new clothes. I hadn't had anything new in months, not that

John noticed or cared." Loraine let out a long sigh on the tape. "After that, I was done. I couldn't take it anymore. Can you blame me?"

Fast-forward.

"...mission trip. Guatemala, I'm pretty sure it was Guatemala. I didn't think ex-cons could leave the country. He did. He went with a group of men from his church for ten days in Guatemala. I think they built a church. Like I said, by that point I was done. I wasn't paying a lot of attention to what he did. While he was on the mission trip, I loaded up Gabe and myself and all our stuff, and moved here. Our house was completely empty when he got back. John's stuff? I gave it to the Salvation Army. I thought it only appropriate. I don't know how he reacted when he found the house all empty. If I cared, I wouldn't have done it like that."

Fast-forward.

"Yes, I found someone else. I needed to be with a man. A real man, not some..."

Rewind.

"...needed to be with a man. A real man, not..."

Rewind.

"...found someone else. I needed to be with a man. A real man, not some, you know... When? The same week; while he was on his mission trip. No, I didn't think that was fast. My husband had been gone for a couple of years. Like I told you, John was no longer the man I married. And I needed a man. I'm sure he knew what I'd done. He had to know. The way I see it, I did him a favor. Since I went out and 'committed fornication,' he's free to find himself a woman more suited to his new tastes. Whatever. I really didn't give a damn what he did. And, no, I never thought he would retaliate like this.

Do you think I would have gone through with it if I thought he would kill my little boy to get back at me?"

Fast-forward.

"He'd threatened me on more than one occasion. You won't have any trouble finding witnesses to back up what I am telling you. It should be in the transcripts from his trial. That's why he went to prison. All I did was talk to the guy. He was nice, and I was just being polite. I'd felt ugly for a long time. I got really big with Gabe. It was our first time to go out after he was born, our first night of letting him stay with a babysitter. But John didn't think the guy was being nice. He said he watched the guy staring at my boobs all night. Like I said, I got really big with Gabe, in more ways than one. The guy said something, I don't even remember what, when I walked past him on my way back from the bathroom. Next thing I know, John has the guy on the ground and has to be drug off."

Fast-forward.

"...hit me in the past."

Rewind.

"...answer to your question, yes, he hit me in the past. Several times. No, it wasn't just when he was drunk. Alcohol gave him a shorter fuse, but sometimes he would just snap. You know, he would just explode and I would sit there and go, where did that come from? When he got really angry, I would try to get away until he cooled down. And, no, he hasn't hit me since he got out of prison. Nor do I recall any threats made after he got out. But I don't see how that matters. He is who he is."

Fast-forward.

"...told me that if I ever left him, I would regret it. Now I do. He killed my little boy to get back at me for what I'd done to him. I never imagined he could hurt me so bad."

Rewind.

"He told me that if I ever left him, I would regret it."

Rewind.

"...if I ever left him, I would regret it."

Rewind.

"...I would regret it."

Andy clicked off the tape and leaned back in his chair. "Christ," he said as he stared at the tape player. "Holy, holy Christ." He ran his hand over the top of his head and tried to think. "Whew." He stood and walked from the kitchen table to the refrigerator and pulled out a beer. "She emptied everything out of the house while he was out of the country?" He shook his head in disbelief and said to his dark and empty house, "I've heard of bitter ex-wives, but, man, she wins the gold medal." Walking from the kitchen through his living room, he opened his beer and took a long drink as he passed on into his bedroom. On the nightstand, next to his bed, lay the picture of Gabe and Loraine. Andy sat down on the bed and picked it up.

I'm not sure how long he sat there staring at the photograph he'd picked up in Gabe's room, but eventually he wound up back at his kitchen table with his Big Chief pad. He flipped it open to the page with the word "why" printed across the top, and began writing. "Why would a woman accuse her son's father of killing his own child?" he wrote on the first line, which was immediately followed by "Can anyone really hate another human being enough to make something like this up????????!" This was, Andy told me, the key question that would determine how far he would go in the investigation. The most incriminating evidence he'd found at this stage were Loraine's words the night of Gabe's death. All of the physical evidence turned on her accusation. Any woman who would empty out the house and move away while her husband was off on a mission trip seemed capable of about anything. But accusing her former husband of murder was more than anything. At the very least, John could end up locked away for a very, very long time. With the recent Supreme Court decision opening the door for executions, it was conceivable that John could receive the death penalty if he had, in fact, killed Gabe in cold blood. Loraine had to know this. He scrawled, "If she were just making this up, why would she take it this far?"

Andy got up, grabbed the Big Chief pad, and moved to the living room. The cuckoo clock on his wall cuckooed three times. Plopping down on the couch, he let out a long yawn, then wrote, "Why would a father kill his only son?" Andy had read accounts of parents who killed children during bitter custody disputes. However, it is far more common for those who do to go ahead and kill themselves as well, rather than wait around to get caught. Or, if someone is driven to kill, it is more likely he would kill the ex-spouse who's making his life a living hell. As his mind tried to wrap itself around these questions, Andy's hand kept writing "why" over and over again. At the end of the page, he added two more sentences: "Why Gabe?" and "Why me?"

He let out a long sigh, then headed to the fridge for one last beer before going to bed.

Even though he fell asleep very quickly, Andy felt like he was still awake. It was like one of those nights when you cram for a test back in college. You study and study and study, and when you finally fall asleep, you feel like you are still studying. That's how Andy's night went. He kept hearing Loraine's voice talking and talking and talking. The sound of her voice took him back to her apartment. He rolled over in her bed and there stood John, staring at him.

The phone ringing broke into his dream. Andy slapped at the phone, unsure of where he was. "Hello," he mumbled.

"Officer Myers?"

"Yeah. Who wants to know?"

"It's Jeanine Martin, the apartment manager at Madison Park. You asked me to call if I heard from John Phillips."

"Uhhh, yeah." Andy looked around his room. Loraine was not there, and neither was John.

"Well, he's here right now. He came by to turn in his keys and sign the papers terminating his lease. I can stall him if you want me to. Otherwise, I think he's in a hurry to leave."

Andy's mind slowly caught up with his body. "Yeah, yeah, do that, please. I'll be right there." He hung up the phone and sat up in his bed. The line between his dream and reality still felt very thin. He yanked the covers up off his bed, just to make sure no one else was in there. "Loraine?" he yelled toward the other end of the house. No answer. Once he was sure he had, in fact, been dreaming, he threw on his uniform and rushed out the door.

The Madison Park Apartments were already familiar territory for Andy. It had always been a place where low-income families, especially single mothers, moved in and out. No one ever stayed there long. Few, if any, of the people who called it home had any kind of deep roots in Trask. (Of course, in a town like this, if you weren't born here, you're a newcomer until the day you die, even if you live to be a hundred. That's just the way it is in little towns in the Midwest. Always has been. Always will be.) Outside the connections kids make with one another in school and sports, most of the people out there don't even make a blip on the rest of the town's radar. The whole complex could get picked up by aliens and hauled off to some galaxy far, far away, and no one outside the guy who runs the liquor store and the woman who hands out the food stamps would notice or care.

And that included Andy. By his third trip out there in less than a week, he was getting pretty sick of the place. Up to this point in his life, the apartment complex had always been a pain in the butt to him. Now it smelled like death. Just pulling into the parking lot was enough to put him in a bad mood. "Man, I hate this stinking hole," he said as he walked through what passed for grass between two of the buildings to look for the manager's office. Even though it was barely 8:30 a.m., a crowd of children had already gathered on the dilapidated playground equipment behind the laundry building. Andy had to step over several bicycles strewn about on the sidewalk leading to the complex office. The office, of course, was empty. "Crap," he mumbled, and walked back into the main parking lot. After standing around, feeling stupid for what felt much longer than it actually was, he played a hunch and walked up the stairs of building three to the Phillips apartment. The door stood open and Andy could hear Jeanine Martin and John talking inside. Apparently, little Miss Martin told John she had to inspect the apartment for damages before he could get out of his lease. She was a pretty good liar for an old lady.

Andy knocked lightly on the door frame. "Mind if I come in?" he asked.

"I was about to leave, so don't mind me," John said. Finishing his conversation with the apartment manager, he said, "Again, thank you so much for your understanding, Miss Martin. I appreciate it more than you can know." He then started walking toward the door. "Good to see you again, Officer Myers."

"Where you going in such a hurry?" Andy asked.

"I'm already late for work," John said. "I had only planned on stopping by here for a minute to drop off my keys. So, if you will excuse me..."

"Sure, sure, sure," Andy said. "Tell you what. Why don't I walk out to your car with you. It will give us a chance to talk. I have a couple of questions I would like to ask you."

"Yeah, that'll be fine. But I really have to hurry," John said. He picked up his pace as he went out the door. Andy followed. "So what do you need to know, Officer?"

"Oh, nothing big. Nothing official, that is. Just wanted to check on you. You know, find out how you are doing since your son died," Andy said.

"I'm fine. I already told you, Officer, I have a hope that is bigger than death." John moved quickly down the building three stairs and started toward his car. "It's you I'm concerned about. How are you doing? You didn't look so good at Gabe's funeral."

"Yeah, yeah, yeah, I'm doing great. But back to you, if you are doing so well, why did you move out of your apartment so fast?"

With that, John stopped a few feet short of his car. He turned to Andy, raised his palms, and said, "The apartment reminds me of a reality that isn't real. My son isn't dead. He's more alive than you or me. Like Jesus said, I don't need to look for the living among the dead." None of this made any sense to my old man. John's talk of his son being alive made Andy think the guy was mental or something. "Now, really, Officer, I have to run. I'm too late already," John said as he turned and started walking to his car.

About the time John reached the car door handle, Andy called out to him, "Why would your ex-wife say you killed your son?" The second the words left his lips, Andy wished he could reel them back in, but he couldn't help himself. That question had been gnawing on him for days and he couldn't keep it in any longer.

To hear Andy tell it, what happened next was huge. Me, I didn't read too much into it, but then again, I wasn't there. Still, I think that even if I had been, I wouldn't have leaped to the same conclusion my old man did. Anyway, Andy threw out his stupid question to John, told him that his wife had accused him of murdering his child. And John's only response was to turn, look Andy right square in the eye, smile, and shake his head. Then he climbed into his car and drove off. Andy took it as a smug, smart-ass, *Oh, wouldn't you like to know?* kind of thing. Keep in mind, Andy thought he had a knack for reading people. The cop in him said he noticed subtle little things other people missed, and he could figure out pretty quickly what someone was all about. And the things that made John look guilty weren't so subtle. From the moment John answered the door talking on the phone, Andy's suspicions were aroused. Then the guy didn't act that upset over his son being dead. To Andy, that just seemed flat-out weird. I don't know what he expected

John to do, maybe go jump off a bridge or something. I'm not sure. But remaining calm and quoting Bible verses was not, in Andy's mind, the appropriate response to the death of a child. And neither were a lot of things Andy saw in John and heard him say.

Andy still didn't have an answer as to why a father would kill his own son, but watching John drive off from the Madison Park Apartments, his gut told him Loraine was right. Proving it would be a much harder proposition. But then again, Andy always liked challenges.

After leaving the apartment complex, Andy drove back to his house, stripped out of his uniform, and climbed into the shower. He didn't have to report to work for several more hours. On his way from the front door to the bathroom, he made one detour. He picked up his beloved Big Chief pad and turned to the only page on which he hadn't done any brainstorming, the "how" page. Quickly he scribbled two sentences. The first simply said: "How did he do it?" The second said: "How can I prove it?" Tossing the pad onto the living-room sofa, he walked back to his bathroom, climbed into the shower, and let the hot water wash over him until his fingers were pruney. The water lubricated the gears in his brain. As he stood there soaking, he kept asking himself, *How am I going to nail you, John Phillips? How am I going to prove you did it?*

As he stood there soaking, another "how" question came to him in the shower. He jumped out and didn't even wait to dry off before finding his Big Chief pad. Water dripped onto the floor as he stood there naked and wrote, "HOW CAN I GET HIM TO ADMIT WHAT I KNOW HE DID?!!!!" Proving he did it wasn't enough for Andy. He wanted to hear with his own ears the sweet sound of John admitting his guilt. Andy wasn't interested in framing an innocent man. No. He was out for justice. And true justice demanded that the guilty man take full responsibility for his crime, and suffer the consequences. Andy needed a confession to feel satisfied that he'd done enough for Gabriel Phillips, and he would not rest until he made it happen.

# CHAPTER

## 5

THE WAY I'VE HEARD the story, and I've heard it many, many times, Loraine Phillips strikes me as the kind of person who never does anything without first thinking it out long and hard. In her taped statement to the police—a copy of which, by the way, I have tucked away in a drawer in my home in Trask—she never once mentioned Andy by name. She talks about going out and finding herself a "real man," but she never says who that real man might be, or how many real men she found. Andy may have been the only one. I don't think he was, although Andy does. Not that it matters. She wasn't looking for anything more than a way to completely emasculate John. I've heard of bitter ex-wives with a taste for conflict, but she outdoes them all.

Whether or not Andy was the only man in her life (and her bed) matters less than the fact that he believed her when she said John killed Gabe as an act of cold-blooded revenge. Any doubts he may have had drove off with John that morning at the Madison Park Apartments.

Andy believed Loraine. But believing something and

having the proof to back it up are two different things entirely. Andy had some circumstantial evidence and a gut feeling, but that's not enough to indict a man, much less convict him. The whole case came down to a "he said, she said" kind of thing. Loraine said John killed their son; John said the boy fell out of bed and hit his head on an open drawer. The evidence could go either way, depending on whose version you believed. Andy also faced the problem that this wasn't his case to prove. He may have been a part of the investigative team, but the sheriff's department took the lead in these things. Their analysis carried far more weight with the district attorney than the opinion of a small-town cop. Andy had friends over there who were working on the case, but they didn't have the same fire for it that he did. Nor had they made up their minds about John's guilt or innocence. Honestly, I think the whole thing would have gone away if not for my dad's persistence. I know it would have. But Andy wouldn't let it go, and he wouldn't let Ted Jackson, Mike Duncan, or anyone else on the Harris County Sheriff's Department forget about it, either.

Andy's search for proof took him back to the Madison Park Apartments. He knew he wouldn't find any new physical evidence there. Anything the initial investigative team might have missed was scrubbed away by the team of women from John's church who descended on his apartment two days after John moved out. Or should I say, after he was moved out. Aside from the brief visit when he encountered Andy there, John never went back to his apartment after Gabe's death. The way I heard it, he didn't want to go back there with all the blood tracked all over the apartment. A friend from church offered to let him move in with him over in

Crosse, and John took him up on it. A group of men moved all his stuff out, while their wives cleaned the apartment like it had never been cleaned before. Moving out of Trask came easy for John. It wasn't like he'd put down any roots in the six months he'd lived there. No one from Madison Park puts down roots. Everyone out there was pretty much invisible until some tragedy forced the rest of the town to take notice. Nothing has changed. It's still that way today.

With no physical evidence to search for, Andy started looking for witnesses who would back up his theory about how Gabe died. In his mind, getting them to talk wouldn't be a problem. Andy once told me that he could get anyone to do just about anything he wanted. Considering how his story ended up, I would have to agree with him. So he went to work on the people of Madison Park. By the time he was done, he must have interviewed every man, woman, and child in the entire place. He didn't find exactly what he was looking for, but what he discovered came close enough.

The interviewing process began at the epicenter of the whole affair, apartment 323. On his first day of playing Perry Mason, Andy went to the apartment next door, where the woman lived who'd called the police the night Gabe died. He already knew from the case file that a sheriff's department team had taken a statement from the woman on the night of Gabe's death, but that didn't stop him. They'd only asked about the noises she'd heard on that night. Andy wanted to know more about John and Gabe's relationship, and whether she'd seen the fits of rage Loraine had described. He had a hunch she had. After all, she was scared to go to John's apartment by herself that night.

Andy knocked a couple of times before the door of

apartment 325 slowly opened wide enough for a pair of eyes standing about four-and-a-half feet off the ground to look out. The chain lock was still latched. The eyes behind the chain didn't say a word.

"Is your mommy or daddy at home?" Andy asked.

"My mom's at work and I ain't got no dad," the boy said.

"Are you here by yourself?"

"I'm not supposed to say. My mother told me to tell anyone who called or came by that she was lying down with a head-ache and to please come back later," the boy said through the crack of a door opening.

"Is she?"

"No," the boy said. "That's just what I'm supposed to say. Then I'm supposed to hang up or close the door. My mom don't want me to talk to strangers."

"She's a smart woman," Andy said. "Then why are you talking to me?"

"It's okay to talk to a policeman. My mother told me that, too."

"That's right. That's right. You can talk to policemen," Andy said as he crouched down to eye level with the boy on the other side of the door. "Can you tell me your name?" Andy asked.

"Brian."

"What's your last name, Brian?"

"Paul. I have two first names," Brian said.

"I guess you do," Andy said as he continued talking through the slit of the door opening. "Brian, did you know Gabe, the boy who used to live next door?" Brian nodded his head yes. As he did, tears started streaming down his face. "Were you friends with Gabe?"

Brian sniffed, wiped his face with the back of his hand, and said very softly, "Best friends."

"Do you know what happened to Gabe?" Andy asked. On the other side of the door, Brian began shaking, his tears flowed even more freely. He didn't say a word. I don't think he could talk even if he wanted. "What's wrong, Brian? Did you see or hear something the night Gabe died?" Brian nodded his head. "What did you see, son?"

"I can't talk no more," Brian said as he shut the door.

Andy could hear the fading sound of Brian crying. It sounded like the boy was running to the back of his apartment. Andy raised his hand and started to knock again, but thought better of it. The mother should have been there for even that small snippet of a conversation, and Andy knew it. Pressing an eight-year-old for information without a parent present could blow up in his face. He turned and walked to apartment 321, on the other side of 323. Before he knocked, he remembered who lived there. "I sure as hell don't feel like talking to Crazy Cathy today," he said to himself.

He decided to check the neighbors who lived across the hall. But first, he wanted to go back into the Phillips apartment for another look around. He'd talked the apartment manager out of a key on his last visit, and let himself in. Like every other trip inside that apartment, he went down the short hall toward Gabe's room. Before he'd taken a step, he heard a sound that nearly made him jump out of his skin. Somewhere in the apartment a child was crying, and it sounded like the child was in Gabe's room. Andy walked slowly into the short hallway. The crying grew louder. When he reached the room, he stuck his head through the door, unsure of what he would find. The room was empty, just like always, but the cries were now louder than before. He stepped into the room, it was more like a tiptoe, and listened. The closer he went toward the closet, the louder the cries became. He opened the closet door, fully expecting to find a little boy in pain, but the closet was empty. The sound came from the opposite side of the apartment wall, from Brian Paul's room. Andy smiled. If he could hear Brian now, then surely Brian heard everything that happened on the night of Gabe's death. The boy may not be an eyewitness, but they didn't get much closer. "Bingo," he said to himself.

Andy sped back to the police station to call Ted Jackson. "Jax," he said when Ted answered the phone. "I think I found a witness to Gabriel Phillips's death. Not really an eyewitness. More of an earwitness."

"A what?" Jackson said.

"I know, it sounds crazy, but I think the kid in the apartment next door heard everything through the paper-thin dividers they call walls in those cheap-ass apartments," Andy said.

"If you are talking about who I think you are talking about, I already got a statement from the mother. The way she talked, something woke the boy, and he immediately woke her up. She said she didn't hear anything more than the three other callers from the complex that night said, and the kid was with her almost the entire time," Jackson said. "Did she tell you anything different?"

"I haven't talked to the mother, only the boy. And I think the kid knows more than his mother is letting on. Hell, she probably doesn't know what he knows. All I did was mention Gabe's name, and the kid fell apart. He started shaking and crying and ran away. I'm telling you, that kid heard more than his best friend falling out of bed. He heard something that scared the crap out of him," Andy said.

"Wait a minute. You talked to the kid without a parent around. Don't you know anything about real police work?" Jackson said.

"Whoa. Whoa. It wasn't like that. I went by the apartment to talk to the mother, and the kid opened the door. I just asked if he knew the kid who used to live next door. That's all. The rest came from him. I swear. But, even then, it wasn't much. Whole conversation lasted maybe a minute, minute and a half tops," Andy said. "I swear."

Ted Jackson let out a sigh in response.

"But here's the deal," Andy said, "here's what you didn't know. The boy's bedroom butts right up against Gabe's. When I was out there just a little bit ago, I could hear the kid crying through the wall, almost like there wasn't a wall there to begin with. Now, if I could hear this kid crying today, I guarantee you he had a front-row seat to everything that happened the night Gabriel Phillips was killed. We need to bring in this kid and his mother together and find out what he knows."

"We? What's this *we* business?" Jackson said.

"We, as in we're on the case and this is my witness, so I ought to be there when you talk to him," Andy said. "This kid might know a few other things, too. He said he and Gabe were best friends. He's probably a good place to start to find out what kind of a father this Phillips guy really was. Loraine Phillips said John used to beat her. If anyone knows whether he had ever hurt Gabe, it would be this kid."

"Possibly. Possibly. But this *we* business still isn't going to happen. Let me set up a time to talk to the boy. Hell, I'll even try to get them to come in here so you can listen from the other side of the glass if you want. But that's as much as I can give you. You seem way too gung ho about this case, almost like it was your kid who died. Like I told you, you need to check your emotions at the door on this one, Andy," Jackson said.

"Come on, Jax. You know me," Andy said.

"Yeah, that's the problem," Jackson replied. "Let me see what I can get set up and I will keep you posted."

"Good enough," Andy said. Then, shifting gears, he asked, "So what's the status on the case? Is this a full homicide investigation yet? I'm curious as to what the D.A. thinks about what you've shown him so far."

"We've notified his office about what's going on, but we are nowhere close to delivering a prosecutable case to him. The investigation has only just started. I know this may sound a little strange to you native Traskites, but we have these little things called rules and procedures we have to go by. We don't have the luxury of making it up as we go along," Jackson said.

"Come on, Jax. You have a guy who acts guilty as hell from the get-go. You have a witness who says he did it. You have his fingerprints on the murder weapon. To top it off, your ex-con suspect has a history of beating his wife. It's not much of a stretch to go from hitting your wife to hitting your kid. What are you waiting on?" Andy said.

"Loraine Phillips doesn't fly as a star witness. Hell, I've got an ex-wife. I know what they're capable of. My ex-wife would make me the evil genius behind the Manson Family if she thought anyone would believe her. All you've got is a bunch of *maybe*'s and *could be*'s. Every bit of evidence we have so far is completely subjective. Sure, it makes Phillips look guilty, if you already think he did it. I've got to give the D.A. more than that or he will hand me my ass on a platter," Jackson said.

"I just gave you a real witness," Andy said. "Talk to the kid, then make up your mind. I'm telling you, Jax, my gut tells me this Phillips guy has blood on his hands. You can't let him get away with killing a little boy who couldn't defend himself."

"Depending on what he says, the kid may be a start, but I'm not about to pin my entire case on the testimony of an eight-year-old. Any defense attorney worth a damn would have a field day with a little kid on cross-examination," Jackson said. I think he heard Andy clicking his tongue or sighing or something over the phone because he went on to say, "Patience, man. Don't rush it. Let the evidence do the talking. Listen to what it says. And if it says John Phillips did it, then we will nail his sorry ass to the wall. But if it doesn't and we still try to nail him, we end up looking like a lynch mob rather than professional law enforcement officers," Jackson said.

"He did it, Jax. You know it. I know it. The kid next door knows it," Andy said.

"Maybe. We'll find out. That's the whole point of an investigation anyway. Right?"

"Yeah, man, whatever you say," Andy said.

Andy hung up the phone, rolled back in his chair, and kicked his desk. "Dammit. You need more evidence? I'll give you evidence. I'll give you so much flipping evidence that you'll choke on it." He grabbed the phone and punched in seven numbers, and when I say punched, I mean punched. He abused that poor phone. After three rings, the other end picked up. "Loraine," Andy said, "this is Andy Myers. Do you have time to answer a couple of questions for me? I'm working on your son's case and I just need to clarify a few things." She couldn't see him until the next day, which was fine for Andy. It was getting late and he needed time to mentally prepare himself to see Loraine.

# CHAPTER

## 6

ANDY FOUND HIMSELF standing next to Gabe's grave. The sun had gone down hours earlier, and the moon cast very little light, but he knew it was Gabe's grave. A layer of dry and shriveled flowers left over from the funeral were scattered across the still-fresh dirt. Andy had a teddy bear in a cop's uniform in his hand, but he couldn't bring himself to drop it on top of the rotting flowers. Instead, he just stood there, breathing in the heavy night air, staring down at the grave, silent. Even if he had been able to think of something to say, the words wouldn't form on his lips. Nor could he cry. His eyes stayed bone-dry the whole time he stood there. Staring.

"Do you really think I would kill my only son because of you?"

Andy turned around to see John Phillips walking up a path between headstones about ten yards behind him. "What did you say?" Andy asked.

"I said, do you really think I would kill my only son *because of you*?" John spit out those last three words like someone had made his lemonade with salt.

"I have a witness," Andy said.

"You don't have anything. You know it, I know it, and the kid next door knows it." John kept walking until he'd closed to within fifteen feet of Andy.

"I know what you did," Andy said, and turned back to Gabe's grave.

"You don't know anything. Do you really think I would kill my only son because of you?" John began laughing. Andy tried to ignore him. "DO YOU REALLY THINK I WOULD KILL MY ONLY SON *BECAUSE OF YOU!*" he shouted.

"Yes," Andy said in almost a whisper.

"Oh, that is rich." John laughed. "That is sooooo rich," he said as he fell to the ground and began rolling around in the grass, laughing uncontrollably.

"Yes," Andy repeated, louder. "Yes, I know you did it. I know you killed Gabe." Andy moved from the grave site to where John lay on the ground, laughing. The sound of his laughter enraged Andy. "I know what you did. I know you killed him." Andy was now standing directly over John.

"Because of *you*?" John could barely get the words out, he was laughing so hard.

"YES!" Andy shouted. "Because of me." His words only made John laugh harder. "BECAUSE OF ME!" Andy yelled as he kicked John hard in the side. "I know you killed HIM!" He kicked John again, and again, and again, but each time Andy kicked him, John only laughed harder. "I KNOW YOU KILLED HIM!" Andy screamed.

*"Because of you?"*

"YES! BECAUSE OF ME. IT WAS ALL BECAUSE OF ME!" he shouted. Andy reared back and kicked John as hard as he could in his face.

"You don't know anything," John said with the same cold tone of the drive-through worker at McDonald's asking if you want fries with that.

Andy sat straight up in bed, his sheets soaked with sweat. "What's wrong?" Loraine asked, lying beside him.

"The dr-dream…," Andy stammered, "it felt so real."

"It was," Loraine said. "Do you really think he would kill my son *because of you?*"

*⸱ ⸱ ⸱*

ANDY AWOKE in a panic, his pulse racing. "Oh, God," he panted. Although neither John nor Loraine had come to him during the night, the question they asked rang in his ears. "This has nothing to do with me," he said to the silence. "I didn't do anything. Hell, I didn't even know she had a kid. And besides, I didn't go looking for her, she came looking for me." He climbed out of bed and went into the bathroom to relieve himself. When he came back to bed, he glanced over at the clock on the nightstand. It was 2:06 in the morning, exactly one week to the minute since the dispatcher sent him on the call where he discovered Gabe's dead body. Andy knew he would never get back to sleep.

A half hour later he was behind the wheel of his 1972 Impala, heading toward the Adamsburg Memorial Gardens. A small bear in a cop uniform lay on the seat beside him. Andy had picked it up the day before, intending to place it on Gabe's grave. Even though cemetery workers cleared off everything except flowers at least once or twice a week, Andy figured it was the thought that counted. And he couldn't stop thinking about Gabe. "Now's as good a time as any," he said to the dashboard. He'd been to the cemetery one other time, the day after Gabe's funeral, but that had been in daylight. He hoped he could find the grave in the dark.

The Impala's headlights shone on the closed gates of the cemetery. Visiting hours officially ended at dusk and would not begin again for another three hours when the sun came up. Shifting the car into park, Andy climbed out, opened the gate (no one ever locked them, and half the time the work crews forgot to close them, but what do you expect from minimum-wage workers?), and drove inside. Driving down the main cemetery drive, Andy counted off one, two, three, four side roads. He turned on the fifth of six roads, which led to the part of the cemetery where they buried babies and children. He went to the very end of the road and parked his car. If memory served him correctly, and who knows at three in the morning, Gabe's grave was somewhere on the fourth row to the south of the road, almost to the end. Thankfully for Andy, Gabe's was the only new grave in this section of the cemetery.

As in his dream, Andy stood over Gabe's grave in silence for nearly fifteen minutes, the bear in his hand. All of the flowers from the funeral had long since been removed. Two vases full of fresh flowers sat where the headstone would eventually go. At least they looked fresh to Andy in the near darkness. The only light came from a streetlight about twenty yards away. Finally Andy crouched down and laid the bear atop the dirt covering the grave. "I got this for you," he said. "It's not much. Just a little something to let you know I'm thinking about you. I think about you a lot. I miss you. I really miss you." He paused and stood silently for a while. "You know, I never really liked kids before I met you. Maybe

I shouldn't tell you that, but you've probably figured it out by now." He paused again before saying, "You were a special boy, Gabriel Phillips. I can't believe you are gone." Tears began to well up in Andy's eyes, but he fought them off. "I don't know why this happened, but I'm trying…I'm trying to fix it." He didn't say anything else for several minutes as he stared down at the grave. "So maybe this will remind you of me," he said. "I don't really know if you can see it or not from where you are now. Like the song says, 'I don't know what happens when people die. I can't seem to grasp it as hard as I try.' Jackson Browne said that. Couldn't have said it better myself." Andy reached down and patted the grave as a way of saying good-bye. "Anyway, I hope you like the bear."

Andy walked back to his car, started it, and drove back through the main entrance. He stopped on the other side, climbed out of his car, and shut the gates. An Adamsburg police car pulled up and shone a spotlight on him. "Everything okay there, buddy?"

"It's okay, Officer, I'm a cop. Andy Myers. Trask P.D."

"What are you doing in the cemetery at this hour?"

"Business. Just taking care of a little business."

"You mind showing me some ID," the policeman asked. Andy flashed his badge, to which the officer said, "I don't know about Trask, but over here we don't spend a lot of time in cemeteries after dark."

"Got it. Yeah, that's fine," Andy said. "I was just leaving anyway." He climbed back into his Impala and drove away. Sleep still wouldn't be too easy to come by, Andy knew that. Once he reached his house, he walked into his kitchen, pulled a bottle of Scotch out of the cabinet, and proceeded to get smashed. He didn't even pretend to drink for any other reason. Pouring a drink into a glass, he tossed it down in one gulp like a teetotaler with a head cold taking NyQuil. Then he gulped down another and another and another until he felt completely numb. Then he took one more drink, lay down on the couch, and passed out.

# CHAPTER

7

LORAINE LOOKED GOOD, *really good,* when she opened her door and invited Andy inside the next afternoon. He struggled to concentrate on why he had come by. His eyes undressed her as she stood in the doorway. It didn't take a lot of effort. She'd opened that door for him on more than one occasion without wearing a stitch of clothing. Not this day. "Hello, Officer," she said coldly, "right on time. Won't you come in." It wasn't so much what she said as the way she said it. Andy felt like he needed to introduce himself, it was almost like they were meeting for the first time.

"Thank you, Ms. Phillips, er, Loraine. This won't take too long," he said as he walked inside. He sat on a chair across from Loraine, who sat on the couch. Andy took a quick glance around the room. The house looked exactly like he remembered it, but Loraine didn't. At least she didn't look at him the way she had just over a week before. Watching the two of them, you could have never guessed they had once been lovers. All of the sexual heat and chemistry Andy said once existed was gone. It was as if it had never been there.

"On the phone you said you had a couple of questions regarding my son's murder," she said, getting right to the point.

"Uh, yes, yeah," he stammered. Given their history, Andy was surprised to find himself so nervous sitting across from her now. "I've, uhhh, been investigating the case and, uhh, I wondered if you could answer a couple of questions for me."

"Yes. I assumed that's why you were here, since that's what you said over the phone. What do you need to know?"

"A couple of things, uh, just a couple of things. Uhhhh, in your taped statement to the sheriff's department investigators, you mentioned how your ex-husband would—"

"Husband," she interrupted.

"Excuse me?" Andy said.

"Technically, he's still my husband. We separated six months ago, but we are still married. The divorce hasn't gone through yet."

"Uh, yeah, okay." He tried to regain his composure. "In your taped statement to the detectives assigned to this case, you said your *husband* would regularly bring home strangers who had nowhere to stay and allow them to sleep on your couch."

"Correct."

Pulling a pad out of his pocket, he flipped it open and said, "And you also said that, and I quote, 'the prostitute was the last straw.'"

"Yes. He brought home a prostitute and allowed her to stay in our home for three or four days. As if that weren't enough, he also bought her new clothes and started the process of finding her a job."

"How did he come into contact with this prostitute?" Andy asked.

"He says he met her when he and a group of people from his church went to downtown Indy and preached on the street," Loraine said.

"Do you believe him?"

Loraine looked Andy in the eye and said with a cold, matter-of-fact tone, "The bastard killed my son. What do you think?"

Andy didn't know exactly what to think, which was why he had asked the question. "Do you recall her name and where she may be now?"

"Why in the bloody hell would I want to know where she is now? Her name? I don't know. Bambi or Angel or something. If you want to find her, his church can probably steer you in the right direction. The Redeemer's House of Deliverance over in Crosse, that's where he goes. He's gone there since he got out of prison. That church takes care of whores and bums all the time. Check with them." Loraine appeared to be getting bored with Andy's questions. She glanced at her watch, tapped her foot, and asked, "Anything else, Officer?"

"Uhh, yes, uhh, the coroner discovered several bruises on your son's body. Most of these were old and clearly did not occur the night of his death. Do you know how he got these?"

"I don't know anything about any bruises," Loraine said. "That makes a couple of questions. Are you finished, Officer?"

"No, not quite. There's just one more thing, one question that's been bothering me since I first started on this case. No matter how hard I try to imagine it, I can't help but wonder why a man would kill his own son."

"You have a son, you tell me," Loraine said. "Is a father's love so strong that he would never do anything to harm his precious child?" Sarcasm dripped from her words.

Andy didn't take the bait. If he wasn't in full cop mode before this point, he was now. "From what I have observed and heard, your husband had a better than average relationship with his son, especially given the fact that the two of you were separated. I can't help but wonder how he moved so quickly from loving father to murderer."

"Don't you?" Loraine said in a hushed tone. Her entire demeanor changed like she'd thrown some internal switch.

"Excuse me?"

"I thought you had probably figured that out by now, Andy." Her eyes dropped to the floor.

"Figured out what, Loraine?"

"That Gabe wasn't John's son." Tears began rolling down her cheeks.

"Did John know this?" Andy asked.

"Yes. I told him the night he killed him. When I dropped Gabe off at his apartment, he started pressing me for more visitation time. He told me how much Gabe missed him and how much he loved his son and that a boy needs his father more than an odd weekend here or there and a random weeknight whenever I might call and ask if he could watch him. He said he was ready to file formal divorce papers and request either full custody or joint physical custody." She looked up at Andy, her eyes red, the harsh tone she'd used earlier now gone. "But he didn't just say it. He started raising his voice and threatening me. He said no court in the state of Indiana would give a child to a two-bit whore like me and that he wanted his son, and he would get him one way or another."

"What did you say?"

"I told him not to bother. I told him the truth. I told him Gabe was not his son."

"What did he do?" Andy asked.

"He pulled up his hand like he was going to backhand me and called me a lying slut. I told him to go ahead and hit me, and I threatened to take Gabe with me right then and there and never let him see him again. Well, that calmed him down. He started pleading with me not to take his son away. He acted all sorry and begged me not to say such horrible lies, that we could work out a way for Gabe to spend time with both of us, that that's all Gabe really wanted. I told him to believe whatever he wanted to believe. And then I told that son of a bitch to never threaten me again."

"Why didn't you tell this to the detectives when you spoke with them?" Andy asked.

"I couldn't, Andy," she answered, her tone almost pleading. "I was telling him the truth. Gabe wasn't his son. But I couldn't admit something like that to complete strangers. I couldn't have them look at me like that, like I am some kind of whore. I'm not a bad person. I swear it. Yes, I was unfaithful to John a long time ago and ended up pregnant, but it was just one time. I'm not that kind of woman. And, yes, I left him for you, but that was completely different. He pushed me to that. He wasn't the same man anymore. I needed a man. Can you understand that?"

Andy didn't know what to say. He muttered something like, "Yeah, I can," and he even started to move over closer to her to comfort her, but he was afraid of where that might lead, and at this point, he knew he couldn't do anything to screw up the investigation.

Here's the part that gets to me: he believed everything she told him. He believed it as if Mother Teresa had been on that couch telling him this story rather than a woman who wasn't exactly the poster child for honesty and integrity.

"I shouldn't have left Gabe with him that night. I knew I shouldn't leave Gabe there, not after what I'd said. But we had plans, you and me, and I didn't want to break them. I didn't want to disappoint you. I never wanted to disappoint you," she said as she stared into his eyes.

A part of Andy thought she was trying to seduce him, but somehow he knew better. "That's all I need, Loraine. Thank you for your time," he said as he got up to leave. "This helps a lot."

"Andy?" she said in that unmistakable tone that got Andy into this mess six months earlier.

"Yes," he said, turning.

"You won't let him get away with this, will you?"

"No, Loraine. If he did it, I will nail him. I already promised you that."

"He did it," she said. "You know he did it."

"Yeah," Andy said as he headed toward the door to leave. "I think he did."

Andy sat in his car for a few minutes and processed what he'd just heard. In his mind, he'd never been able to figure out how a father, even a bad one, could willingly kill his child. But if the child wasn't his, that changed everything. That also provided the missing piece to the puzzle as to why John would flip out and kill Gabe when he did. Loraine left him six months earlier, and by her own admission, she'd let John know she'd found someone else. Even if she hadn't, Gabe had surely told him about the new man in his mother's life. If John was going to fly into a jealous rage, it surely would have come earlier, during one of these other milestones in their breakup. But it wasn't just jealousy that drove him to kill. If John wasn't Gabe's father, that little boy now represented everything that had destroyed John's life. It all started to make perfect sense to Andy. Now he just needed to find enough evidence to convince Ted Jackson to go to the D.A.'s office for an indictment.

◢ ◢ ◢

LIFE GOT IN the way of Andy building his case, specifically, life as a cop in a small town. The first week of August marked the annual Goat Cheese Festival in Trask. Apparently, back in the early twentieth century, one of Trask's leading families had a large goat cheese operation. They opened a goat-cheese-processing plant just outside of town, and for a while it employed more people than anything else around. As ridiculous as it sounds, at its peak, Trask became known as the "Goat Cheese Capital of Indiana." The goat cheese craze didn't last, but the Goat Cheese Festival did. On the first week of August, the town blocks off the town square, brings in carnival rides and booths selling elephant ears and lemon shake-ups, and celebrates goat cheese. Back in the 1930s or '40s, every food booth had to sell only foods made out of goat cheese, but that didn't last. The festival, however, got bigger every year. By the 1970s, they had a Goat Cheese Festival Queen contest, along with a parade that featured Shriners on minibikes and all the Goat Cheese Queen candidates in convertibles, along with fire trucks from every fire department in the county. Everyone in town loves the Goat Cheese Festival, even if it doesn't have much goat cheese left in it.

Everyone, that is, except the Trask Police Department. The Goat Cheese Festival means pulling double duty for a week straight, along with setting up nonstop nightly patrols across from the bar to watch the carnie workers. At least half a dozen carnies end up in the drunk tank every year. The festival also increases the reports of burglary, assault, and shoplifting. All in all, it is a really fun week for the already overworked police department.

Andy's Goat Cheese Festival week kicked off on Tuesday afternoon around four with a complaint from Harlan Masters, who lived in a house on the northwest corner just off the town square. He called in claiming that some carnies were urinating in his bushes. Andy couldn't drive straight up the square because the road was already blocked with a Tilt-A-Whirl, haunted house, and some kind of a caterpillar ride, so he walked the one block from the station to the square, then up the square to Harlan's house. Andy figured the sight of a cop in uniform might send a message to the carnies putting the rides together that they were being watched. Walking past the carousel, he shot a look at the greasy thirty-something man hanging horses on the poles. *You and these other sons of bitches better watch yourselves, because I am,* Andy said without speaking a word.

"Andy, you've got to do something about these damned carnies," Harlan said as Andy walked up onto his porch. "Every year it's the same damn thing. I don't know why we still have this damn festival. There hasn't been one damn piece of goat cheese eaten in this damn town in fifty damn years." When it came to profanity, Harlan had a rather limited vocabulary.

"I know, I know, Harlan," Andy said. He'd had this same conversation with Harlan every year since he'd joined the force. "You know we'll put on extra patrols, try to keep them off your property."

"That's damn right. This is my property. That damn town square doesn't come over to this side of the street. I should have never bought this damn house. Thanks to this damn goat cheese, I can't sell it. What kind of damn fool wants to live next door to the goat cheese festival." Andy heard the same rant every year. "HEY! You damn carnie, get away from there. Don't you go pissing on my tree," Harlan yelled to a carnival worker walking down the street.

"Now, Harlan, if you want, you can put up a sign that says 'private property,' and ask people politely not to come up into your yard. The carnival workers who come here every year already know to stay off your property. I will make sure they get the word out to the newbies," Andy said.

"I would like that," Harlan said. "Thanks, Andy. I know you're the only one around here who hates this damned festival as much as I do." Then, turning his attention to another worker walking down the street, he yelled from his porch, "Stay off my yard. This is private property, not some damn public restroom."

"I'll see you, Mr. Masters," Andy said as he walked off Harlan's porch and made his way down the other side of the town square.

The festival didn't officially begin until the next day, but the square was already filled with activity as the carnival workers put the finishing touches on the rides. "Hi, how are you?" Andy posed to two men working on the motor of the Ferris wheel. They did not respond. "How are you this afternoon?" he said to a familiar-looking heavyset woman cleaning the glass on the dunk tank. She wore a flower print blouse whose flowers had long since faded into something more like light spots than flowers, along with a well-worn denim skirt that was frayed along the hemline.

"Fine, thank you," she said with a smile that hadn't seen a dentist's chair in years. "And you, Officer?"

"Couldn't be better," Andy lied. After five years on the force, and five years of Goat Cheese Festivals, Andy recognized the faces of many of the workers. The same carnival company came through year after year, and they retained a surprising number of their employees.

Halfway down the west side of the square, another crew had set up an open-sided tent in a town parking lot. Under the tent were tables and chairs. It looked like a food booth, only larger. Andy walked over to check it out, but stopped short at a sign hung on the flap of the tent: REDEEMER'S HOUSE OF DELIVERANCE. WELCOME. Ducking under the tent, he discovered that the group was indeed serving food, but this wasn't another elephant ear and lemon shake-up booth. A group of men and women were preparing meals for the carnival workers. Looking around, Andy noticed there wasn't a cash register anywhere. The meal was free. He walked up to the serving counter to find out more about what was going on, when the man dishing ice into plastic cups said, "Hello, Officer Myers. I was hoping I might run into you here today."

The sight of John Phillips took Andy aback. It was his first time seeing him, much less speaking to him, since John had moved from *suspicious* to *guilty* in Andy's mind. Andy could feel his heart beating in his ears, his face flushed red. *Dammit,* he cursed to himself, *don't give too much away.* He wanted to drag John out from behind the counter and beat the crap out of him; he wanted to yell, *Yeah, I'd hoped I would run into you, you child-killing son of a bitch, wanted to run into you at about seventy miles per hour.* He wanted to do and say all kinds of things, but he didn't. Andy kept his composure and asked, "So what are you guys doing here, this afternoon?"

"We're out here for the carnies," John said. "They spend so much time on the road that we wanted to give them a good, home-cooked meal. Just a simple way to show them how much God loves them."

"Well, that sounds real nice." Andy laid it on thick. "I'm sure they will appreciate it."

"I think they will. It's our first year to do something like this in Trask. About five years ago someone got the idea of giving the carnival workers a meal on the night they set everything up over in Crosse during their September Apple Festival. That's the last stop of the season for a lot of the carnies. The meal went over so well, we thought we ought to try doing the same thing for some small-town festivals. This is our first year in Trask. Hopefully, it won't be our last," John said.

*If I have anything to do with it, it will be* your *last,* Andy thought, but he didn't say it. He just smiled and said, "That's great. That's a real nice thing you're doing. Most people look at the carnies as a nuisance, if they look at them at all."

"That's right, that's right," John said. "You're welcome to come back over in a half hour when we start serving, if you would like. I know you're a single man. There are some great cooks in our church. We've got fried chicken and mashed potatoes and gravy and sweet potato pie. You don't want to miss a meal like this."

John's statement took Andy by surprise. *How in the hell did he know I'm single,* Andy wondered. "Er, what? Uh…yeah, yeah, I might just do that. Nothing I like more than a hunk of sweet potato pie," he lied. "Well, John, I've got to get back to the station. It sure was good seeing you again, and under better circumstances at that. By the way, are you doing okay? It must be hell, I mean, heck, to lose your son the way you did. Walking in and finding him lying there in all that blood could sure haunt a man for a long time. How are you getting along?"

"Thank you for your concern, Officer," John said, smiling. "That means a lot to me that you're worried about me. It's been tough, but I'm hanging in there. I don't know where I would be without God's promises and the hope they give me."

"Good. Good," Andy said. "Well, if you ever need to talk to anyone, I'm always around."

"The same goes for me, Officer. I'm available if you need to talk. I have the hope that God gives through Jesus to carry me through. I'm afraid you don't have that, and I don't know how you can see the things you see on your job without it," John said.

Andy couldn't maintain the little show any longer. He'd gone past his tolerance for small talk with murderers, and his eyes showed it. "That's very nice of you. I will keep that in mind," Andy said as he turned and walked back onto the town square heading toward the police station.

# CHAPTER

THE FIRST COUPLE days of the Goat Cheese Festival passed without any major incidents. Andy had to make another visit to Harlan Master's house after someone stole his Private Property, No Trespassing sign and he had to break up a fight between a couple of fifteen-year-old boys. Testosterone and Mountain Dew are never a good combination. Other than that, Wednesday and Thursday of the festival were pretty much business as usual for this time of year.

Friday night, however, was "Wristband Night," and "Wristband Night" was always the biggest night for both attendance and trouble. You could buy a wristband for three bucks and ride all of the rides for free. Every Trask police officer had to work that Friday night. Since Andy had more seniority than anyone other than the chief, he pulled the plum assignment, working undercover at the festival. Undercover didn't exactly mean undercover, since everyone in town knew him. All this meant was that Andy and three other officers didn't have to wear their uniforms. Instead, Andy got to wear his favorite pair of Levi's and a Trask Tigers T-shirt and walk around the festival gorging himself on hot dogs, corn dogs, and Pepsi, like any other good resident of Trask. Two uniformed officers were also on duty, but the chief didn't want to flood the place with cops and take away from the townspeople's ability to have a good time.

The carnival opened at 4:00 and closed at 11:00 p.m., with wristbands going on sale at 5:00 p.m. Andy arrived at four-thirty and checked in with the other undercover officers and the Trask police chief, a sad-eyed Trask native named Ed Spence. Spence assigned each of them a quadrant of the town square, which they would work for an hour, before rotating counterclockwise to the next quadrant. "The Goat Cheese Queen is supposed to show up around six," Spence reminded them, "so everyone keep your eyes open for her. Remember last year when one of the girls who lost came up and pelted her with dog poop. We don't want that to happen to our queen again. So keep your eyes open." After the briefing, Spence went home. I guess he figured, since he was the chief, that was his privilege.

Andy's night started in the northeast corner of the town square, which placed him right between the kettle corn booth (his favorite) and old man Master's house (the royal pain in the butt). He stuck pretty close to the kettle corn, but by his third bag, he thought he ought to walk around a little more before he made himself sick. Most of the people in this quadrant of the carnival were under four feet tall, since it was the kiddy-ride section. He walked across the street to the pony ride on the vacant lot on the far east side of the square, sat on a bench, and watched. His stomach ached from too much kettle corn, but that didn't stop him from daydreaming about a corn dog. The crowd had steadily grown over the past hour, and although it would be larger still by seven, it was already large enough that you couldn't walk far without bumping into someone. He hadn't sat on the bench long before someone's butt knocked his arm off the bench seat back. "Excuse me," a young woman said, a boy in tow beside her, "I didn't see you there."

"That's all right, miss." That's when Andy recognized the boy. "Miss Paul, isn't it?" he said.

"Yes?" she said in a voice that hinted that she should recognize him, but she was also suspicious of any stranger who called her by name.

"I'm sorry. I'm Andy Myers. You probably don't recognize me out of my uniform. We met a couple of weeks ago at your apartment complex in the middle of the night. I was the first police officer on the scene for—"

She cut him off. Andy figured it was because she didn't want the sound of Gabe's name to upset her son. "Oh, yes, I do remember you. It's good to see you again."

"So, are the two of you here by yourselves?"

"Yes, sir." She called him "sir," like Andy was an old man. I guess he looked that way to her. "My son loves coming to the carnival. This is the only night I could get off to take him."

Andy smiled. "I'm not that thrilled at being here, but I have to be. Duty calls. I'm stuck here at the festival until it closes." Then an idea popped into his head. "If you wouldn't mind, I could sure use some company," he said. "Time drags by with no one to talk to."

Miss Paul looked down at her son, Brian, who clutched her hand. To Andy, the kid acted a lot younger than Gabe. He seemed very skittish, unnaturally so. "What do you think, Brian? Would you mind if the officer tags along with us?"

Before Brian could answer, Andy said, "Tell you what, it will be my treat. And you can tell me to get lost if I overstay my welcome. Have you ridden anything yet, Brian?"

The boy shook his head no.

"What would you like to ride first?"

Brian pointed toward the Tilt-A-Whirl.

"That sounds great. Why don't we go get ourselves some wristbands and ride the Tilt-A-Whirl?" Andy threw the whole "watch one quadrant for an hour and rotate counterclockwise" thing out the window. He had more important things to do than guard the Goat Cheese Queen from getting sprayed with poop.

The boy still acted hesitant, but he and his mother walked with Andy over to the ticket booth. "Three wristbands, please," Andy said as he plunked down a ten-dollar bill. He handed bands to Brian and his mother. "You know, in all the confusion the other night, I didn't catch your first name," Andy said to her.

"Kim," she replied.

"Okay, Kim, do you feel up to the Tilt-A-Whirl?" Andy asked.

"Not really," she said. "Those round-and-round rides make me sick. I think I'll just watch, and the two of you can ride it."

"Fair enough. What do you think about that, Brian?" Andy offered. The boy nodded his head yes. I think the Tilt-A-Whirl helped him warm up to my old man, since he wouldn't have been able to ride it without him. The kid's mother wasn't going to get on it, and she probably didn't have enough money on her to spring for the wristbands. Andy took the kid's hand, and the two got in line. It had been a long time since Andy had ridden any of these rides, but he remembered that getting on anything wilder than a park bench probably wasn't a good idea with a belly full of kettle corn. Of course, by this point it was too late. Besides, he needed something more than company. This boy might well hold the key to proving John Phillips killed Gabe.

The line moved quickly. Within five minutes Andy and Brian were strapped into the red car with the curved roof hanging over the top of them. Andy's stomach began to gurgle as the round ride top began to slowly move. The faster it went, the more the kettle corn started moving, and the more Brian started squealing and laughing. "Make it spin, make it spin," he yelled to Andy. They grabbed the wheel in front of them and set the car in even more motion than the inertia of the ride produced. A couple of minutes into the ride, they had their car spinning around and around, as the entire ride moved faster and faster. *Oh, God, I think I'm going to hurl,* Andy kept thinking. He could feel the upper sides of his cheeks pushing in and his gag reflex springing into motion. "This is great," Brian yelled as he threw his arms straight over his head, and his body pushed up tight to Andy's from the centrifugal force of the ride. "Wheeeeeeeeeee," Brian said. *Oh, God, make it stop*, Andy thought.

Finally the ride slowed to a stop. Brian sprang up out of his seat and darted over to his mother. Andy staggered off the ride, his head and stomach still spinning in opposite directions from one another. "Been a while since you've been on the Tilt-A-Whirl, Officer Myers?" Kim Paul laughed.

"Uhh, yeah," Andy said. He pulled his hand up to his mouth, trying to regain his composure and his stomach. "Yeah, that's a great ride, if you're eight. And call me Andy." He and Kim both laughed. "Well," he said slowly, "what's it going to be next, Brian? And please, nothing that spins around in a circle for a while."

"I'm hungry," Brian said. "Can we get something to eat?"

Andy grabbed his mouth and suppressed a belch. "Sure," he said, "anything you want."

Neither Kim nor Brian ever told Andy to get lost. Brian was having so much fun that his mother let him stay at the carnival until it closed at eleven, rather than taking him home at nine, like she'd originally planned. By the end of the evening, Brian was pulling Andy toward different rides. It seemed pretty clear to Andy that the kid didn't get a lot of attention from a father figure, and the kid ate up the attention Andy gave him. The way the mother talked, she'd gotten pregnant in high school, and the boy's father had never shown much interest in him. She had to drop out of school, but the father graduated and went to Indiana University, in Bloomington, on a scholarship. Four years later he took a job in Colorado, and she never heard from him again. Now she had to work two jobs to keep a roof over their heads, which meant Brian spent a lot of time by himself. Andy just listened to her story without sharing any of his own. As far as fathers went, he wasn't any better than Brian's, but Kim didn't need to know that.

When the carnival closed, Andy offered to drive Kim and Brian back to their apartment. She declined his offer, but Brian asked if they could see one another again sometime. "Sure," Andy said, "I can guarantee that." Brian smiled, never suspecting Andy had any other motives. And Andy kept his word. Over the next few weeks he showed up more and more often at the Paul apartment. He began showering on Brian some of the attention he once showed Gabe. And by the time Ted Jackson finally got around to interviewing Brian in the presence of the boy's mother, Andy's efforts paid off.

# CHAPTER

## 9

ABOUT THREE WEEKS after the Goat Cheese Festival, Ted Jackson called Andy and invited him to lunch. The two hadn't talked since Ted told Andy he needed more evidence, which really didn't fit the obsessive way my old man had approached this case. That doesn't mean Andy let it rest. No. He was simply trying a little more subtle approach with Ted and the other detectives assigned to this case. Ted's reaction to Andy's news that there was an "earwitness" to the murder pretty much convinced my old man no one in the sheriff's department wanted to do the heavy lifting in the investigation. It wasn't enough to point them in the right direction and hope they followed the trail. Andy knew he had to drop the evidence right in their lap. Even then, they would need a little extra encouragement to even see what he'd given them.

Ted drove over to Trask and met Andy at the Bluebird Diner on Main Street. At least that's what it's called now. I'm not sure what they called it back then. Ted arrived first, and ended up waiting nearly fifteen minutes for Andy.

"Sorry. I got called out right before I was headed in this direction," Andy said. That was a lie. He'd been in the back of the police station watching Bob Barker give away fabulous prizes on that day's showcase. Making Ted wait was nothing more than a little mind game Andy decided to play with his old friend.

"That's all right, I know how that goes," Ted said. "So what's good in this place these days?" He glanced at the stain-encrusted menu.

"Everything," Andy said, laughing.

"They still have those giant tenderloin sandwiches, where the meat is three times the size of the bun?" Ted asked.

"Always. And the breading on the tenderloin is thicker than the meat itself."

"Sounds good and healthy. Think I'll have that." Ted shoved the menu back behind the napkin holder.

"Mmmm, why not?" Andy motioned toward the waitress, who came over and greeted them with a big "hi, y'all" in a thick Kentucky accent. Sometimes the line between Indiana and Kentucky gets pretty blurry. Andy ordered their tenderloin sandwiches along with fries and iced teas.

After the waitress left, Ted said, "I've got some bad news for you, Andy."

"That's a hell of a lunchtime conversation starter. Really sets the old taste buds on edge."

"Yeah, whatever. I'm serious. The case against John Phillips doesn't look so good," Ted said.

"What? Why?" Andy said.

"The guy's a frickin' Eagle Scout, that's why. I must have talked to everybody in this dumpy little town who ever met him, and they all say the same thing."

"Have you talked to Brian Paul, like I asked you to?" Andy asked.

Ted sighed. "Not yet. I will. I will. I promise. But I don't know what good it will do. Everything I've uncovered about John Phillips says the guy would cross the street to keep from stepping on a ladybug."

"I'm not buying that, Jax," Andy said.

"Suit yourself. But you ought to hear the stories. Hell, I know how much time you've spent out at Madison Park, you've probably heard the stories," Ted said.

"Like the guy whose old Pinto broke down and he didn't have a way to work, which meant he would lose his job and his apartment, and he and his girlfriend had a baby on the way and he would have probably started selling drugs or breaking into rich people's houses to make ends meet if John Phillips hadn't stepped in and offered to take the guy to work every day, even though it was way out of his way and he even paid to get the guy's car fixed? Yeah. I heard that one," Andy said.

"And did you hear the one about the single mom that was about to get tossed out for not paying her rent, and John paid it for her?" Ted asked.

"And how he fed carnival workers. And how he volunteers in a weekend youth basketball program in inner-city Indy. And how he walks on water and leaps tall buildings with a single bound. Hell yes, I've heard them all. So what?" Andy said.

"So what? I'll tell you so what. A guy who carries an old lady's groceries in for her during a thunderstorm doesn't exactly fit the picture of a man who could smash his son's head in with a dresser drawer. You wanted me to investigate the case. I've investigated the case. I followed the evidence. And the evidence tells me this guy is not a killer," Ted said.

"I think you're missing the whole point, Jax," Andy said.

"Great. The chief detective of the *Trask* Police Department is going to lecture me on following the evidence," Ted said.

"Go to hell. You don't have that much more experience than me. I could have jumped over to county the same time you did—hell, even before you did—but I chose to stay here. I *chose* to stay," Andy said.

"I know, I know, I was out of line," Ted said.

"That's all right. But think about it, Jax. It doesn't mean a rat's ass how many poor, starving people John Phillips feeds or how much good work he does. The guy's history, his own police record, shows he is prone to fits of rage where he is capable of doing anything. *Anything.* If his buddies in the bar in Pendleton eight years ago hadn't pulled him off some guy back then, he would already have one murder rap, and wouldn't have had an opportunity to commit a second," Andy said.

"But the man has changed," Ted protested.

"Yeah, he's cleaned up his act. Cut out the booze. Got all religious. Gone respectable. But are you telling me that something couldn't still set him off, something that would make him so mad that there is no limit to what he could do? The guy still has a trigger. He may have buried it pretty deep, but it is still there. If someone hit him hard enough, hurt him bad enough, they could set it off," Andy said with a self-confidence that spoke more than his words.

"What? Do you know something you haven't told me yet?" Ted asked, taking the bait.

"You need to talk to Loraine Phillips again. Ask her to tell you everything that happened that night."

"I think we got a pretty full statement from her already," Ted said.

"No. Ask her about the argument she had with John when she dropped Gabe off earlier that evening. Ask her very specifically about what she said about Gabe's relationship to John," Andy said.

"Andy, I've already told you, bitter ex-wives are capable of saying anything. You're lucky. Your ex-wife quietly left the state and leaves you alone. We all aren't that fortunate."

"Ask her, Jax. I don't care how much of a mister nice guy someone is, anyone who hears what she told him would probably lose it. The old rageaholic in him had to come storming back with a vengeance. And I do mean vengeance."

"What did she say?" Ted asked.

"Nah, I won't tell you. You have to ask her yourself." The waitress placed two iced teas, two straws, and a handful of sugar packets on the table, then walked away. Andy took a long drink of his tea, without sugar. He always drank his tea without sugar, I'm not sure how he could stomach it. Then he said, "And before you go crowning John Phillips as Boy Scout of the year, you need to talk to a Miss Angela Peters."

"Who's that?" Ted asked.

"A hooker. At least she used to be a hooker. She's off the streets now, thanks to John," Andy said.

"Doesn't that just confirm what I've already said about him?" Ted countered.

"Not exactly. Talk to her. Here's her address and phone number," Andy said as he slid a piece of paper across the table. "She lives over on the west side of Indy now. Used to walk the streets downtown. She was one of the lost souls John brought home to save."

"Oh, yeah, the last straw Loraine Phillips talked about in her statement," Ted said.

"Yep. 'The hooker was the last straw.' That's her," Andy said.

Now it was Ted's turn to ask, "So what?"

"So she was very appreciative of John's efforts to save her," Andy said.

"And…"

"And she showed it, shall we say, in ways which she'd refined during her professional career, if you catch my drift," Andy said.

"How did you find this out?" Ted asked.

"She told me. Said she would swear to it in court."

"Holy crap," Ted said.

"Exactly," Andy replied as their sandwiches arrived.

"One more thing," Andy said.

Ted shook his head. "What now?"

"Talk to the kid Brian Paul. You have to talk to this kid."

"Don't tell me you've interrogated him already? I thought you were going to leave that to me," Ted said as he dumped ketchup on the fries that came with his tenderloin sandwich.

"I ran into him and his mother the other day. They brought it up, not me. I told them to call you. You need to hear what this boy wants to say," Andy said.

"Which is…?"

"Three words," Andy said, "pattern of abuse. It seems our Mr. Phillips really does lead two lives. And that second life is going to land his ass in jail for a very long time."

"Are you sure about all of this, Andy? And if you are, why haven't you come to me with it before now?" Ted said.

"Why do you think? I gave you a lead on a witness almost a month ago, and you haven't done a damn thing with it yet. Yes, I'm sure. Check it out. Talk to these people, then put it together with the physical evidence you have, and tell me what you've got," Andy said.

"It sounds like we would have a pretty good case," Ted said.

Andy just smiled in response, then took a big bite of his tenderloin.

◂ ◂ ◂

ANDY HAD ANOTHER ACE in the hole that he didn't mention to Ted Jackson because Jackson already knew about it. Jackson just didn't know that he knew it. And that ace was named Reginald Chambliss, the Harris County district attorney. Chambliss grew up in a tiny wide spot in the road called Silver City, in very rural Harris County. The town sounds like it ought to be out in Nevada or California or anyplace where they actually mine silver. But Silver City got its name from some guy with the last name of Silver that thought he ought to have a town named after himself. The last of the Silvers died off eons ago, and the fourteen houses, one post office, and two used-car lots that make up the town bear zero resemblance to a city, but that's what they call the place. Chambliss grew up there, and I guess he took the jokes about his hometown pretty personally, because after graduating from Indiana University School of Law, he came back to the area determined to make a name for himself. He had that air of self-importance that made him refuse to allow anyone to call him Reggie or Reg. He was Reginald Chambliss, Esquire. Honestly, I think his entire goal in life was to see a sign go up on the way into his hometown that said: SILVER CITY, HOME OF REGINALD CHAMBLISS, BENEVOLENT

DICTATOR OF THE WORLD, or, at least, PAST GOVERNOR OF THE
GREAT STATE OF INDIANA. I guess what I'm trying to say is, the
guy had political ambitions that went way beyond the Harris County District Attorney's Office. And everybody knew
it, especially every cop in the county.

There's only one problem with political ambitions in a
place like Harris County, Indiana. No one outside the county
knows or cares about who runs what. Even the people living
in the county don't really care. I would say nine out of ten
people who vote for any office smaller than lieutenant governor don't have a clue about who they are voting for. They see
a familiar name or party under the heading of county com-
missioner or cemetery board of directors, and they punch
the hole next to it. Any politician who wants to expand his
field of influence has to get noticed in a big way. And the best
way for a district attorney to get noticed is by successfully
prosecuting a case that captures the attention and imagination of those living beyond their little slice of paradise.
Andy knew this case had that kind of potential. And he was
right. Heck, if Geraldo had heard about it, the case might
have gained national attention.

Unlike their previous meetings, Ted Jackson didn't ignore
Andy's leads this time around. And neither did the D.A.'s
office. Two weeks to the day after their lunch at the Bluebird,
Andy was called in out of the field and told to report to the
Trask police station. He knew something big was up when
the dispatcher didn't make that call. The big chief himself
radioed Andy and asked him to come to his office. Reporting to the Trask police chief's office isn't nearly as big a deal
as it might sound. The entire police station consists of three
rooms and two holding cells (yes, just like Mayberry). The

chief's office isn't much bigger than a converted walk-in closet.

"What's up, Ed?" Andy asked as he tapped on the door frame of the chief's office door. Andy was the only person on the force who called the chief by his first name. They'd known each other forever, and Andy had been on the force longer than anyone else, except for Ed Spence. Formal titles just didn't seem to fit.

"Yeah, Andy, come on in," Spence said. "I've got someone here who needs to talk to you."

As he stepped inside, Andy was surprised to see Reginald Chambliss in the flesh sitting in the far chair in front of the chief's desk. Chambliss stood and stuck out his hand. "It's good to finally meet you, Officer Myers. I've heard a lot about you."

Andy was struck by how Chambliss appeared so much smaller than his reputation. That's not to say he was a short man, but from all the talk Andy had heard about him, both in inner-office gossip and through the newspaper, he expected to see a combination of John Wayne and "Iron" Mike Ditka. Instead, he discovered a very average-looking lawyer, maybe five feet, ten inches tall, 170 pounds, wearing a blue off-the-rack JCPenney suit, with a yellow paisley tie and black wingtip shoes. He was hardly the overwhelming physical presence Andy expected.

"No, sir, the pleasure is all mine," Andy said as he shook his hand.

"Sit down, sit down, both of you," Chief Spence said. Turning to Andy, he said, "Mr. Chambliss and I have been discussing that incident out at Madison Park a couple of months ago. He tells me that the sheriff's department nearly dropped the ball on it, that they were ready to dismiss it as an accident and let it go at that, but you wouldn't let it go. He said you suspected something more and you kept digging until you found—"

Chambliss interrupted. He wasn't the kind of man who could allow a conversation to drag on very long without contributing to it. "That's right, Officer Myers. I've spent a lot of time with Ted Jackson the past couple of weeks and he brought me up to date on both the evidence and the testimony he has uncovered thus far. Good man, that Jackson. Gave you most of the credit for the leads he's been following."

"Ted's a good guy," Andy said. "He and I started on the force right here in Trask together an eternity ago."

"That's what he said," Chambliss said. "Now listen, Andy, I don't have a lot of time so I'm going to cut right to the chase. I'm ready to issue an arrest warrant for John Phillips for murder one. I don't even think this one will be close. The real kicker came yesterday. I listened in as Ted questioned that boy from next door, what's his name?"

"Brian Paul," Andy said.

"Yeah, that's it, Brian. He's a brave little boy. My heart went out to him. Can you imagine it, watching his best friend being murdered by his friend's own father? I was a little skeptical about how much he would be able to see through that hole he said he and the Phillips boy had bored through the wall between their closets. Then I looked through it myself this morning…" Chambliss shook his head in disbelief. "Open-and-shut case, I would say. If the guy's smart, he will plead out. If he doesn't, I plan on going after a death sentence."

"We've never had anything like that around here," Chief Spence said. "Hell, this is our first murder in nearly fifty years."

"I hope it's another fifty years before you have another one," the D.A. said.

"Amen to that," the chief replied. These two guys had political schmoozing down to an art form.

"Anyway, Officer Myers, I just stopped by on my way back to the office to thank you for your diligence in this case." The D.A. stood to leave. "Oh, and I almost forgot. Since Phillips lives over in Crosse in the next county, the state police will have to be present for the arrest after the warrants have been issued. How would you like to be there when they bring him in? I can probably arrange that for you."

"I would like that very much," Andy said. "All I've ever wanted was justice for Gabriel Phillips. I want to be there when it happens."

"An arrest is a long way from a conviction," the D.A. said, "but I'll make sure you're there. The warrant should be issued by tomorrow morning, and I'd like to bring him in sometime early in the afternoon." Turning to the chief, he said, "You think you can live without Officer Myers here tomorrow afternoon, say between noon and three?" The times didn't surprise Andy. If you wanted a story to get maximum exposure on the local television newscasts, you planned it for early afternoon. That way, the news crews could get their videotapes back to the station for editing in time for the six o'clock news. If the story broke much earlier, it might get buried on the noon news with the farm reports and all the other excitement of the morning. Much later, and it wouldn't air until the late news after half the voters had gone to bed. For a guy from a nothing little town in the middle of nowhere, Chambliss had pretty good media savvy.

Ed Spence smiled. "Not a problem."

"Good. I'll make it happen." Chambliss did some farewell handshaking as he exited. Like any good politician, he never left a room without pressing some flesh.

"Why the hell didn't you keep me posted on what you were doing with the Phillips case," Spence said to Andy after Chambliss was out of earshot. "Damned D.A. came in here talking about the case like I knew what was going on. Hell, I didn't know anything. I just had to smile and fake it." The chief's ears turned red when he was mad, and now they looked like they were glowing. "Don't ever pull that kind of Lone Ranger crap again. Got it, Andy?"

"Sorry, Chief," Andy said. "This one was pretty personal to me. I guess I was a little uneasy about sharing too much information."

"Well, you sure as hell didn't have any trouble sharing it with your buddies over in Adamsburg, now did ya? If you want to go to work for Taylor Van Dyne [which was the sheriff's name] I can probably arrange that."

"No, sir. You know I like it here just fine. I'm sorry." Andy kicked it into full butt-kissing mode. "It won't happen again."

"You're damn right it won't," Spence growled.

# CHAPTER

## 10

THE NEXT DAY was like Christmas and the Fourth of July rolled into one for Andy. He bounced out of bed before his alarm went off, cranked up Boston on his home stereo, and started getting ready for work. The music was loud enough for him to sing along to "More than a Feeling" in the shower, but he turned it down once "Long Time" came on so he could hear the phone if it started ringing. It did, right on cue between sides one and two of the album. "Mr. Andy Myers?" a female secretary's voice said.

"Speaking," Andy replied.

"Please hold for the district attorney."

Less than a minute later the big man himself got on the phone. "Good morning, Andy," Reginald Chambliss said. "I trust you slept well."

"Like a baby, sir," Andy said.

"Good, good. You must be a little like me. There's nothing that sets my spirits to soaring like the thought of finally getting to nail some son of a bitch that I know is guilty as sin."

Andy smiled. "That's exactly right, sir. Last night was the best night's sleep I've had since I walked into that apartment and found that kid lying there dead."

"Just wait until we get our conviction. You talk about sweet. Ahhh, there's nothing quite like it. But I'm not telling you anything you probably don't already know. How long have you been a policeman there in Trask?" Chambliss said.

"Just under seven years, sir."

"Then you know what I'm talking about. You've put away your share of bad guys over the years, haven't you, Andy?"

"But none as big as this one," Andy said.

Although he couldn't see it, since they were on the phone, Andy imagined a huge smile just broke across the D.A.'s lips. "No, they don't get much bigger than this in terms of the splash they make when they fall," Chambliss said. "Our Mr. Phillips thought he'd cooked up quite a clever scheme, thought he could get away with murder. I guess we're about to show him, aren't we?"

"Yes, sir," Andy said.

"Well, listen, the reason I called, you need to be at the Harris County sheriff's office by noon this afternoon. You're going to ride over with Ted Jackson. The state police will lead the way, but our guys will make the actual arrest. I also would like for you to stand behind me during my news conference after we have him in custody back here in Adamsburg," Chambliss said. These guys always liked to have cops as a backdrop when they made headlines. It gave them that real law-and-order image voters are so wild about.

"I'll be there, sir. And again, I cannot tell you how much I appreciate your letting me be a part of this today," Andy said.

"You've earned it," Chambliss replied. "We wouldn't even have a case if it weren't for you."

"That's very kind of you to say," Andy replied. Their conversation ended with more nauseating small talk.

The one thing that gave Andy a charge more than anything else about John Phillips's arrest was the fact that the guy never saw it coming. He never had a clue. Of course, he should have. It didn't exactly take a Ben Matlock (I'm sorry for all the old television references. I'm nuts about old shows) to figure out that he was the prime suspect from the word "go." In addition to his interrogation the night of Gabe's death, or should I say the morning of his death, sheriff's department detectives had questioned him more than a half-dozen times. They'd asked him about his argument with Loraine earlier the evening of Gabe's death; he acted shocked that anyone would think such a thing had happened. They'd asked him about his fingerprints on the back of the drawer; he had some story about fixing it the day before. They'd asked him about the former prostitute's allegations that he'd demanded sex from her in repayment for getting her off the streets; he said anyone who knows him knows that is impossible.

But most of all, they asked him about the night Gabe died and the things the neighbors said they heard. Both Brian Paul and Crazy Cathy, the two neighbors on either side of John's apartment, said they heard Gabe let out a bloodcurdling cry of "No, Daddy. Please, no, Daddy," just before the banging and bumping started. John teared up on that one. He said something about how nightmares terrorized his little boy and how he wished he could have set him free from them. In all the times the detectives questioned John, not once did he ever ask to have an attorney with him. They read him his rights. They asked if he understood them and if he had any questions about them, but he always said the same thing in response, "I have absolutely nothing to hide."

You would think after so much questioning, John would have figured out that the police had him in their sights, but he didn't. It didn't dawn on him until four state police cruisers pulled up in front of the window factory where he worked on Highway 8, between Crosse and Indianapolis. A Harris County sheriff's car pulled in behind them, along with a couple of Crosse city cops. One of the guys John worked with, some stoner named Sonny, thought it was a raid and shot up to the rafters to hide. I don't think he came down for a couple of days. But John never moved from his workstation, not when he saw through the large windows in the front of the plant police cars pulling up, and not when he saw the parade of police officers come through the factory's doors and start walking toward him. And not when he saw Andy Myers looking directly at him as he made his way toward John with the rest of the crowd.

"John Phillips?" Ted Jackson said as he walked up to John.

"Yes, Detective Jackson, you know that's who I am. We've talked several times," John said. And then he added something that shows just how clueless he really was, "Hello, Officer Myers. It's good to see you today."

"John Phillips," Ted Jackson continued, "I have a warrant for your arrest for the murder of Gabriel Phillips."

Andy lived off the high of that moment for a long time. He said John's face went completely white and his jaw nearly hit the floor. "What?" John asked. "There has to be some kind of mistake. I didn't kill my son. I've told you that many, many times. My son died when he struck his head falling out of bed . . ."

A state trooper walked behind John, pulled his arms back, and handcuffed him as Ted Jackson said, "Mr. Phillips, you have the right to remain silent. If you give up the right to remain silent, anything you say can and will be used against you in a court of law. You have the right to have an attorney present during questioning. If you cannot afford an attorney, the state will assign one to your case. Do you understand these rights, Mr. Phillips?"

"I don't understand how you can think I killed my son. Officer Myers, you were there that night. Tell them. You saw how my son had fallen out of his bed and struck his head against a drawer." John's voice had a pleading quality to it, but he didn't sound desperate. Andy wanted him to sound desperate. He didn't answer John's request. Andy just stood back and took the whole thing in, like a Yankee fan enjoying a September sweep of the Red Sox.

"I'm afraid you gentlemen have made a terrible mistake," John said.

"Do you understand your rights as they have been explained to you, Mr. Phillips?" Jackson asked.

"How did you ever conclude that I could have harmed my little boy? I love my son," John said.

"Mr. Phillips, do you understand your rights as they have been explained to you?" Jackson asked again, firmer this time.

"Yes. Yes," John said. "I understand them." He turned and looked at Andy. "Officer Myers, please. You knew my son. Tell them that this is a mistake. Tell them that I would never do anything to harm Gabe." Andy ignored his request. Instead, he walked toward the door, following the lead of the other police officers.

The state trooper who'd cuffed John took him by his shoulder. "Please come with me," he said as he led John out the factory door. As soon as they walked out into the sunshine, camera crews from all three local network affiliate Indianapolis television stations jumped in front of them. The cameras followed John down the sidewalk from the factory door to the parking lot, across the lot, and up to a waiting police car. Their microphones recorded the trooper saying, "Watch your head" as he pushed down on John's head, placing him in the backseat. Unlike the classic arrest scenes that play out on the local news, John didn't try to hide his face or block the cameras with his hand. He walked with his head held high, a confident look on his face. Andy took the look on his face as one more example of John's arrogance, as though he'd covered his tracks so well that no one would ever be able to prove what he'd done.

Once John was in the state trooper's car, one of the reporters yelled, "Mr. Phillips, do you have anything to say about the very serious charges brought against you?"

His response became his basic defense throughout his trial. "I've done nothing wrong, and I have nothing to hide. The people who know me know I could never do anything like this. But ultimately, God is my judge. He's in control. He will take care of me through this." Andy remembered that line because this wasn't the last time he heard it. Far from it.

The camera crews were back out in force for Reginald Chambliss's news conference, along with print reporters from both Indianapolis papers, as well as the daily papers from Adamsburg and Crosse. The owner/editor/chief reporter from the weekly Trask paper also showed up. Good ole Chambliss; he was quite the politician. He went out of his way to take questions from the little Trask one-man operation. I guess he wanted to bill himself as the friend of the little man in his still-unannounced, but already planned, upcoming campaign.

But the print guys weren't Chambliss's first concern. He held his news conference for the cameras, and once they started rolling, he hit his groove. After walking up to the podium—and he wore a much nicer suit than the one he'd had on when Andy met him—Chambliss introduced all of the "fine law enforcement officers" behind him "who worked so diligently to make sure justice was served for poor little Gabriel Phillips." He then proceeded to brief all those in attendance on the basics of the case. If the version I heard of this day was correct, the guy used the phrase "poor little Gabriel Phillips" a couple dozen times before he ever took his first question. Poor little Gabriel Phillips was "a small boy who'd suffered a lifetime of abuse," a boy "too small to defend himself," and a child "who suffered the misfortune of becoming the means by which the man he considered to be his father exacted his revenge against poor little Gabriel Phillips's mother."

As if on cue, the reporters asked if the prosecutor's office would seek the death penalty. "I believe the facts of the case will show that this appalling, vicious act of violence was a premeditated act that will, under the Supreme Court guidelines, qualify as a capital murder case. Therefore, yes, I will seek the ultimate punishment and deterrent the state of

Indiana has to offer: the electric chair," Chambliss replied. All in all, it made for great theater. Andy soaked it all in as he stood behind Chambliss on the podium. He'd waited for this day for a long time and he wanted to enjoy every moment of it.

One incident occurred later, however, that took some of the luster off that afternoon for Andy. After the news conference, he walked down to Ted Jackson's office to try to talk his old friend into going out and getting a drink after they were both off duty. By this point, Andy had completely given up the charade of sticking to the twelve steps. Ted wasn't in his office, and his secretary thought he may be over in the processing room checking on the status of a couple of prisoners from cases on which he'd been working. Andy went off to find him. As he walked through the main door of the processing area, his eyes caught those of John Phillips, who was in the far side of the room. John was now wearing the distinctive orange jumpsuit inmates love so much. Yeah, I'm being sarcastic. John was just standing there, his hands cuffed in front of him, although his legs were not in irons. He appeared to Andy to be waiting for one of the officers to finish some paperwork before taking him back to a cell.

The sight of John sort of surprised Andy. He hadn't expected to see him again so soon. When their eyes met, a funny thing happened. Andy had hoped to see the pangs of guilt eating away at the guy. Instead, John gave him the kind of look that passes from one friend to another who is hurting to let him know he is there whenever needed. That's how Andy described it when he told me about it. I don't really know what that look might look like, but Andy apparently caught the message right off. Or maybe it was just his conscience talking. Guilt pretty much drove him throughout the investigative phase of the case. Andy reminded himself, though, that he hadn't done anything wrong. He didn't go looking for any of this. All of these events found him. I guess that's how life works out sometimes. Like I said before, life is funny. Just when Andy thought he had everything figured out, he was already starting to doubt himself. He should have let it go. But if he had, I wouldn't be here now.

# CHAPTER

## *11*

ANDY HAD JUST WATCHED John's arrest and the high-lights of the press conference on the eleven o'clock news when his phone rang. "Hello," he said.

"Hi, Andy. Loraine. I was wondering if you might have time to drop by this evening. I would like to thank you for all you've done for Gabe."

He hadn't had a phone call like this in what felt like a much longer time than it actually had been. Two months earlier he would have been out the door before she could get her words out. But not that night.

"There's no need to thank me, Loraine. I was just doing my job," he said.

"That may be true, but I really want to show you how much I appreciate all you did. I heard the D.A. mention you by name and how you'd taken the initiative to see this case through to an arrest. I think you should be rewarded," she said.

Andy swallowed hard. Self-control had never exactly been his strong suit, but he could hear the sound of Ted Jackson's voice in his head saying, *Don't do something stupid and blow this* case. *Think like a cop, not with your pants.* And in spite of all the D.A.'s blustering, the case against John Phillips wasn't exactly airtight. Most of it still came down to a matter of interpretation. The evidence could be made to say whatever a really smart attorney wanted it to say. Even Brian Paul's testimony was anything but a slam dunk. Ted Jackson had already privately asked Andy if he'd coached the kid in what to say, and Andy didn't think Ted was convinced when he said no. If some reporter or defense team investigator saw him going over to the dead kid's mother's house on the night the dad was arrested for murder one, the whole case could blow up.

"Please don't think that I don't appreciate your gratitude, Loraine. Lord knows there's nothing I would like more than to see you right now, but it's all a little premature. An arrest isn't the same as a conviction. This case still has a long way to go before justice is served. I'm afraid if we saw one another now, we might needlessly jeopardize it. I hope you understand," Andy said.

"We'll call it a rain check, then," Loraine said.

"You can count on it," Andy said.

After he hung up the phone, a wave of anxiety swept over Andy. *An arrest is a long way from a conviction,* he thought. *And a conviction is a long way from a confession.* And that's all he ever really wanted. He wanted John Phillips to confess. Deep down he thought it would have already happened. In his mind he pictured John's arrest playing out like a scene from a television lawyer show, like *Perry Mason.* Perry would always figure out who the real killer was, and then he'd get the guy up on the witness stand to nail him. About halfway through his testimony, Perry would spring the real evidence on him, and the guy would crack. All the pent-up guilt would come pouring out and the guy would confess right then and there. Most of the time Perry could even get them to break down in tears.

That's what Andy fantasized would happen when the police descended upon the window factory earlier that afternoon. He'd already played the whole scene out in his head. The second Ted Jackson said, "John Phillips, you are under arrest for the murder of Gabriel Phillips," John was supposed to fall to his knees, crying. Then he would say, "I confess. I did it. I did it. I can't live with the guilt any longer. I killed my son." Andy was a little disappointed when it didn't play out that way, disappointed but not surprised. After all, this wasn't the movies. He hoped that by the time John's preliminary hearing rolled around the day after tomorrow, John would realize that the jig was up, and plead guilty. If the case went to trial, the D.A. would press, and press hard, for a death sentence. Surely, John would value his own life enough to accept the inevitable and take responsibility for what he had done.

*Are there any loose ends floating around that might trip this case up?* he wondered. He looked back over a list he'd made in his Big Chief pad of what he considered the strongest parts of the case against John. At the top of his list, Andy had written, "He did it. Case closed." You have to keep in mind that this was a list he'd made for himself, and not anyone else. Below this, he'd listed key parts of Loraine's testimony, with a big circle drawn around the statement "Argument at the door. Not his son." He'd also underlined the word "not" three or four times. Farther down were the words "Brian Paul, earwitness." I've read over this list several times, and

I'm always amazed that Andy never called Brian an eyewitness, even though Brian told Ted Jackson and later testified in court that he saw John slam the drawer onto Gabe's head. Down on the bottom of the page were the words "Not the man he claims to be." Andy read through this list several times before pushing it aside, grabbing the keys to his patrol car, and walking out the door.

Would you be surprised if I told you he ended up at Madison Park Apartments? I didn't think so. Andy pulled into the parking lot under the only working streetlight, just like the night Gabe died. He shut off the engine and lights, rolled down his window, and just sat there. Listening. At first, he didn't hear anything except the sound of the occasional car going up and down State Street. He climbed out of his car, walked around to the front, and leaned against the passenger-side fender. This gave him a direct view of building three. His mind tried to go racing around to the events of the night Gabe died; then it jumped over to Loraine's apartment and reminded Andy of how stupid he was to turn her down tonight. It kept jumping all over, until Andy finally quieted his thoughts enough to just listen to the night at Madison Park.

The night was a little cool for mid-September, but a few people had their windows open. Andy could hear Ed McMahon's laugh and Doc Severinsen make up a ridiculous song as Johnny Carson played "Stump the Band" on NBC. A baby was crying over on the east side of the complex, and doors slammed on the west side. Another door slammed louder somewhere close by, which was immediately followed by the sound of the door reopening, and a woman yelling, "Don't you walk out on me."

"Leave me alone," the man yelled back. "I need a drink."

"Would you people keep it down!" another woman yelled out an open window.

"I'm trying to sleep over here," someone else yelled.

"Mind your own business," the man who had just stormed out of his apartment yelled back.

Andy got back in his car and drove home. The next morning he was back at the complex, but this time on duty. From the day Loraine told him about the argument she'd had with John while dropping off Gabe the night of his death, something hadn't sat right with him. He had been so busy running with what she told him, that he never stopped and paid attention to the uneasiness floating around in his brain. That is, until his late-night listening session. Reading back over his list, he'd felt uneasy. Then the night sounds of the lovely Madison Park Apartments sharpened the uneasiness into a full-blown question, one that he should have asked himself a long time before: if Loraine and John had argued at the door of John's apartment that night, why hadn't anyone else reported hearing it? He'd talked to nearly every resident of the complex and asked them so many questions about that night that most of them locked their doors and pretended not to be home when they saw his car pull into the parking lot. But no one, not any of the neighbors or anyone from anywhere else in the complex, had said a word about hearing an argument earlier in the evening. Why?

Now, the fact that no one reported hearing the argument didn't mean it hadn't happened. Most people are so caught up in their own little world that a nuclear bomb could go off next door, and they wouldn't notice until the walls blew in. Quite a few people reported hearing Gabe screaming in the night, but that happened around two in the morning when he didn't have a lot of other sounds with which to compete. Loraine said she dropped Gabe off around six in the evening. Six o'clock on a summer night is a crazy time for most families. The fact that no one noticed two separated parents arguing over their child's visitation schedule didn't mean much.

However, as Andy walked from his car to building three, he knew he would feel a lot better if he could find someone to back up Loraine's story. Any defense attorney worth his fee would jump on the fact that she had not included this detail in her original statement to the police. She claimed she left it out because she was ashamed of her past actions. Considering some of the things she'd done with him, Andy wondered if she even knew what shame meant. "Okay, Loraine, let's see if anyone can back you up."

He started at the door he'd avoided up to now, apartment 321, home to one Crazy Cathy. He only had to knock once, and the door swung open wide and there stood Crazy Cathy in what appeared to Andy to be the same oversized shirt she'd worn the night of Gabe's death. She held a Schlitz Malt Liquor in one hand, and a cigarette hung off the other. "Wadda you want?" Crazy Cathy asked. "Don't tell me you're here to run me in again." Now that I think about it, I don't think Andy ever told me her real name. She had to have one, but no one ever told me what it was.

"I would like to ask you a couple of quick questions about the night earlier this summer when you called the police about the disturbance next door," Andy said.

"You mean when that kid got his brains bashed in? Yeah, wadda ya wanna know? I've already answered so many questions from you damn cops about that kid that you'd think he was related to the president or something. What makes that kid so special, huh?"

"It's an ongoing investigation. However, we have made an arrest and are trying to finalize all the details in the case…"

"Well, whoop-dee-crap," Crazy Cathy said. "You made an arrest. What's the matter, sweetheart, ya run outta old ladies to hassle?"

Andy could see this was leading nowhere. Crazy Cathy was already on the D.A.'s witness list. He didn't see much point in further antagonizing her. "I'm sorry to have disturbed you, ma'am. My questions, they aren't that important. Thank you for your time," he said as he started walking away from her door.

"If they weren't that important, then why in the hell did you come knocking on my door? Geez," she said as she turned to close the door, "you would think that the damned police department that my tax dollars supports would have better things to do than…" The door slammed behind her.

"Weeeelllll, that was certainly productive," Andy said as he walked farther down the hall. He could hear a television blaring from apartment 323. A new tenant had moved in on the first of the month, a sixty-eight-year-old man with severe hearing loss. Crazy Cathy would love that. He paused at the door for a moment, then turned to the apartment directly across the hall and sniffed a couple of times. The distinctive odor of burning rope could only mean one of two things. Either a rope fire had broken out and he needed to contact the fire department, or the people in apartment 324 had decided to get stoned at five after nine in the morning.

He knocked once. No answer. He knocked again, firmer this time. The door opened just a crack and a woman said, "Now's not a real good time."

"I don't care. Open the door. Police," Andy said.

"Why the hell did you answer the door?" someone yelled from farther back in the apartment.

"You know, Officer, I was just getting ready for work," the woman's voice said through the crack. "If you could maybe, like, come back later this evening, that would be great."

Andy pushed the door open. "No, I think now is a real good time," he said. A heavy brown haze hung in the living room, which was illuminated by a single lamp with a beat-up shade. Three shapes that appeared to be human beings were flung over the sofa and love seat. Jefferson Airplane played in the background. The woman who'd answered the door shifted her weight from side to side like she was trying to regain her balance. Her Kansas concert T-shirt was stretched out of shape, while her faded jeans with holes in the knees were partially unzipped, revealing more than Andy wanted to see. From the looks of her clothes, she'd been wearing them for a couple of days. Her eyes were red and bloodshot.

"All four of you live here?" Andy asked.

"No," the woman replied. "Just me. I live here with my daughter."

Andy's head snapped around to her. "You telling me you have a kid in here with you now?"

"No, man, she's at her dad's. I'm a good mother. I don't do this crap when she's here."

"Yeah, I'm sure of that," Andy replied. The shapes on the couch and love seat started moving. Andy glanced around the room. Empty pizza boxes covered what might have been the dining-room table. The apartment floor had a layer of beer cans, cigarette butts, and other assorted trash. He walked over toward the shapes on the couch, when his foot slipped on something that could have been a used condom. "Nice party you have going on here," he said. "Hey, sleeping beauties," he shouted to the shapes lying on the living-room furniture. "Time to go home. Party's over." The shapes began moving, tugging at their clothes, and struggling to get up on their feet. By the time they made it to the door, Andy could tell the shapes belonged to two men and one woman. All three of them reeked of pot, alcohol, and BO.

"Hey, Em, I'll call you later," one of the male shapes said as he stumbled out the door.

"Don't do her any favors, Ringo," Andy said as he placed his boot on the male shape's backside and helped him out the door.

"What's your problem, man?" the male shape said.

"Nothing, nothing at all," Andy said as he pushed the door shut in his face. Then, turning to the woman who lived in the apartment, he said, "Call it a hunch, but I've got a feeling you have some things here in this apartment that you would rather I not find. Would that be a safe assumption?"

"All right, fine. What do you want?" she asked.

"I came by just to ask you a few questions. And your name is?" Andy said.

"Emily," the woman replied without giving a last name.

"How long have you lived here, Emily?"

"Six months. Why?"

"A little boy was killed right across the hall from your apartment a couple of months back," Andy said.

"Yeah, I remember that night. So," Emily said. From the

look on her face, it appeared she wouldn't be able to keep standing much longer, but Andy didn't offer to let her sit down. She kept standing while he continued his questions.

"A witness said that earlier that evening the man who lived in the apartment, John Phillips, had an argument with a woman that became rather heated. I'm just having a little trouble finding any other witnesses who also heard them arguing. I was wondering, did you hear anything like that on the night of the murder?"

Emily's body had started to sway. She looked like she would be down for the count any second now. "What do you need to hear?" she asked.

Andy just smiled in return.

# CHAPTER

## 12

JOHN'S PRELIMINARY HEARING took all of ten minutes, and for Andy, they were ten of the more disappointing minutes of his life. The D.A. seemed pleased the case would go to trial; Andy was anything but. The hearing began with two deputies escorting John into the courtroom, his hands cuffed and his feet shackled. Both restraints were removed prior to the judge walking into the courtroom. Unlike the trial phase, which was to come, John was not allowed to dress for court. He had on the same county lockup orange jumpsuit that Andy had seen him in a couple of days earlier. The deputies led John to a table where a heavyset, gray-haired, balding man sat. The orange jumpsuit would have been an improvement over this guy's lime green blazer, grayish shirt, which was probably white at one time, and red-and-blue-striped tie. He stood as John came over, revealing a pair of yellow slacks. Apparently, this was John's court-appointed attorney. From the sound of things, John was in real good hands. Again, I'm being sarcastic.

Sitting across from John Phillips's crack legal team, Regi-

nald Chambliss appeared to be the picture of professionalism and confidence. The contrast between him and the
public defender assigned to John's case couldn't be starker.
Two other younger attorneys sat at the table with the D.A.,
both sharply dressed. As he watched the way they worked,
even in something as simple as a preliminary hearing, it
quickly became apparent to Andy that these attorneys did
the legwork, while Reginald Chambliss took care of the
showmanship. Juries were his specialty.

The bailiff announced the judge's arrival, and Andy stood
up from his seat in the back of the courtroom, along with
everyone else in attendance. The crowd was rather sparse,
although several reporters sat in the row directly in front of
Andy. At least he assumed they were reporters. All of them
had small notebooks in which they took copious notes.

The Honorable George Houk ambled in, wearing the usual
black robes over what appeared to Andy to be blue jeans and
cowboy boots. His salt-and-pepper hair had a pressed-down
indention that looked like Houk had been wearing a hat up
until the moment he walked through the courtroom door.
Andy assumed it was a cowboy hat. The cowboy image fit
because Houk had a reputation as a no-nonsense kind of guy
who didn't suffer fools in his courtroom. Andy had observed
this firsthand. About a year earlier, Andy had to testify against
an eighteen-year-old kid who'd been caught breaking into
homes where teenage girls lived. Apparently, the kid was on
some kind of sex-offender-training program. For two summers the Trask police received complaints that the kid was
peeping into bedroom windows. Finally he graduated from
window peeper to underwear thief and junior stalker. Andy
finally caught the kid late one night walking out of a house

a couple of blocks from the police station with two handfuls of panties. In the boy's trial the kid's mother yelled and carried on from the back of the courtroom, challenging every witness and scoffing loudly at every piece of evidence against her son. Houk warned her twice, then locked her up for a week for contempt of court. She actually ended up spending more time behind bars than her son, although he did serve six months of house arrest.

"You may be seated," the judge announced, and the courtroom complied.

"John Phillips, will you please rise," Judge Houk said. John did so. His dapper attorney stood next to him. "Mr. Phillips, the state has charged you with one count of murder in the first degree. How do you plead?"

"Your Honor, my client—" the attorney began to say before John cut him off.

"Not guilty, Your Honor. I am completely innocent," John said with a clear, firm voice.

"Let it be recorded that Mr. John Phillips has entered a plea of not guilty. Mr. Edmonds," he said to the public defender, "have you had an opportunity to meet with your client?"

"Only briefly, sir. I've also had trouble obtaining all the pertinent documents from the prosecutor's office that I need to begin to prepare my defense. In fact, I feel as though I should have had more time to study the prosecution's case so that I could have fully counseled my client regarding his options with this hearing today," Mr. Edmonds said.

"Duly noted, Mr. Edmonds. Now there's the matter of—"

"It wouldn't have mattered," John interrupted the judge.

"Excuse me?" Judge Houk said, looking up from the papers in front of him. He shot a look at John's attorney that I think has been banned in thirteen states.

"It wouldn't have mattered how much time my attorney would have had to go over the evidence. The fact is I did nothing wrong. I am not guilty. In fact, I wish I could represent myself in these proceedings. I believe—"

"Mr. Phillips"—now it was the judge's turn to interrupt—"Indiana state law does not allow people like yourself to represent themselves in capital murder cases. I don't think you grasp the gravity of the charges brought against you. If you are convicted, the district attorney here plans to push for a death sentence. Death, Mr. Phillips. I believe you need to listen to your counsel's advice."

"My life is in God's hands," John said.

"That may be true, but your ass is in mine" Judge Houk said. "Now, as I was saying, to the matter of bail. Mr. Chambliss, you had a recommendation to make."

"Yes, Your Honor. The people request that bail be denied due to the nature of these charges," the D.A. said.

"Duly noted, Mr. Chambliss. Mr. Edmonds, your response."

"Your Honor, my client has shown no risk of flight. Denying him bail would, I believe, hamper our efforts to mount a viable defense," Mr. Edmonds said.

"Thank you, Mr. Edmonds," the judge said. As Andy watched the two attorneys with the judge, the entire scene almost seemed staged, as if this were a game both attorneys had played many times. "In light of the circumstances, I believe that there is some cause for concern of flight. Bail is set at two hundred thousand dollars. And now for the question of the date of the trial. Mr. Chambliss, is the state ready to proceed to trial?"

"Yes, Your Honor."

"I'm sure you are," Houk said. "Mr. Edmonds, how much time do you need to plan your client's defense?"

"Your Honor, I have just been brought on to this case this week. My client did not retain counsel at any time while he was being investigated in regard to these charges. I believe I need a minimum of two months to adequately prepare," Edmonds said.

"Very well, the trial date is set for December fourth, at nine a.m., with jury selection to begin one week prior. This hearing is adjourned." With that, Houk slammed down his gavel. The deputies returned for John, and everyone else got up to leave.

Andy walked over to Reginald Chambliss. "Is that it?" he asked, more than a little annoyed.

Chambliss laughed. "What did you expect? You've sat in on prelims before. You know the drill. All in all, I thought this went quite well. There's not much risk of flight because I would be shocked if anyone could scrape together the two hundred grand for the guy's bail. We got a good court date, close enough to the holidays to make sure the judge keeps the thing moving along and the jury won't drag its feet. I've argued cases in front of Judge Houk many times, and I've always been pleased. I would say things couldn't be better."

Andy laughed nervously. "No, I guess not," he said.

Now here's the thing you need to understand about Andy and the way he'd built his case. The D.A. was focused on the jury, but Andy was obsessed with John. He didn't give two winds to Monday about the jury. He had hardly even given the jury much thought. In his mind everything was about forcing John to admit to what Andy knew he had done. Yes. Andy expected a confession. He wanted an admission of guilt. Again, Andy approached this whole thing like a television cop show. His plan all along had been to overwhelm John with the evidence, to make it crystal clear to him he could not carry out this charade any longer, and then watch him crack. But John hadn't taken the bait. He hadn't broken under the pressure. Not yet, at least.

The D.A.? Well, the D.A. was absolutely giddy. He'd never had the opportunity to actually send someone to death row. The Supreme Court effectively banned the death penalty for much of the 1970s. Indiana was a little slow getting back into the execution business after it was reinstated in 1977. Only a handful of death penalty cases had gone to trial, and all of them stirred up a storm of media attention. Throw in the fact that the victim was an eight-year-old boy, and the murderer was his father, and you have just what the doctor ordered for Reginald Chambliss, Esquire. I think he would have keeled over with disappointment if John had entered a guilty plea. He was going to be in heaven for the next two months.

Not Andy. He had already started thinking of what he would do, now that finding justice for Gabe was behind him. He had to put those plans on hold. In fact, when it came to John Phillips, Andy was just getting started.

◦   ◦   ◦

ANDY PLANNED ON ignoring everything that had to do with John Phillips until the trial began. Sure, he wanted a confession, but there wasn't a lot he could do about that now. Periodically, which in this case meant at least two times a week, he double-checked to see if anyone had posted John's bail. No one ever did, which meant John remained locked up in the Harris County Jail until his trial. As a favor to Andy, the D.A. had recommended John be kept in isolation, ostensibly for his own protection. The general jail population doesn't always look too kindly on a child killer. Andy's real reason was to force John to be alone with his guilty conscience, with nothing else to distract him for days and weeks at a time. He stuck to this plan for the first five weeks between the preliminary hearing and the trial. Eventually, however, his obsession with getting a confession out of John pushed him to go talk with John face-to-face.

The county jail didn't exactly roll out the welcome mat for everyone who wanted to stop by and visit with a capital murder suspect under security lockdown. All visitation requests had to be submitted at least twenty-four hours in advance for the sheriff's approval. It was his call who got in or didn't, since the sheriff's department ran the jail. Of course, the sheriff himself didn't handle this personally. One of his flunkies did. And that flunky had to report every name to Ted Jackson. As lead detective on the case, he wanted to keep an eye on everyone who showed even the slightest interest in John Phillips.

Ted showed up at Trask police headquarters at eleven at night, just as Andy was walking out to his patrol car to start his rotation on the graveyard shift. "Jax? What brings you out to this neck of the woods in the middle of the night. Janey kick you out and you can't afford a hotel room, so you want to stay in one of our cells for a while?" Andy joked.

"Yeah, right, smart-ass," Jackson said. "One ex-wife is enough. I don't plan on having another. No, it's been a while since my patrolman days. I was wondering if you would mind if I rode along with you tonight for a while."

"Knock yourself out," Andy said, "and you must think I'm a complete idiot if you think I am buying that explanation. Climb in."

Andy pulled out of the police parking lot and started on his usual patrol loop. He and Ted talked about the Yankees winning the World Series and about how the Bears might do during the upcoming season and about why the old ABA was so much better than the NBA. They talked high school football and high school basketball and about a whole lot of nothing for over an hour and a half. During that time Andy had to respond to exactly zero calls. He did help a guy stuck out on Highway 8 in a broken-down car. The timing chain had snapped in the poor guy's motor, which would be bad enough even if the man and his wife hadn't been traveling from Wheeling, West Virginia, to Springfield, Illinois. Andy called a tow truck for them and arranged for them to stay in the local negative-four-star motel.

After the broken-down car was off the highway, and the motorist and his wife were safely deposited at the Pelican Motel, Andy asked Jackson, "You ever going to tell me why you are out here tonight?"

"I saw your name on the John Phillips visitation request list," Jackson said.

"So?"

"So why do you need to see him? What is it with this guy and this case that's turned you into such a psycho spaz?" Jackson asked.

"No reason," Andy said.

"Yeah, right," Jackson said.

Neither said anything for several minutes. Andy turned off Highway 318 onto Main Street. He drove through four flashing traffic lights (they turn off the traffic lights in Trask at ten every night, and they flash yellow until six the next morning). He pulled into the First National Bank parking lot. Driving slowly around the back of the building, he shone his spotlight on each of the doors, checking for signs of forced entry. If Ted hadn't been with him, Andy probably would have gone back to the station and shot the breeze with the dispatcher for a couple of hours. It beat driving the streets late at night alone.

"You ever going to tell me?" Jackson asked.

"Tell you what?" Andy replied.

"What made you grab onto this case like a pit bull. What haven't you told me? Because you care too damn much for this to be nothing more than finding a dead kid in an apartment and getting a hunch something wasn't right?" Jackson said.

"Not a thing," Andy said.

"Cut the crap," Jackson said. "What is your connection to this case?"

"The mother," Andy finally admitted.

"What about the mother?"

"I've been seeing her for quite a while. Or at least I was, up until Gabe died," Andy said.

"Don't tell me you're the 'real man' she went out looking for," Jackson said.

Andy looked at him and shrugged his shoulders.

"Holy crap. I cannot believe you, man. You know you

should have told me this from the very beginning," Jackson said. "So how well did you know the boy? I mean, come on, I know you. I know how you hate kids." Andy just looked at him again. "I should have known. So that's what this whole thing has been, your own personal campaign for vengeance."

"Justice, Jax, not vengeance. He did it; you know he did it," Andy said.

"Oh, and I'm sure you aren't biased at all." Jackson let out a long sigh. "So tell me about the evidence you found; all these witnesses no one else knew anything about."

"What about them?" Andy asked.

"You know what about them. Are they legit?"

"What do you think?"

"You don't want to know what I think," Jackson said. "You realize if I go to the D.A. with this now, it's my ass."

"Just let the evidence speak," Andy said. "Let it play out in court. That's all you have to do. Come on, Jax. I didn't do anything I shouldn't have done."

"Yeah, and I really believe you." Jackson shook his head in disgust. "Okay, here's what we are going to do. I'm going to keep working the case and try to verify your witnesses' stories. And you," he said, shooting a look at Andy, "you stay the hell away from John Phillips and everything else associated with this case. I don't want to see you at the jail. I don't want you talking to any of these witnesses. Hell, I don't want you to even read a story in the newspaper pertaining to this trial. You got it?"

Andy nodded his head.

"I'll get out here," Jackson said, and reached down for the door handle.

"Come on, Jax, let me drive you back to the station. You don't want to be out walking the mean streets of Trask at this hour."

"I'm willing to take my chances," Jackson said. Andy stopped the car in the bank parking lot and Ted climbed out. "I'm serious," he said to Andy as he got out. "Butt out. You are officially off this case. I may even recommend to the D.A. that you not testify. If Phillips's attorney gets you up on that stand under oath, he could have a field day with our case."

"I don't think it will have to go that far," Andy said.

"Like hell it won't," Jackson said as he slammed the door shut.

"Fine," Andy said. "Whatever you say."

# CHAPTER

## 13

DECEMBER 4 ROLLED around, and the trial started. But Andy didn't get to sit in on it like he had hoped. If it were up to him, he would have taken time off from work, found a front-row seat, and enjoyed the show. He wanted a seat with a good view of John Phillips, just to watch him sweat. Unfortunately for Andy, as a key witness to the prosecution's case, he would only be allowed in the courtroom while he was on the witness stand. There's a law about the separation of witnesses that basically says one witness cannot listen to the testimony of another. The court needs each witness to give his or her account of what he or she saw and heard, without having a witness's memories contaminated by the memories of someone else. Once a witness is off the stand, he could stay in the courtroom for the rest of that session, but only if both sides waived their right to recall the witness later. That never happens with someone as vital to the case as Andy. Ole Reginald Chambliss wasn't about to jeopardize his case just so Andy could watch John Phillips's reaction to all the testimony against him.

Because he was the first officer to arrive on the scene the

night of Gabe's death, Andy was the prosecution's first witness. However, he didn't testify until the second day of the trial. The first day, which ended up not starting until one in the afternoon, was filled with all sorts of procedural matters and opening statements. Reginald Chambliss had turned opening statements in front of the jury into his own Shakespearean moment, and he refused to rush through them. He was so long-winded it pushed any actual testimony into the next day.

Andy arrived at the courthouse about a half hour before the trial was set to resume. One of the assistant D.A.'s, a twenty-three-year-old, fresh-out-of-law-school whiz kid named Rachel Maris, met Andy in the foyer to ask him if he had any questions regarding what would take place in the trial that day. They didn't discuss his testimony, although she did give him a general range of the types of questions Chambliss would ask. "You will get no surprises from us," she said. "We've gone over the transcripts of your taped statements about a million times and highlighted the parts most vital to this case. All of Mr. Chambliss's questions will try to bring out the best of what you've already told us."

Andy nodded. "That shouldn't be too painful, then."

Maris laughed. "Don't worry. You'll do fine," she said. "I'm sure you've done this many, many times in your tenure on the force. There's absolutely nothing to worry about. You couldn't be in better hands."

"I hope so," Andy said. He and Rachel Maris exchanged more small talk before going to their assigned places. Maris walked into the courtroom, where, Andy assumed, she took her seat at the prosecutor's table. Andy went into one of the side rooms designated for those called to testify. No other witnesses were in the room, which, again, is by design.

After what seemed like an eternity, a bailiff walked into the holding area and said, "Officer Myers, they're ready for you now." Andy walked into the courtroom and walked down the center aisle up to the witness stand. The room was a lot smaller than its televison counterparts looked, and outside of reporters from all the local TV stations and newspapers, there weren't many people in attendance. Andy couldn't scope out the whole room while he was walking in (this wasn't like walking into a bar), but he did notice John had turned around in his seat to make eye contact with him as he walked by. That made Andy feel a little uneasy, but he passed it off as the same kind of butterflies he always felt when called to testify in court.

"Do you swear that the testimony you are about to give is the truth, the whole truth, and nothing but the truth, so help you God," the bailiff said.

"I do," Andy replied.

"Please be seated," the bailiff said.

Reginald Chambliss rose from behind the prosecutor's table, buttoned his suit jacket, and moved into the open area in the front of the courtroom. Andy noticed that he'd ditched his off-the-rack suit for one that looked far more expensive than anything that would ever hang in Andy's closet. Of course, the suit was dark blue, with a white shirt and a red tie. He looked like he'd been shopping at the power politicians' clothing outlet. "Officer, for the record, would you please state your full name," he said.

"Andrew Eugene Myers." Yeah, Eugene. I always thought that was a funny middle name.

"And, Officer, what is your official position?"

"I am a senior patrolman for the City of Trask Police Department."

"How long have you been a Trask police officer?" Chambliss asked with a relaxed, very informal tone.

"Six years, ten months," Andy replied.

"Now, Officer Myers, can you tell us what took place on the morning of Tuesday, July seventh?"

"I was working the graveyard shift, and I received a call from the Trask dispatcher with a report of a 10-16, that is, a domestic disturbance, from the Madison Park Apartments. The call came in a little after two in the morning—two-oh-six to be precise."

"Was this unusual, getting a call like that in the middle of the night?" Chambliss asked, lobbing another softball of a question toward Andy.

"Not at all. I probably go out to that apartment complex two or three times a week for some sort of disturbance or another when I work the overnight. Usually, the calls turn out to be nothing, at least nothing major. I didn't think much about getting a call on that night. I figured it would be more of the same, either a television cranked up too loud with someone asleep on the couch in front of it, or some couple arguing with one another. That's all," Andy said. He'd rehearsed this little speech in his head a few thousand times over the past two months. He knew exactly what he wanted to say.

"What did you discover when you arrived?" Chambliss asked.

"Several residents were waiting for me in the parking lot. They seemed pretty agitated about something. Another resident greeted me at the top of the stairs of building three as I made my way up to apartment 323, the apartment about which three separate calls had been made to the police department. Still, I didn't think too much of any of this. The people out there tend to be easily excitable. Sometimes I think calling the cops is their favorite form of entertainment."

"Objection," John's attorney, Donald Edmonds, said. "The witness is making a judgment that has little bearing on this case." Andy figured the guy just wanted to remind the court that he was there and he was paying attention.

"Sustained," Judge Houk said. "The entertainment habits of the residents of the Madison Park Apartments has little bearing on the events of the night in question."

"I apologize, Your Honor," Andy said.

"What did you find when you went to the Phillips apartment?" Chambliss asked.

"I had to knock several times before anyone opened the door. When the door finally did open, I found John Phillips talking on the telephone. He waved me into the apartment, and kept on talking on the telephone," Andy said.

"Is there anything unusual about that?" Chambliss asked, again, setting up Andy to make a point.

"Absolutely. When accidents occur, those who come upon the accident usually drop everything to try to help the accident victim or they call for outside help. This is especially true when a child is injured. In my experience, parents don't let anything come between them and their child in need. Sometimes we almost have to pry the child out of the parent's arms. Mr. Phillips, however, appeared very nonchalant, as if I had arrived at the wrong apartment. I have never before observed a parent react to the injury or death of a child as I saw Mr. Phillips act. I had to insist that he get off the phone before he would hang up," Andy said. He thought he noticed a visible reaction from the jury as he said this. *Good*, Andy thought. He wanted the jury to feel the same apprehension about John as he felt from the first time he met the guy.

"Then what happened?" Chambliss asked.

"Then Mr. Phillips said, 'He's back here,' in a way that sounded like a waiter showing me to a table. He also said something about how he was just about to call the police. I followed him down the apartment hallway, to where he motioned into a room and said, 'He's in there.'"

"What did you discover in the room into which Mr. Phillips led you?" Chambliss asked. His tone had become very serious.

"The room was very small, but the floor looked like it had been painted in blood. And on the bottom bunk lay a small boy. There was blood smeared on the side of the mattress as well. I rushed over to the boy to try to start CPR, and the linoleum floor was pretty slick from all the blood, which, as it turned out, was not all blood but also water from a broken goldfish bowl. I moved the boy from the bunk bed to the floor to start doing mouth-to-mouth, but he was unresponsive," Andy said.

"What was Mr. Phillips doing while you were working on his son?" Chambliss asked.

"Nothing. He stood in the doorway and watched. I asked him what had happened and he told me his son fell out of the top bunk and hit his head on the bottom drawer of the dresser that was right next to the boy's bed," Andy said.

"Was this a normal response from a parent in a situation like this?" Chambliss asked.

"Objection," Edmonds said. "The prosecutor is leading the witness."

"Sustained," Judge Houk said.

"In your nearly seven years of experience as a police officer, what manner of behavior have you observed in other parents when their child has been injured?" Chambliss asked, rephrasing his question.

"Nothing like this. A lot of parents rush over and try to be so close to their child that it prevents us from working on them. Others, when they give you the distance you need to administer help, cry and weep and carry on or show extreme anxiety in some other way. Mr. Phillips not only kept his distance, he seemed very detached from the situation. He began talking about what his son's name meant. At one point he even offered to pray for me. I have never before observed a parent who demonstrated so little emotional response to the injury or death of a child," Andy said.

"You said the floor was covered with blood. Was the child bleeding?"

"Yes, sir. From the back of his head. Although the blood wasn't flowing freely like it obviously had earlier, it still dripped from the back of his head. The pillow on which he'd been laid was soaked with blood, and the mixture of blood and water covered the floor. It pretty much ruined the uniform I had on that night," Andy said.

"Were the defendant's clothes covered with blood as well?"

"No. He freely admitted later he had changed clothes between the time Gabe died and when I arrived."

"Is there anything unusual about that?"

"In my experience, yes. Mr. Phillips took the time to

change his clothes, but he never called the police or fire departments for help. I've never seen that in a parent. Usually, a mother or father is so upset by their child's injury and so focused on trying to help them, they lose sight of everything else. I found this quite odd," Andy said.

"Objection," Edmonds said. "This is nothing but conjecture on the part of the witness."

"On the contrary," Chambliss said. "The unusual nature of the defendant's response on the night in question calls into doubt the defendant's explanation of Gabriel Phillips's death. His actions aroused the suspicions of law enforcement professionals from the very beginning. This is not conjecture on the officer's part, but a clear observation of an abnormal emotional reaction to this traumatic event."

"Objection overruled. You may continue, Mr. Chambliss," the judge said.

"What did you do after unsuccessfully trying CPR?" Chambliss asked.

"I radioed in for the coroner and the Harris County Sheriff's Department to come to the scene. The sheriff's department takes the lead in investigating potential crime scenes like this. I also agreed to let the dispatcher call out the fire department paramedics and an ambulance. To me, it was apparent that the boy was dead. However, I wanted to make sure we gave him every possible chance to survive," Andy said.

"Did the defendant say how long it had been since the accident occurred when you arrived?" Chambliss asked.

"He said ten or fifteen minutes."

"Would that ten or fifteen minutes have made a difference in saving Gabriel Phillips's life?" Chambliss asked.

"Objection," Edmonds said. "The witness is a police officer, not a doctor."

"Sustained," the judge said.

"I withdraw the question. What happened after you radioed in for help?" Chambliss queried.

"I led Mr. Phillips back into the living room, where we waited. I left him there after the fire department arrived. I had to show the paramedics back into the boy's bedroom, where some of them didn't do too well. A couple of them knew Gabriel through their sons and became very distraught. Once Detective Ted Jackson and the sheriff's department investigative team arrived, I turned the scene over to him and rejoined Mr. Phillips in the living room. He never said anything else. Most of the time he sat with his head down and his eyes closed," Andy said.

"Thank you, Officer. No further questions," Chambliss said.

"Your witness, Mr. Edmonds," the judge said.

Before Donald Edmonds stood up, John whispered something in his ear. Andy didn't know what he said, but it was pretty clear Edmonds didn't like it. He let out a loud sigh, then stood and said, "Officer Myers, did you know the deceased child?"

"Yes, sir."

"And how did you know him?"

"I am a friend of his mother," Andy said without offering any further information.

Edmonds looked down at a sheet of paper in his hand, then glanced back at John. "No further questions," he said in an agitated voice.

"Would the prosecution like to ask anything further at this time?" Judge Houk said.

"No, Your Honor," Chambliss said.

"Your Honor," Edmonds said, "the defense would like to reserve the right to recall the witness at a later time." Andy couldn't read minds, but the look on the attorney's face looked like he said this in spite of what his client had told him.

"Mr. Chambliss?" the judge said.

"I have no objections to that, Your Honor. In fact, the prosecution would also like to reserve the right to recall the witness." That was a lie. The prosecution let out a huge sigh of relief that John's public defender didn't hammer Andy about his relationship with Loraine. The D.A. reserved the right to recall Andy only as a way of keeping him as far from the courtroom as possible.

"Very well," the judge said. "Thank you, Officer Myers, you may step down." As Andy walked out of the courtroom, he heard the judge say, "Next witness."

And that was it. Andy had to leave the courtroom and he couldn't go back until the day the judge read the verdict. For the rest of the trial, Andy had to content himself with getting his information from the local news. Every night for a week and a half, some reporter would stand out in front of the courthouse in the cold and tell what had happened that day. When they cut to the courtroom scene, they showed those hokey artist's renditions that were as close as you could get to the action inside. Cameras wouldn't be allowed in courtrooms for quite a while yet. The cartoon caricatures of John didn't squirm and sweat like Andy wanted to see him squirm and sweat, but it was as close as he could get to the courtroom.

Even as the trial proceeded, Andy held out hope that John would change his plea and admit to what he had done. From the way the news reporters described the action inside the courtroom, John wasn't doing too well. Sandy Jacobs, the perky little twenty-something blond reporter from channel six's *Action News,* described the forensic evidence as "damning" and she called the ex-hooker's testimony a "bombshell" that severely damaged the image the Phillips defense team presented of their client. "Phillips," the reporter said, "pressured the former prostitute for sex in repayment for helping her off the street. This hardly fits the picture of a deeply religious man the defense maintains John Phillips is." Andy stood up from his couch and cheered when the reporter said the defense barely challenged Ms. Peters's claims.

Christopher Brilliant, the channel eight field reporter who came across like Geraldo on steroids, described Loraine's testimony as "gripping" and "heart wrenching." He told how several members of the jury had tears running down their faces as Loraine described the anguish and guilt she carried since the day her little boy died. Reading from his script, the reporter said she closed her testimony by saying, "He told me that if I ever left him, I would regret it. Well, I regret it now. I wish I'd died instead of my son." When they switched back to the studio, the female news anchor called the story "tragic," before moving to a report about a local farmer and his giant beet.

But all the reporters nearly had a cow right there on the television screen after Brian Paul testified. Andy couldn't believe his ears when he heard Pamela Martinez, of News Team Thirteen, say that the defense did not even bother to cross-examine "little Brian Paul after his tearful account of the murder of his bestest friend." After hearing that one,

Andy immediately called Ted Jackson to get the scoop on what had happened. As the lead detective on the case, Ted Jackson sat at the prosecutor's table throughout the trial.

"What happened in the courtroom today?!" Andy asked the moment Ted answered the phone.

"And hello to you, too," Ted said. "I figured you would probably call tonight, once the word got out about Brian Paul's testimony."

"So what happened?" Andy asked.

"Chambliss put the kid on the witness stand, and we each just sort of held our breath. I told you how nervous we were about pinning the case on the testimony of an eight-year-old kid. But the kid had to testify. I'm not telling you anything you don't already know. So Brian tells the court that Gabe was afraid of his father because he'd beaten him in the past. At this point Chambliss introduces the pictures of the bruises on Gabe's body to back up the Paul kid's story. Everything's going pretty smooth and I'm thinking we may actually get through this without a hitch. I'm always nervous when kids testify. No matter how many times you talk to them ahead of time, you never know what's going to come out of their mouths.

"But when Brian got to the night of the murder, he almost started contradicting himself. He told how he woke up to the sound of Gabe screaming, 'No, Daddy. Stop it, Daddy. No.' You know the kid's story better than I do, you know how it goes. When he gets to the part about running over to his closet, he never said anything about seeing John hit the Phillips boy, through the hole the two of them had bored in the wall. Chambliss almost had to spell that part out for the kid. The boy finally did say the words 'I saw him do it,' but he could barely get the words out. The tears started flowing and he began to stutter and stammer. I looked over to the two little hotshot attorneys at the table with me, and we all hoped the jury took Brian's fumbling around as an indication of how upset he was because of what happened to his best friend, but who knows what they will think? When Chambliss said the words 'your witness,' I just knew that Edmonds would tear the kid apart," Jackson said.

"So what happened?" Andy said.

"Nothing. Edmonds didn't even cross-examine the boy. John leaned over and whispered something in his ear, just like he did when you testified, and Edmonds said, 'No questions, Your Honor.' That's pretty much been the pattern through the first week of this thing. I would say the defense attorney has spent maybe twenty minutes combined cross-examining all of our witnesses. He probably asked you more questions than he's asked anyone, and even then he didn't press. I really thought he would go after Loraine Phillips. I mean, come on, she's the most bitter ex-wife I've ever met, including my own. But Edmonds barely asked her anything and even then he didn't ask anything that really mattered. I don't know what his strategy is, but whatever it might be, it sure as hell ain't working," Jackson said.

Now I would be lying if I told you Andy wasn't relieved when he heard that the defense left Brian Paul alone. He'd tossed and turned several nights over the thought of what might happen to the boy when he testified. The case wasn't nearly as strong without the kid. "What was Phillips doing while the boy was talking?" Andy asked.

"Not much. I think I saw him wipe away a couple of tears, but he didn't break, if that's what you want to know."

"So what's next?" Andy said.

"The prosecution's finished. We saved Brian Paul for the last, sort of the icing on the cake. The judge sequestered the jury, so we wanted them to leave the courtroom for the weekend with the kid's words ringing in their ears. The defense is supposed to get started on Monday. I've seen their list of witnesses. It's pretty short. I bet the whole thing is wrapped up by the middle of next week," Jackson said.

"What's your read on the jury?" Andy asked.

"I'm not the expert people reader that you are," Jackson said, "but I would say based on how the first week has gone, Phillips doesn't stand a snowball's chance in hell of walking away from this one."

"That's what I wanted to hear," Andy said.

"Yeah, I know," Jackson said.

◢ ◢ ◢

TED JACKSON WAS RIGHT. The defense didn't take long, not in comparison to the prosecution's case. From what Andy could gather from the bits and pieces of information on the news, and from the little bit he could squeeze out of Ted Jackson, all John's attorney called were character witnesses. His pastor testified on his behalf, as did the prison chaplain and a few people from John's church. One name piqued Andy's attention. Ted mentioned that someone named Eli took the stand. Andy recognized the name as the same as the person to whom John was talking on the phone when Andy arrived on the night of Gabe's death. However, he didn't tell Ted or anyone else he recognized the name. It turns out that Eli was the inmate John nearly killed in the fight in the yard, then turned around and saved his life. From the way they described him on the news, Eli told quite a story from that day in the prison yard. I guess his point was that John would never hurt anyone, especially someone he loved. However, it had little to do with the night of Gabe's death.

The defense rested late Monday afternoon with John testifying on his own behalf. Ted Jackson told him later that John never got too far away from his basic defense of "I didn't do it. I have nothing to hide. God is my witness that I loved my son and would never harm him." As for the testimony against him, he dismissed Angela Peters by saying that anyone who knows him knows he would never do anything like she described. He called Loraine a good mother, and said he could understand how her pain over the loss of their son pushed her to make up these accusations against him. And he showed his only hint of emotion when he addressed Brian Paul's assertion that he had seen John kill Gabe. According to Ted Jackson, John said he did not know why Brian would make up a story like this. Brian, he said, was Gabe's best friend and that he had always tried to be like a father to the little boy. John believed the child had to be confused because of the trauma of that night.

Reginald Chambliss didn't spend too much time cross-examining John. His case was already so strong that trying to break John on the witness stand could work against him, especially if John didn't break. Ted said, instead, Chambliss asked Phillips that if all these testimonies against him were inaccurate, why didn't he press his attorney to more fiercely cross-examine them? John said, "The truth will always prevail," or something like that. Chambliss followed up by saying, "Don't you realize that your failure to challenge these witnesses only makes you look guilty." John didn't deviate from his script. He went back to saying, "I have nothing to hide. I am innocent. God will make sure the truth prevails." Ted called it the weakest defense he'd ever seen, especially in a murder case.

Tuesday was filled with closing remarks from both attorneys and instructions to the jury. The jury started their deliberations on Tuesday, right after lunch. Andy took the rest of the week off so that he could be there when the verdict was read. He didn't have to wait long. Wednesday morning at eleven, Ted Jackson called. "The jury's done," he said. "Court reconvenes at one, if you want to be there."

"Does a cat have climbing gear?" Andy said. "Of course, I want to be there." He hung up the phone, got dressed, and drove to the local liquor store to pick up a bottle of champagne with which to toast the victory. Returning home, he put the champagne on ice, parked his Impala, and drove his patrol car to the Harris County Courthouse in Adamsburg.

Andy arrived at the courthouse about ten minutes before one. He parked in the police lot and headed through the side entrance. In the hall outside of the courtroom, he ran into Rachel Maris. "So," he asked, "what do you think are our chances?"

Rachel broke out into a big grin. "Nothing is ever a slam dunk because you never know what a jury will do, but...," she said, and made a dunking motion with her right arm.

"I hope so," Andy said.

"You worry too much. Relax," she said as she pushed the door to enter the courtroom.

"I'm trying," Andy said as he followed her.

Rachel Maris took her usual spot in the front between the district attorney and Ted Jackson. Ted turned as she sat down and made eye contact with Andy as Andy looked for a seat. He smiled and waved. Andy gave him a nervous wave back. As he did, the bailiff walked in and said, "All rise." At that, Andy ducked into a spot to his immediate left. He'd hoped to sit on the opposite side of the courtroom, where he could watch John's face as the verdict was read, but this place would have to do. "Superior Court of Harris County, State of Indiana, is now in session. The Honorable George Houk presiding," the bailiff said. After the judge took his place behind the bench, he said, "You may be seated."

Andy took his seat on the aisle about eight rows behind John Phillips and Donald Edmonds. Edmonds was his usual dapper self, wearing an orange blazer and white pants. John leaned over to his attorney as the jury walked in, placing his arm around his shoulder as if to encourage his court-appointed lawyer. Andy turned his attention from John to the jury as they filed in. He studied each face, looking for a clue as to what they might have decided, but all he saw were looks of relief that this was over.

"Ladies and gentlemen of the jury, have you reached a verdict?" Judge Houk asked. Andy could feel his heart beating in his ears.

"We have, Your Honor," the jury foreman replied. Later, Andy couldn't remember if the foreman was a man or a woman. His eyes were glued to John Phillips.

"Would the defendant please rise," the judge said. The hair on the back of Andy's neck stood on end, and his sweat poured off his palms. John Phillips stood up, as did his attorney, whose orange blazer was the same color as the prisoner jumpsuits. John wore a light blue leisure suit.

"We find the defendant guilty of murder in the first degree," the foreman said. Andy could feel fireworks shoot off from his shoulders. He couldn't see John Phillips's face, only his back. That was enough, for now. With the trial over, Andy had already planned on a face-to-face meeting with John Phillips so that he could see his reaction up close and personal. A woman began wailing on the other side of the courtroom. Andy turned and saw that it was Loraine Phillips. She collapsed in her seat and the man next to her wrapped his arms around her and held her up. Andy had never seen him before, but he assumed he must be her newest love interest. A group of people just to Andy's left also began making noise, but all of them were saying things like, "This ain't right, this just ain't right." *Fools,* Andy thought.

Judge Houk slammed his gavel down a couple of times, saying "Order, order" in a firm voice. He then went down the line, asking each juror individually if the verdict was indeed unanimous. It was. *Yes!!!* Andy yelled inside. The judge thanked them for their service, and dismissed them. He then said, "Mr. Phillips, you will be held in the Harris County Jail without bond until your sentence is determined. The laws of the state of Indiana dictate that murder in the first degree is punishable by death or by life in prison. Do you understand this?"

"Death holds no fear for me, Your Honor," John said.

"A simple yes or no will be sufficient, Mr. Phillips," the judge said.

"Yes, Your Honor, I understand the possible sentences I may receive because of this guilty verdict. I place it all in God's hands and trust He will do what is best," John said.

The judge raised an eyebrow at John. "Since God isn't in the habit of walking into this courtroom and pronouncing sentences, this decision will be up to me. The sentencing hearing will hereby commence in two weeks on January 4, 1979. This court is adjourned," he said with a slam of his gavel.

The reporters inside the courtroom lunged forward to try to get a sound bite from John Phillips. And he gave them one. Andy heard him say, "As I have said from the beginning, I did not harm my son. I loved my little boy very, very much. I don't understand how I could even be charged with this crime, much less convicted of it, but God is still God. He's in control. If He wants me to go to prison, so be it. I can serve Him there as well as I can on the outside. I'm not worried about the verdict or any possible sentence. God is a just God. I'm entrusting my life to Him. He is the only judge I care anything about."

Andy laughed as he listened. *You're delusional, John Phillips. And you're a bigger idiot than I thought if you are anxious for God to get hold of you after what you've done,* he thought. John's supporters shouted out words of encouragement to him as the bailiff handcuffed him and led him out of the courtroom. Andy looked around. His eyes met Loraine's. Her cheeks were bright red and wet from tears. "Thank you," she mouthed from across the courtroom. Andy just nodded his head in return. *I didn't do it for you,* he thought, *this was for Gabe.*

He drove home, uncorked the champagne, and started to polish off the bottle all by himself. No sooner had he opened it than Loraine called. She wondered if she might stop by his place to express her appreciation for all Andy had done. Unlike her call after John's arrest, Andy didn't turn her down. They shared the champagne, then shared his bed for only the second time. Except for their first night together, they'd always met at her place. Funny. Sleeping with Loraine in his own home formed the bookends for their relationship. They'd started out there the night they met in a bar, and they ended up there on the last night he met with or spoke to her. Theirs was a very strange relationship from the beginning. I guess it only makes sense that it ended the way it did.

# CHAPTER

14

LIFE SEEMED TO STAND STILL for Andy even after John's guilty verdict. He couldn't get away from the place where he'd been since the day Gabe died. A jury may have convicted John, but for Andy, the saga still wasn't over. A guilty verdict wasn't enough. It had never been enough. He didn't want a jury to say John killed Gabe. Andy wanted John to admit it. He had to hear with his own ears the words "I did it." Anything short of that would never satisfy his demand for justice for Gabriel Phillips. That's not to say Andy didn't try to let it. I think he may have actually succeeded for the first forty-eight hours after he heard the verdict. Of course, his little celebration party helped. But after he sobered up, and his house became empty once again, images of Gabe lying in a pool of his own blood started haunting Andy again. Every time he closed his eyes, he saw Gabe's lifeless face while Andy tried to start CPR. He could hear his own voice on the radio requesting the coroner to take the body away. And he could hear John Phillips claiming Gabe fell out of the top bunk with a bad dream.

The more these sights and sounds haunted Andy, the more he realized he hadn't won anything yet. There could be no justice for Gabriel Phillips until the man who took his life confessed his guilt and accepted the consequences of his actions. And Andy would never have peace until justice was done. These thoughts slowly consumed him, which made Andy's mood grow darker by the day. From the way he acted, you would think the jury had come back with a completely different verdict. His coworkers noticed. They all expected him to be ecstatic. He was anything but. After a couple of days Ed Spence changed the department schedule around and stuck Andy on the graveyard shift so no one except the night dispatcher would have to be around him. Working the graveyard shift during the holidays only made things worse. Especially on Christmas Eve.

Since moving back to Indiana, I've found we get a white Christmas about every third year. Apparently, that year was the third year, because it started snowing early in the day on Christmas Eve and didn't stop until early the next morning. Andy hated snow. He hated driving in snow. He hated walking in snow. He hated people who got excited about playing in snow. All in all, he hated snow. And it had snowed all day and it was still snowing at night when he fishtailed his patrol car out of the Trask Police Department parking lot and started his appointed rounds through town. He reported for duty earlier than normal to allow the guys with families to spend more time at home.

About half an hour into his shift, Andy was driving up Main Street when he noticed a Chevy Citation headed the opposite direction that appeared to him to be driving erratically. So he flips on his red lights, does a U-turn, and takes off after the guy. The city snowplows had the streets pretty clean, but with the snow still falling, the streets were too slick for this to be a real high-speed chase. I don't know if whoever was driving the Chevy didn't see him or what, but they didn't pull over. Instead, the Chevy kept on going, making turns through the neighborhood until pulling into a driveway. This particular Chevy was one of GM's first front-wheel-drive cars, which is why it got so far ahead before Andy could catch up. His big old Mercury police cruiser had rear-wheel drive, which meant he spent more time fishtailing and spinning out than pursuing.

By the time Andy pulled up to the house where the car parked, the driver had already climbed out and started trudging through the snow up to the house, his arms full of gifts. Since it was Christmas Eve, you guessed it, the guy was dressed like Santa Claus. Andy pulled up in front of the house, his red and blue lights flashing, and he gave a quick blow of the siren, just to get the guy's attention. And it worked. It worked so well that half the neighborhood looked out its doors and windows as Andy jumped out of his car, pulled out his sidearm, and yelled at Santa, "On the ground!" Santa tromped around in the snow to where his entire body faced Andy, and he said something like, "What?" and Andy went nuts. He yelled at Santa, "On the ground. NOW!" Since it had snowed most of the day, the ground had about six or seven inches of snow on it, except, of course, next to the sidewalk leading to the front door of the house. So Santa threw the gifts to the side, and you could hear glass breaking, and fell facedown into a snowbank. Andy tried running up to him, but he fell face-first into the snow himself. By this point the people in the house were out on their front porch, along with all the neighbors who'd been watching out their windows. Adding an audience to his frustration set off Andy, and he walked over to Santa and planted his knee in the middle of his back while fumbling for his handcuffs—which he dropped in the snow. Finally Andy dug the cuffs out, but, of course, they are now so cold that skin will nearly freeze to them, but he slaps them on Santa anyway. While Andy pulled the guy up out of the snow by his wrists, Santa's beard and hat stayed attached to the ground. A little five-year-old girl on the porch let out a scream and said, "That's not Santa. That's Daddy." She started crying. The mother pleaded with Andy to find out what was going on. He just dragged Santa back through the snow to his patrol car, shoved him in the backseat, and told him he was under arrest for driving under the influence. No field sobriety test. Nothing. As ole Rosco P. Coltrane used to say on *The Dukes of Hazzard,* he cuffed him and stuffed him.

If Andy had stopped for just a moment, he might have recognized Santa as the pastor of the local Methodist church, which just happens to be the largest church in town. Every business leader in the community goes there. Andy had met the pastor a couple of weeks earlier when the pastor delivered a huge can of caramel corn to the police department as a way of showing the church's appreciation for the officers. Now this poor clergyman sat in the back of Andy's car, cold and wet, with wrists that were slowly freezing to a set of ice-cold handcuffs. To make matters worse, if they could get any worse, he never even bothered to check for ID until he'd hauled the guy all the way over to Adamsburg to book him in the county jail. The pastor, in shock in the backseat, could hardly talk. It wasn't exactly Andy's finest hour.

The pastor didn't get angry, like you would expect, once they cleared up the situation, even though that took nearly twelve hours. I think he was just grateful to get out of jail before Christmas ended. Chief Ed Spence, however, was not nearly as forgiving, and neither were the community leaders who happened to be parishioners of the pastor's church. Andy ended up suspended without pay for two weeks, and he was lucky he didn't lose his job. He probably would have been fired if the pastor had pressed a wrongful-arrest lawsuit against the town, but he didn't. It wasn't just the wrongful arrest that got Andy in hot water. It was the excessive force he'd used when arresting one of the spiritual leaders of the town dressed as an icon of the Christmas season. I don't know if the Trask Police Department ever fully recovered from that public relations disaster.

Ted Jackson invited Andy to come over on New Year's Day to watch Notre Dame play in the Cotton Bowl on television. Andy hadn't left his house since his suspension, so he was glad to finally have a little company. He didn't feel he could show his face in Trask, not yet at least. Maybe not ever. Ted's wife, Janey, had made them a bunch of snacks before leaving the house to go shopping. She hated football. Ted's son spent the day at his mother's house, which left Ted and Andy alone. Not long after the second quarter started, Ted finally worked up the nerve to ask Andy, "What's going on with you? A two-week suspension for excessive force, that's not like you. Although, I do have to say that collar of Santa was some fine police work. Every force around the world's been trying to catch that bastard, but you're the one who finally nailed him. Good work."

"What can I say? I wasn't going to let him slip down any chimneys on my watch," Andy said as he grabbed a handful of potato chips and washed it down with a swig of Pepsi.

"And nabbing a pastor all at the same time. Most people would be fooled by that whole clerical collar and Bible thing. You got him for what? Driving under the influence of the Spirit? Way to go, Baretta."

"I show favoritism to no man," Andy said.

"Yeah, but seriously, man. What's going on? You haven't been yourself the past couple of weeks," Ted said.

"Ahh, it's nothing. Haven't you ever read how people get depressed during the holidays? That's all it is," Andy said.

"I know better. I thought you'd be on cloud nine for at least a month after the Phillips verdict. You got what you wanted. You nailed the guy. We wouldn't have even had a case if it weren't for you. Hell, we wouldn't have even pursued it if you hadn't dogged us about it. Why are you so down?"

"I don't know," Andy said.

Ted didn't say anything for a while. The two of them sat back and watched the game. During the next Gatorade commercial Ted looked over at Andy and said, "You're not feeling guilty, are you?"

"Me. Hell no. For what?" Andy said.

Ted looked at him.

"What?" Andy asked.

"You sure had a way of finding the right witnesses at just the right time. And their testimonies were exactly what we needed to put Phillips away. It sure was convenient, the way they just sort of turned up like that," Ted said.

"You trying to say I coached those witnesses on what to say?" Andy said.

"You tell me. I mean, come on, Andy. I heard that Paul kid's testimony a thousand times, and he always said the exact same thing in the exact same order using the exact same words. No variation, ever. You know that never happens."

"Other people backed up what he said," Andy said.

Ted shook his head. "Don't play me for a fool. We've known each other way too long for that. Sure, other people backed up his story about what he heard. But the kid said he saw John Phillips smash Gabe's head in. He didn't just hear something on the other side of his wall. He steps forward as an eyewitness, which was the one thing we had to have to nail this guy for murder one. That's awfully convenient."

"Then why did you still use him as a witness? No one put a gun to your head. If you had doubts about whether or not he was telling the truth, why did you take him to the D.A.? Why did you make him your climactic witness to drop the hammer on Phillips?" Andy pressed.

Ted didn't say anything in return.

"I'll tell you why. Because you know Phillips did it and you didn't want to take a chance that he might get off. Am I right?" Andy said.

"Go to hell," Ted said.

"Sounds like we're both going to hell if what you say is true. If you think I instructed Brian Paul or any other witness on what to say, go investigate it. Nail my sorry ass to the wall. Hell, I don't have much of a career left anyway, not after busting Santa Claus in front of the whole freakin' town. What do I care? If you think I crossed some line, if you think I did something wrong, prove it. But I can tell you why you won't. You don't want to let some guy who killed his own kid in cold blood get away with it on a technicality. Am I right?"

"Let's just watch the game," Ted replied.

"That proves it. You know I'm right," Andy said.

"Fine. I know John Phillips killed his son and I didn't want to take a chance on the case falling apart. You may be correct about that, but that doesn't make you right. The evidence would have taken us there; it would have given us a conviction. You didn't have to massage the truth to make it more damning," Ted said.

"Massage, hell. If you think I crossed the line, why don't you prove it?" Andy asked. "Go ahead. I don't care. I've got nothing to hide."

"Need a new Pepsi?" Ted changed the subject as he got up and walked off to the kitchen, completely ignoring Andy's question.

Andy took the hint and didn't bring up John Phillips again until long after Joe Montana led Notre Dame to a victory in one of the greatest college football games of all time and shortly before USC kicked off to Michigan to start the second half of the Rose Bowl. Then he said, "I need to talk to him face-to-face."

"Him who?" Ted replied.

"You know him who. Phillips," Andy said.

"Holy crap, don't tell me we're back to that," Ted said.

"I just need to talk to him. And not over those visiting-room phones. I need to talk to him face-to-face. I have a couple of questions that still haven't been answered. I need it, Jax," Andy said.

"Why? What more could you possibly want from this guy? Hell, he's already been convicted of killing his kid. I wouldn't be surprised if the judge gives the guy death. In fact, given the circumstances, I would be shocked if the guy doesn't fry. Isn't that enough? What more could you need?"

"I need to look him in the eye and ask him straight up why he did it."

"Okay, John Wayne. Then what? You gonna get your posse and take him outside of town and string him up yourself?" Ted joked.

"You didn't know Gabriel Phillips, Ted. You never…" Andy choked back tears and swallowed hard. "I don't understand…" He could barely get the words out. "I don't understand how anyone could hurt that little boy. He didn't deserve…" Andy wiped away tears from his face and tried to continue but couldn't. Finally he said in almost a whisper, "I just need to talk to this guy."

Ted Jackson let out a long sigh. "Okay. I'll set it up. But I want to be in the room with you."

Andy shook his head. "No. I need to talk to him alone." He looked over at Ted, his eyes and cheeks red.

Jackson growled out, "Dammit, Andy, you just have to make this even harder for me. All right. Fine. You can talk to him alone, but I'm going to be on the other side of the glass listening in. If you even so much as put your pinky toe over the line, if you give me the slightest hint that you are going to do something more than talk, then I will be in there in half a second and I don't give a damn about how long we have been friends, you will pay the consequences."

"Understood," Andy said. He sat silently for nearly a minute. "Thanks. You won't have to worry about me, Jax. I'm not the Charles Bronson type." That's a *Death Wish* reference, just in case you didn't catch it. Most guys back in the 1970s loved that movie where Charles Bronson goes out and takes out the murdering punks who killed his wife and raped his daughter.

# CHAPTER

## 15

Two days after that conversation, Andy found himself sitting behind a wooden table in interrogation room three in the Harris County Sheriff's Department headquarters. The sheriff's office and the county lockup were all together, and both sat across a parking lot from the county courthouse. Andy was not wearing his uniform. He still had a few days to go on his suspension. Not that it really mattered. Every county officer knew he was a cop and they figured he was on official business, since Ted Jackson had set up this meeting. If they knew about Andy's suspension, and they probably did, since nothing stays a secret long in small towns, they didn't seem to care.

Andy did not rise out of his chair when a deputy brought John into the room. He just sat there at the far end of a wooden table, a cup of coffee in front of him. The chains running from John's handcuffs to his leg irons jingled and jangled as he shuffled in, the sound of which fit the time of year, but not the setting. "Take a seat," Andy said with the cold, calculating voice of an executioner, and pointed to the chair on the other end of the table.

"Would it be possible to remove these handcuffs and leg irons? I promise I won't try to get away," John said with a smile.

"No," Andy said without expounding. Then, turning to the deputy, he said, "You don't have to stick around. I'll be all right in here by myself."

"You sure, man? I ain't got nothing else to do." Andy thought the deputy sounded like he'd just moved off the farm.

"Yeah, I'm sure," Andy said.

After the door closed behind the deputy, John laughed, then said, "I thought all the interrogations ended with the trial."

Andy glared at him. "I'm glad you can laugh about this. I was right about you. You are a smug son of a bitch."

John shook his head. "You really don't know me, Officer. You confuse peace with smugness and you don't know what to make of it."

"Peace? Hah." Andy laughed. "Nice act. Save it for the sentencing hearing."

"It's not an act," John said. He looked across the table at Andy, looked at him without saying a word for so long, it made Andy very uncomfortable. It was one of those looks that made Andy feel as though John were looking right into his soul. This wasn't how Andy had this little confrontation planned. "I'm worried about you," John said to Andy. "I have been since the night I met you. I thought perhaps the verdict against me might give you some peace. Actually, I prayed that it would, but obviously it hasn't."

"This isn't about me," Andy said.

"Isn't it?" John said.

"What the hell is that supposed to mean?" Andy said.

"You already know. Don't you?" John replied with a gentle tone in his voice.

Andy stared across the table at John. "What are you talking about?" he said.

"Can I ask you a question, Officer Myers? Can you tell me why my son's death haunts you?" John asked. "Would it have been easier on you if I'd screamed and cried and carried on the night you arrived at my apartment?"

"It would have been easier on me if you hadn't killed him," Andy said in a way that was colder than the temperature outside, which in Indiana at the beginning of January is pretty darn cold.

"Do you really think I could kill my own flesh and blood?" John said.

"That's an odd question for a man waiting around for a judge to give him a death sentence. And from what I understand, he wasn't your flesh and blood. You only thought he was," Andy said.

"Oh, he was my son, all right. And I'm not worried about a death sentence. We all live with a death sentence hanging over our heads. No one lives forever, at least not in this life," John said. "But you didn't answer my question."

Andy said in a tone dripping with sarcasm: "Yes, I not only think you could kill Gabriel, I know that you *did,* in fact, kill him. I know it, and the state of Indiana proved it beyond a reasonable doubt. Yet, for some reason, you can't seem to climb out from behind your wall of delusion to own up to what you've done. You will probably maintain your innocence until the moment they strap you into the chair and flip the switch. Being the religious man you claim to be, you should want to confess what you've done and get things right with your God before you go and see him. I guess I was wrong."

"Why does my son's death haunt you so?" John asked, seemingly ignoring everything Andy had just said. "I know that it does. I found the bear you left on his grave."

"How dense are you? Why do you think it haunts me?" Andy said.

"That doesn't answer my question. Do *you* even know why it haunts you? Do you know why you can't get past that night? Do you understand what made you come here today?" John said.

Andy leaned across the table and said, "The only thing that haunts me is my desire for justice for Gabriel. He didn't deserve what you did to him. That's what haunts me. Justice. I want to see that Gabe gets justice."

"Then you should already be satisfied. A jury said I am guilty as charged. The murderer didn't get away with his crime and justice has been served. Case closed. So why isn't that enough for you? Do you know?"

"Why did you do it, John? Why did you kill Gabe?"

"Can I ask you a question, Officer Myers?" John replied.

Andy slammed the table, rose up out of his chair, and said, "NO. DAMMIT. Answer the damn question. WHY DID YOU KILL HIM!?" He heard a tap on the one-way glass on the back wall and sat back down. "Why did you kill Gabriel?" Andy repeated, much calmer this time.

John slowly shook his head. "It doesn't matter what I say, does it?"

"Like hell it doesn't," Andy said.

"What is it that you want to hear?" John asked.

"The truth," Andy replied.

"You already know the truth, but somehow that doesn't seem to be enough for you. Can you tell me why?" John said.

Andy rubbed his forehead and let out a long sigh. He had envisioned a completely different conversation, with different results. John's insistence on turning every question around caused Andy to become more and more frustrated. Finally he looked up at John, fire blazing in his eyes, and said, "I need to hear the truth from you."

"The truth is I loved my son more than you can understand. I still do. The truth is he never understood why his mother and I couldn't live together any longer. I couldn't explain it to him without destroying his image of his mother, so I didn't try. The truth is his mother could never do anything to hurt me so bad that I would ever even consider harming my little boy. The truth is I forgave her for what she did, I forgave her for the lies she threw at me, and I forgave her for accusing me of something I didn't do. And the truth is...I forgive you for believing her and pushing so hard to convict me of murder," John said.

"I don't need your forgiveness," Andy said. He paused for a moment, took a deep breath, and said, "I'm just going to ask you one more time, why did you do it?"

"This won't be the last time, we both know that." John laughed. "You are going to keep asking me until I tell you what you want to hear, but even then it won't give you the peace you're looking for. I've had similar conversations with my wife. She didn't just accuse me to the police. She called me a baby killer to my face, many, many times. Nothing I can say will satisfy her. Finally I had to ask her, do you really think I would kill my only son because of you?"

John's words stopped Andy dead in his tracks. "What did you say?"

"I said I told her, do you really think I would kill my only son because of you?" John said.

Andy looked at him like he'd seen a ghost. He'd heard John say these same words a few months earlier in the dream that haunted him to this day. "Yes," Andy said softly.

"Excuse me, Officer," John said.

"Yes, I think you would," Andy said.

"Then there's nothing else I can say," John said.

This line of questioning wasn't getting Andy anywhere. The room was filled with silence for several minutes, both men looking across the table at one another. Finally Andy said, "I'm going to be there tomorrow. I'm going to be there to see the look on your face when the judge tells you he's giving you the chair. And then I'm going to be there to watch you fry. I am going to be there to see you get what you deserve, and I'm going to enjoy every minute of it."

"Whether I live or die doesn't really matter. To me, to live is Christ, and to die is gain. When the worst thing that can possibly happen to me is that I get to leave this earth and go home to be with my God, who loves me, and to see my son again, I would say my future looks pretty good. God has me where He wants me, and I trust Him completely. He knows what He is doing," John said.

Without responding, Andy turned toward the one-way glass and said, "I'm through. Come and get him."

After John had been led back to his cell, Ted Jackson walked into the room and said, "Well?"

"Well, what?"

"Andy, this isn't some cop show. This is the real world. And in the real world bad guys don't crack and cry for mercy. According to the people I've put away, not a one of those I arrested was guilty. They all claim they're innocent. The prison system is stuffed to the gills with innocent people. You know that. Every trial that ends with a guilty verdict is nothing but a huge miscarriage of justice. They don't call these guys cons for nothing. You got your guilty verdict, and you'll probably get your death sentence. Let that be enough. He's guilty, we proved that. He doesn't have to admit it to make it real. Hell, the more he denies doing anything wrong, the more likely he will actually have to serve whatever sentence he gets. Accept it. Enjoy it. And move on," Jackson said.

"I'm trying," Andy said. "After I hear the judge hand down his sentence, I think I will be able to. I've never had a case affect me like this. I guess that's what I get for breaking my own rules about women with kids," he said with a nervous laugh.

"These cases…anytime there's a child involved, they suck you in, even if you don't know the kid ahead of time," Jackson said. "Here's some free advice. Go home. Go out in your garage and build something. Or just pound nails into a piece of wood. Or take your lawn mower apart and put it back together. Even if you screw it up, the price of a new lawn mower is nothing compared to what this case is doing to you. Go home and do something with your hands and let your mind relax. And while you're at it, do me another favor. Get back on the twelve steps. The alcohol's not doing you any favors."

Andy knew Ted was right, and took his advice. He went

home, spent the afternoon in his garage, and got busy. Now, my old man was never much of a mechanic. And he never claimed to be a carpenter. So he combined his lack of skills in both by taking out a hammer and beating on his lawn mower until both arms ached. By the time he was finished, he felt much better. He also went to an AA meeting that night, his first in over a year. He quit drinking completely, although he didn't throw out all of his booze. He stashed one bottle away as sort of an emergency bender kit, just in case he needed it.

# CHAPTER

## 16

THE SENTENCING HEARING commenced at nine the next morning. Andy woke up before his alarm went off, and bounced out of bed for the first time since his suspension. Every other day of his unpaid vacation found him dragging out of bed around noon with a hangover. On this day his head felt clear, clearer than it had in months. His arms and hands ached from his afternoon swinging a hammer in the garage, but it was worth it. He had slept well. He'd almost forgotten what it was like to get a good night's sleep. Of course, it helps when no one haunts you in your dreams. And he'd had a lot of dreams since John's conviction. He never told me what they were. For all I know, he may not have been able to remember anything about them except the panic they left him in when he woke up. Or maybe they were just too weird to tell anyone about. Whatever they had been, they left him alone that night, for which he was thankful.

Andy arrived at the courthouse nearly an hour early, mainly because he was cheap. He hated putting money into parking meters, which he never had to do when he drove his patrol car. But he couldn't drive his patrol car while he was suspended, which left him behind the wheel of his old Impala. However, since he was a cop and had friends on the Adamsburg city force, as well as the sheriff's department, he knew the location of the three meters near the courthouse that did not work. He had to make a few trips around the block while he waited for one of them to open up, and when one finally did, he pulled his car into the spot, locked it, and headed toward Judge Houk's courtroom.

Unlike the day when the judge read the jury's verdict, Andy had his choice of any seat in the house when he walked into the courtroom. That is, almost any seat. To his surprise, he wasn't the first observer in the courtroom that morning. A solitary black man with muscles that bulged under the long sleeves of his white dress shirt sat in the front row, directly behind the defendant's table. He didn't move when Andy walked in, nor did he acknowledge Andy's presence when he asked, "Hi, how ya doing?" The man kept his shaved head bowed down, with his eyes closed, and Andy noticed his lips were moving. "Whatever," Andy said as he sat in the second row on the prosecution's side of the room. He thought it would give him the perfect vantage point to watch John as his sentence was read.

Pulling out a newspaper, Andy soon lost himself in the previous day's college basketball scores and an article about the Indiana Hoosiers' chances as they entered conference play. Over the next forty-five minutes, the courtroom filled to about two-thirds capacity. Occasionally Andy would look up to see if he recognized anyone. Loraine came in about ten minutes before the hearing began, accompanied by the same man who'd sat with her on the day John was found guilty. The two held hands as they entered, and he put his arm around her shoulder after they sat down. She glanced at Andy as she walked in, but she did not acknowledge him in any way. It was as though she did not know him. Andy followed her lead and went back to his newspaper. By now he'd read every story on the sports page, as well as the front-page section. With nothing else to do, he was now reading the classifieds. It doesn't take long to read the daily Adamsburg paper.

About the time he'd read the last of the day's real estate listings, Rachel Maris walked over to him to say hello. "This shouldn't take too long," she said. "Both sides filed briefs with the judge earlier, and he's read the sentencing investigator's report, so he should have already made up his mind on how he is going to rule today. If we have to, we're prepared to call the boy's mother to the stand to remind him of the cold-blooded nature of this crime. This judge usually doesn't want a rehash of what's already been said, so I don't think it will be necessary. Of course, if the other side starts trying to flood the hearing with so-called character witnesses, then all bets are off. But from what I've heard about George Houk, the only thing that really moves him are signs of genuine remorse from the guilty party. If that happens, he may give Phillips a life sentence. Without it, this guy will probably fry."

"All I want is justice," Andy said.

"Well, get ready," she replied, "because you are about to see it in action."

"All rise," the bailiff said just as he did every time he called court into session. "Superior Court of Harris County, State of Indiana, is now in session. The Honorable George Houk presiding." The judge walked in, his cowboy boots clicking on the floor, his hair still showing that distinctive hat line as he sat down behind the bench, and told everyone to be seated. Then he clanked his gavel, and the hearing began. The jury box remained empty because, back when all this took place, the judge, not the jury, decided on the sentence even in death penalty cases.

"I've read the briefs filed by both the prosecution and the defense, as well as the investigator's report. Because the prosecution has asked for a death sentence, I went back over the transcripts of the testimony of the witnesses both sides called during the trial phase of this case," the judge said. "Would either side like to call any additional witnesses before I render my ruling?" Andy watched John closely as the judge spoke. There wasn't much to see. John displayed very little emotion. He appeared almost disinterested, as though he were sitting in the back of the courtroom and someone else's fate was about to be determined. The man sitting directly behind John, the only person to arrive in the courtroom before Andy, had not moved. His head remained down, his lips continued to move.

"No, Your Honor," Donald Edmonds said, rising.

"The people also waive their right to call additional witnesses, Your Honor," Reginald Chambliss said.

"Very well," Judge Houk said. "Mr. Phillips, would you like to say anything on your own behalf before I pass sentence?" Andy thought he saw John's attorney cringe at the question.

"Yes, sir," John said.

"You may proceed," the judge said.

Standing up from his seat behind the defendant's table, he said, "In Job chapter two and verse ten, Job asks his wife,

'Shall we accept good from God and not accept adversity?' He said this after he'd lost everything he held dear, including his children. I believe I understand Job a little better now than I ever have before. The most precious thing I had in this world, outside of the gift of my Savior, has been taken from me. And just when I didn't think life could get any worse, I find myself convicted of taking his life. I do not understand why my son had to die, nor do I understand how anyone could believe I killed him. All along I've maintained my innocence, and that does not change now. But more than that, I believe God is still God. He is still in control. I don't have to understand these things to accept them and trust that God has a plan.

"However you may judge me does not matter. I have a Judge in heaven, and I know how I stand before Him. I do not fear prison. I have been there before, and I discovered God was there waiting for me. He's walked with me every day since. If His path leads back to where He found me, so be it. His will be done. Nor do I fear death. Jesus said, 'I am the resurrection and the life; he who believes in Me will live even if he dies.' He lived, died, and rose again to deliver us from the fear of death and the captivity that fear brings. He has set me free, and nothing can change that, whether I am living my life here among you or sitting in a jail cell. Wherever I may be, I am free, even in my chains.

"You asked, Your Honor, if I wished to say anything on my own behalf. I'm not sure what others say when they stand in this position. Perhaps they plead for mercy, or maybe they defiantly thumb their nose at you and dare you to throw the book at them. I won't do either. When I stood before you for the first time, you told me that you held my life in your hands.

You are mistaken. My life rests in the hands of my Lord and Savior, Jesus Christ. I entrusted myself to him nearly eight years ago, and He has not failed me yet. All I ask is for His will to be done. I prayed for you as you considered my sentence. I asked God to give you wisdom, and I asked that whatever you now decide, it will work to give God glory.

"That's all I know to say. I thank you for letting me speak freely. I pray that you and all of the others in this courtroom will experience the peace and freedom that only Christ can give. Amen. And amen."

Andy didn't really know what to think as John spoke. At first, he became angry at John's audacity to rattle off a sermon while still refusing to accept responsibility for what he had done. But, as John kept talking, Andy's anger gave way to pity. He could tell John really believed what he said, yet he wondered how someone could believe this so strongly and do what John had done. Of course, Ted said it best. *They don't call these guys cons for nothing. Most are really good at fooling other people, and they are all experts at fooling themselves.*

By the time John got to the end of his little speech, Andy just wanted the guy to shut up so the judge could pronounce his sentence and everyone could get back to their lives. *Gabe Phillips's death consumed my father for a very long time. He was long past ready to crawl out of the jaws of this beast and reclaim something approaching normalcy.* That's not to say Andy didn't listen to John. He did, even as he tried not to. The things John said about being free struck a chord with him, and Andy got mad at himself for letting it. He'd wrestled with his own demons for a while, and he felt anything but free. A thought jumped into his mind so quickly that he let it take root like a dandelion in a lawn before he could pull it out. The little thought said, *"I wish I could be free like that."* He quickly squashed it and reminded himself that the man talking was a convicted murderer who most likely was on his way to death row. Even so, the thought stuck around, like a sliver in his brain.

Andy also watched the other people in the courtroom while John went on and on. The man directly behind John never moved even one of his very large and very numerous muscles. He sat stock-still, head down, eyes closed, lips moving. Judge Houk just looked annoyed. Leaning back in his chair, with a pen tapping his desk, his body language seemed to say, *Let's get this over with.* Reginald Chambliss, Esquire, seemed to enjoy John's speech. He turned in his chair and watched John, a little smile on his lips. Rachel Maris had told Andy that the only thing that might persuade the judge to go easy on John would be some sign of genuine remorse. The more John talked, the less remorse he showed, and the happier Reginald Chambliss became. Loraine was another story. She never once looked in John's direction. From where Andy sat, she looked like she'd gone to another world. At one point she laid her head on her male companion's shoulders, and he gently stroked her hair. The sight didn't make Andy jealous. In fact, he felt a little relieved by it.

Once John finally finished talking and sat down, the judge straightened himself in his chair and said, "Does either counsel wish to address the court before the sentence is pronounced?" Andy loved it. Here John gives his grand oration, and the judge basically passes it off with a "Yeah, whatever. Next."

"No, Your Honor," Chambliss said.

"No, Your Honor," Donald Edmonds also said.

"Very well," Judge Houk said. "Mr. Phillips, would you please rise?" John stood up, as did his attorney. Only then did Andy notice that the public defender had actually dressed himself in what appeared to be professional attire. He wore a navy blue suit, the kind a real lawyer wears. "Mr. Phillips, the state of Indiana mandates that murder in the first degree be punishable by life in prison or by death. Given the nature of this case, both the cold-blooded premeditation that you showed, as well as the tender age of the victim and your relationship with him, it is the opinion of this court that you have shown a complete disregard for life, as well as for the proceedings within this courtroom. Therefore, I hereby sentence you to be remanded to the state penitentiary in Michigan City, where you will be put to death in the electric chair at the soonest date possible. May the God about which you talk so freely have mercy on your soul."

"He already has, Your Honor," John said.

"You better hope so," the judge replied. "Court dismissed."

The gavel fell, and that was the end of it. The ensuing scene in the courtroom wasn't nearly as chaotic as one might expect. John's supporters wailed in protest while the prosecution team shook one another's hands and slapped each other on the back. Chambliss's face could barely contain his smile. One look at the guy and you knew he couldn't wait to get outside and speak to the camera crews. He had his headline case that would make his name known from right here on the shore of Lake Michigan all the way down to the Ohio River, and Terre Haute to Richmond, and every point in between. If he'd scripted the case himself, it couldn't have gone any better. He'd probably already started writing out his change of address cards for the big move he planned to make into the governor's mansion after the next election. Voters love the tough, law-and-order types.

Andy fully expected to see or hear some sign of joy from Loraine, but he didn't. She didn't let out a peep when the judge pronounced John's sentence, and she didn't say a word as she got up out of her seat and walked out of the courtroom, her male companion in tow. At one point she passed very close to Andy. He started to say something, but thought better of it. They seemed to be exactly what they were back before they met that night in a bar: strangers, nothing but strangers. Deep down Andy wished that was all they'd ever been.

Ted came over and shook Andy's hand. They exchanged some small talk, nothing important. Before he left, Ted asked Andy, "So what are you going to do now that this is all behind you?"

"I haven't thought that far ahead," Andy said. "I'm just glad it's done. I go back to work next week. Hopefully, life can get back to normal pretty quick."

"I hope so. For your sake, I hope so," Ted said as he patted his friend on the back and they walked out of the courtroom together.

You would think my story would end here. John Phillips goes off to prison for killing his son, the only child my father ever loved. In a perfect world, Gabe's death would make my dad reconsider how he'd walked away from me before I was ever born. After seeing the error of his ways, he would drive over to Saint Louis, where he and I would have a tearful reunion that would be the beginning of a beautiful father-son relationship. Sorry. This world is far from perfect and that's not how the rest of the story played out. I wish it had. But then again, life is funny. You never know where it's going to take you.

# CHAPTER

## 17

TED JACKSON HAD TOLD my old man to put this case behind him. It didn't take long for Andy to realize that the only way he could do that was to get a completely fresh start. He put his house up for sale and started looking for a place in the country with some acreage around it, but that didn't feel like enough of a change. Driving to work one day, he decided he should quit the Trask police force to become a Harris County deputy sheriff, but the more he thought about it, the more he realized he needed to do something bigger. He found himself attracted to one of the women in his AA group, and even went so far as to get her phone number. Yet on the afternoon he picked up the phone and punched in six numbers, he hung up before he dialed the seventh and threw her number away. A new relationship wouldn't take him as far as he knew he needed to go, especially a relationship with someone who potentially had as many problems as he had.

That is why in the spring after John's conviction, Andy applied for a job as a trooper with the Indiana state police. Ed Spence gave him the highest of recommendations, as did his friends on the Harris County sheriff's department. Good ole Reginald Chambliss, Esquire, even wrote a letter of recommendation for him. It may have been overkill, but Andy didn't want to take any chances. He officially resigned from Trask the week before the Indy 500 (which is always the last Sunday in May) and started basic training with the state police the first of June.

I don't know about other states, but in Indiana, the six months of training to become a state trooper is tougher than military boot camp. Laugh if you want, but that's what Andy told me. And since he went through both, he ought to know. For twenty-four weeks he ran and trained and sweat off more pounds than he thought he had to spare. Every day of training was basically like the day before in that it left him so exhausted he didn't have time to think about John or Gabriel or anyone else with the last name of Phillips. On his occasional weekend off, he was only home long enough to wash his uniforms; then it was back to Bloomington and more training.

Halfway through basic he had to fill out a form requesting where in the state of Indiana he would like to be stationed. Andy put down anywhere but Harris County, and the state gave him his wish. He was assigned to the Columbus area, down in southern Indiana, which meant he could look forward to days spent patrolling Interstate 65 and State Highway 46. After graduation from the academy, he sold his house in Trask for less than market value, furniture and all. He didn't just want to put the Phillips case behind him. He wanted to be free of everything that was his life the night he found Gabe's body. In early January he moved to Brown County, the tourist center of the state, which lies just to the west of Columbus. People come from all over Indiana, Illinois, Kentucky, and Ohio to see the leaves change in Brown County every fall. It was cold and snowy when Andy moved in to his one-thousand-square-foot house that was more cabin than house, halfway between Nashville and Columbus. By this point he'd also gone nearly a year without a drink, which was the longest stretch he'd managed to put together in fifteen years. Andy had his fresh start. From his job to his circle of friends and even the sheets on his bed, everything in his life was new.

About the time the snow finally melted and farmers started plowing their fields to get them ready to plant corn, Andy stopped at a Denny's just off mile marker 43 of Interstate 65 for a Grand Slam breakfast. It may have been half past two in the afternoon, but that didn't matter. Denny's served the Grand Slam all day. Since he was in uniform and on duty, he received great service. Businesses along the interstate liked having state troopers drop by. The sight of their car in the parking lots made the management feel a little safer.

As he walked into the restaurant, Andy stopped and bought an *Indianapolis Star* from the vending machine next to the front door. He intended to read the sports page with his meal. Baseball season would begin soon, which would help fill the void the Hoosiers' failure to make the NCAA tourney had created in his life. He tossed the paper on the table of a corner booth and sat down.

"How are you this afternoon, sir?" a smiling, rail-thin, middle-aged waitress asked. She smelled of coffee and cigarette smoke. "Can I get you something to drink?"

"Pepsi, please," Andy said.

"Is Coke all right?" she asked.

"Sure, Coke's fine," he said. "And I don't need a menu. Give me a Grand Slam breakfast, eggs over medium."

"Bacon or sausage?"

"Sausage."

"All right, sir, we'll get that right out to you," she said, and walked away.

After she was gone, Andy opened up the paper and started to peel away the top few sections when a front-page story caught his eye. The headline read: "APPEAL PRO-CESS BEGINS FOR CONVICTED CHILD KILLER." Andy decided the recap of yesterday's Reds-Dodgers exhibition game could wait. He dropped the rest of the paper back onto the table and began reading. The story started off with a line that said something like, "The first of the state-mandated appeal hearings is scheduled to begin Monday in Indiana-polis for John Phillips who was convicted of the June 1978 killing of his son, Gabriel Phillips." What followed was a brief recap of the Phillips case, along with an explanation of the new death penalty laws the state had adopted to put it in compliance with recent Supreme Court rulings. Nothing in the story was particularly earth shattering, and Andy almost stopped reading until he came to a quote from a death pen-alty opponent who said something along the lines of, "John Phillips is a classic example of everything that is wrong with capital punishment. The poor guy got railroaded in the courts, and now he will hardly cooperate with his court-appointed attorneys who are fighting on his behalf. Since he won't fight to save his own life, we're going to fight to save it for him."

Andy finished reading the story about the time his glass

of Coke arrived. He took a long drink, grimaced (he much preferred Pepsi), and picked up the sports section. Before he got to the Reds score, he put the sports section back on the table, and went back to the quote from the death penalty opponent. "He won't fight to save his own life," he read again. "Who was there to fight for Gabe on the night he killed him?" Andy asked.

"Excuse me?" the coffee-and-cigarette-odor-emitting waitress asked as she passed by his table.

"Sorry, ma'am, I was just thinking out loud," he said.

"Well, if you need anything, you just let me know," she said.

"Don't worry, I will," he said.

The waitress walked away, and Andy went back to the quote. "He won't fight to save his own life." Those words seemed to jump off the page at him. *I wonder if he's finally cracked? I mean, come on, how long can this guy live in denial?* A smile crossed his lips as he took another long drink of his Coke. *Maybe, just maybe...* The thought made the two eggs, two links of sausage, and two pancakes the waitress slid in front of him taste even better. For over a year Andy had convinced himself that justice had been served with John's conviction, but now he realized he hadn't so much convinced himself as he had pushed the whole case out of his mind. Once he started thinking about it again, he realized he still wanted to hear a confession. He still needed John Phillips to say the words "I did it and I deserve whatever happens to me now." Gabe's killer didn't just need to be caught and convicted. He had to feel the full weight of the guilt for what he had done, and that weight had to break him in two. *A year on death row just might have been the trick,* he thought as he placed the eggs in between the pancakes and covered them with syrup. *And even if it didn't, the sooner the appeal process runs its course, the sooner justice can be served.* He smiled and wolfed down his meal.

After Andy finished his afternoon breakfast, he told himself he wouldn't give John Phillips another thought. And he didn't. At least not while he wrote a ticket to the driver of a red 1966 Mustang convertible he clocked doing seventy-two in the southbound lanes of I-65.

And he didn't think about John while he assisted a car filled with Indiana University coeds whose car had run out of gas just north of the Bloomington exit. Andy had to work hard to keep his eyes from wandering to places they shouldn't go and to think like a cop. Their shorts were way too short and their shirts were way too tight and Andy was way too old to stare at eighteen-year-olds the way his eyes wanted. He called for a wrecker and stayed with them while they waited for it to arrive. However, he spent most of that time in his patrol car filling out paperwork, or doing anything to keep his mind on his job.

And Andy didn't think about John Phillips or the events that caused him, Andy Myers, to completely remake his life at the age of thirty-two as he assisted the Brown County Sheriff's Department search for twin four-year-old boys who had disappeared from a mobile home that sat at the end of a dirt road, which was at the end of a gravel road, which was at the end of a single-lane, barely paved road off a remote state highway. I guess what I am saying is, these people lived out in the middle of nowhere. An uncle was supposed to be watching the twins, but he fell asleep on the couch. When he woke up, the boys were gone. The house was surrounded by fields that might have grown corn if anyone had ever bothered to plow them. No one had in years, which meant the weeds were tall enough for anyone shorter than the minimum height required to ride the Beast roller coaster at Kings Island to get lost inside. A creek also meandered through the property. This time of year, the water ran high enough that it stretched from grassy bank to grassy bank. If the boys had wandered over close enough to it to fall in, they wouldn't leave any footprints.

The volunteer fire departments from two local towns arrived to join in the search, as did the neighbors. Everyone wanted to help, but with so many people descending on such a small place at once, chaos ensued. Andy took charge of the scene. He broke the volunteers into groups. He sent one set of firemen to the fields to the south of the house, and another group to those on the north. Andy had them search in a grid pattern. Rescuers lined up an arm's length from one another and walked through the field, side by side, first north to south, then east to west. If the boys were crouched down hiding, one of the volunteers would step on them if they didn't see them first. He had a couple of the other groups of volunteers walk in the tall grass and ditches beside the road for a mile in each direction. A few men with fishing boats had already started cruising up and down the creek. The boys' mother showed up at the house about forty-five minutes into the search, and she was hysterical. Andy switched gears from search coordinator to chaplain. He calmed her down the best that he could until a real chaplain arrived from one of the local police departments. "Thank God," Andy said as he passed her off. Hysterical mothers were not his forte.

No one had found as much as a lost shoe from the two boys after an hour and a half. About the time everyone began to fear the worst, a loud shout came up from behind the mobile home. "I've got 'em! I've got 'em!" he yelled.

All of the rescue workers moved quickly toward the house. Andy dropped his mic and ran over toward the yelling man, along with the sheriff. The boys' uncle came out from around the corner of the mobile home, a boy in each arm. "They'd climbed into the shed out back of the house and were playing," he said. "All of these police cars and fire trucks pulling in scared 'em so bad that they hid down under some boxes. That's why no one seen 'em when we looked in there."

The boys' mother came running out of the mobile home, tears running down her face. "Mommy, Mommy," the boys said as they reached out for their mother. She pulled them out of her brother's arms, hugged them so tight Andy thought she might crack their ribs, and started kissing them repeatedly. The joy of finding them alive quickly gave way to her motherly instincts. "Don't ever do that to me again," she scolded. "You scared me half to death." The boys started crying, and the mother cried even more, and even some of the crusty volunteers started tearing up.

Watching the mother with her sons, a random thought popped into Andy's head, the kind of thought he hadn't had for a long time. He thought, *I wish I could have given Loraine a reunion with her little boy.* Now, he hadn't thought about Loraine since the day he turned in his resignation at the Trask police force. And he hadn't really thought about Gabe since the last time he drove past the Adamsburg cemetery, right before he started his state police training. This one random thought, along with the sight of a grateful but frantic mother, opened a door and all of the old thoughts and feelings he'd successfully ignored for over a year came flooding back. He had his fresh start, all right, but deep down Andy Myers was still Andy Myers. And the old demons that haunted him in his former life hunted him down in his new one.

Just because they'd found him didn't mean Andy surrendered willingly. He tried to push the feelings and obsession with Gabe's case back out of his mind. Staying busy had held them at bay before, and that was the tactic he tried this time as well. He threw himself into his work and found extra tasks to keep himself busy. Even during the monotony of sitting alongside the highway pointing a radar gun at cars and trucks zipping down the highway, he created mind games to keep his thoughts busy. He calculated the time it would take a car to reach Indianapolis from his mile marker, dividing the mileage by the car's speed. When the mind games didn't work, he lowered his threshold of speed over the limit that would make him pull someone over. That month he wrote more speeding tickets than any trooper in the state of Indiana. On his off days he ran, but these weren't little jogs in the park. Andy drove over to Brown County State Park and began running the hilly trails that leave ordinary, middle-aged weekend hikers sucking for air. When images of Gabe lying on a bloody floor tried to squeeze past Andy's defenses, he ran harder and faster until he was too tired to think about anything at all.

His strategy worked for a while. One day, however, he was done in by the smallest of acts. During breakfast on June 3, he was sitting in his kitchen, eating a bowl of Wheaties, when he looked up and noticed he hadn't changed his calendar since April. He had this cheap-looking calendar he picked up from the local hardware store hanging right next to the kitchen wall phone. So he slid his bowl of Wheaties aside, went over to the calendar, and pulled it off the nail sticking through the hole that was just above the landscape photo. He flipped from April to May just to look at the picture, which I think was some mountain scene from California. Then he turned the page from May to June and pushed it back on the nail. As he stepped back from the calendar, his eyes glanced down at the grid of days and one number popped out at him. Yeah, you guessed it. It was the second anniversary date of Gabe's death. He stood staring at the square on the calendar with the number in the middle until he couldn't see the number any longer because of the tears welling up in his eyes. "Two years. My God, has it really been *two* years?"

He sat back down at his table and kept staring up at the calendar, wiping tears away. Memories came flooding back, especially the memory of his last time with Gabe. Andy could see the two of them, sitting up high in the red seats of the upper deck in Cincinnati's old Riverfront Stadium, munching on hot dogs, while the "Big Red Machine" played far down below. It was the longest continuous time Andy had spent with a child since he was a kid himself. For a guy who didn't like children, he had the time of his life. Gabe kept peppering Andy with questions, most of them completely unrelated to one another. I like kids, but that kind of conversation gets old fast for me. Somehow, when it came to Gabe, nothing got old for Andy. Even two years later he could hear Gabe asking, "Why did you become a policeman, Andy?" A moment later it was "What do you think they put in hot dogs that make them taste so good?" Then it was

"What was your favorite baseball team when you were my age?"

But the one question that Andy could now hear above all the others was Gabe asking, "Do you believe in God?"

"I guess so," Andy said.

"I believe in God," Gabe said, "but I don't think my mom does."

"Really? Why do you think that?"

"She won't go to church anymore. She used to go all the time, when my mom and dad still lived together. Now she drops me off at the door, but she won't go inside."

"Just because she doesn't go to church doesn't mean she doesn't believe in God," Andy said.

"Yeah, I know. But she doesn't just not go. She gets kind of mad when I bring church up. And she doesn't pray before we eat. And one day I went outside to empty the trash, and when I pulled the lid off the trash can, I saw my mom's Bible in there. My dad gave it to her one year for Christmas. I think if someone throws their Bible away, they don't believe in God," Gabe said. Then he added, "I worry about my mom. I pray for her every day. She always seems sad."

Andy sat in his kitchen, staring at the calendar, replaying Gabe's words over and over in his head. Memories of Gabe and all the feelings they stirred up about Loraine and John had invaded this place, and they would not leave. Andy's reprieve was now officially over.

# CHAPTER

## 18

ALTHOUGH THE OLD MEMORIES had found him, Andy did his best to keep from obsessing over Gabe's death. The change of scenery helped, as did his job. Back when he lived in Trask, he did basically the same things in the same places and saw the same people every day. Once that place became infected by the Phillips case, he had to get away from it. His new surroundings did not have that smell of death. He didn't have to answer calls at the Madison Park Apartments two or three days a week or drive past the Adamsburg cemetery every time he went to the Harris County Courthouse. With enough effort, he could push Gabe and John and Loraine completely out of his mind for weeks at a time. I'm not so sure that was any better. The questions that haunted him never really went away. I think he just got used to their voices.

Sometime I think it was August because it was still hot. Andy was out on patrol on Interstate 65. He was cruising south, to be exact. The grass on the sides of the highway had turned brown and dry (it was a pretty dry summer that year) but another colorful sight had sprung up in its place. All along the highway, very large, very bright billboards had popped out like dandelions in May. You couldn't get away from them. Up on the billboard was the smiling face of one Mr. Reginald Chambliss, Esquire, the infamous Harris County prosecutor turned Republican nominee for governor. Good ole Reginald Chambliss was leaning against a broom, and underneath the billboard read: SWEEP OUT CRIME AND CORRUPTION. VOTE REGGIE CHAMBLISS, GOVERNOR. His high-profile murder case had proved to be the real broom, sweeping him right past Harris County and into statewide politics. Reginald Chambliss couldn't have plotted it out any better if he'd written the story of his life himself. Andy laughed when he saw one of the billboards for the first time. After a while he got where he hardly noticed them.

But on this particular hot August day, Andy pulled his police cruiser off the interstate and parked underneath a Chambliss billboard. He kept the engine running, and the AC cranked up on high. Pulling out his radar gun, he started clocking southbound motorists. Traffic was light, and he'd parked in a rather conspicuous place, which meant most people slowed down before they ever got to him. The red digital numbers that flashed on the gun dropped as the cars came closer to his location. He didn't really feel like getting out in the heat anyway, which meant he let anything under sixty-four miles per hour slide. The gun registered a couple of sixty-fives and one 66, but those numbers dropped so fast that by the time the cars reached him, they were down to fifty-three or fifty-four. He figured they got the point without having to be pulled over, so Andy left them alone.

All of a sudden, a green Ford Maverick went flying by. A

large 8-3 flashed on his radar gun. "Holy crap, I didn't think those cars could go that fast," Andy said. He dropped the radar gun onto the passenger seat and reached down to turn on his lights and sirens. Suddenly a black blur flew past that had to be going at least ninety. He yanked the shifter down to drive and pulled out after them. In a matter of moments Andy had his cruiser up to nearly one hundred and was closing in fast on the black blur, which he could now see was some kind of Plymouth. While Andy closed in on the Plymouth, the Plymouth closed in on the Maverick. It pulled up to the side of the green car and started trying to force it off the road. Andy couldn't see anyone but the driver in the Maverick, and from the way his hands were flying around, he looked to be scared out of his mind. Suddenly the Maverick slowed down and pulled over onto the shoulder, which Andy assumed was because the driver had spotted him in his mirror. The Plymouth stomped on the gas and took off. Andy stayed on its tail.

"Columbus dispatch, this is Indiana 2-3. I am in pursuit of a black Plymouth Fury, Indiana license three-three-C-one-eight-zero-three. We're southbound on I-65, mile marker five-two. I need another unit to check on a green Ford Maverick on the shoulder approximately one half mile north of this location."

"10-4, Indiana 2-3."

The Fury yanked from the passing lane to the right-hand lane to avoid hitting a VW Bug in the left lane, then swerved back left. Andy had to slow down due to the Bug's interference. Andy passed it on the left-hand side, his tires throwing up gravel from the edge of the median. He closed in on the Fury's bumper again, his siren blaring. Up ahead, Andy could see traffic starting to build just past a road construction sign. The Fury's brake lights lit up, and the right-hand blinker came on. It slowed and pulled over onto the right-hand shoulder, then stopped.

Andy pulled his cruiser behind the stopped car, and turned off his siren. Over his PA mic he called out to the driver of the Plymouth, "Get out of the vehicle and lie down on the ground behind your car." Slowly the driver's-side door opened, and a heavyset man, who looked to be in his forties, climbed out, his hands shaking as he held them up in the air over his head. "Facedown on the ground, sir," Andy called out again over the PA mic.

"Yes, sir. I will, sir," the man said as he lowered himself to his knees and lay down on the hot asphalt highway shoulder.

Andy stepped out of his cruiser, his hand on the .38 pistol, waiting in its holster. "Place your hands behind your back, please, sir."

"Yes, sir," the man said, his voice cracking.

Pulling his handcuffs out of a compartment on his belt, Andy secured the man's hands, then helped him to his feet. Bits of gravel stuck to the man's cheeks and tears ran down his face. "Would you like to tell me what was going on back there?" Andy asked.

"I caught them together," the man said. "I walked into my house after work and I found them in bed together, right there in my own bed."

Andy already had a pretty good idea of the answer, but he asked anyway. "Who are 'they,' sir?"

"My wife. We've been married seven-and-a-half years, and I walk in and find her doing our next-door neighbor. If I could have caught up to him, I would have killed the son of a bitch." Then he looked up at Andy, his shoulders slumped forward, his voice breaking. "I'm really sorry, Officer, running from you like that. I can't believe this is happening. I thought the guy was my friend. I loaned him my Weedeater last week. If I'd known he was screwing my wife, I would have used it on him. Can you blame me?"

Andy patted the man on the shoulder as he led him to the back of his police cruiser. "What's your name, sir?"

"Ken. Ken Chamberlain. I'm in a lot of trouble, aren't I, Officer?"

"Yeah, I'm afraid so, Ken. Do you have your driver's license on you?" Andy asked.

"In my back pocket," the man replied.

When Andy ran Chamberlain's license, he found the man hadn't had as much as a speeding ticket since he was sixteen. He was from Henry County, over sixty miles away. He'd been after the man in the Maverick for nearly an hour by the time they sped past Andy. As much as he hated to do it, Andy had to take the guy in. Later he learned the unit that responded to his call for help couldn't find the green Maverick. Apparently, the driver headed toward home as soon as the black Fury left him alone. *That's a hell of a way for your marriage to end,* Andy thought as he finished his reports and went back out on patrol.

Long after his shift ended, Andy walked out on his back deck, a Pepsi in his hand, and stared out, the daylight fading away from the trees. Believe me, there wasn't much else for him to do. Cable television hadn't arrived in Brown County, and the rabbit ears on his old black-and-white set could only pick up one channel. As he stood on his deck, watching the trees sway in the wind and listening to the tree frogs, he started thinking about Ken Chamberlain sitting in the Bartholomew County Jail. *The poor dumb bastard,* Andy thought. But he couldn't leave it at that. He started pondering Ken's question: *can you blame me?* It made Andy ask himself what he would have done in the guy's place. And he had to admit he would have probably done the same thing. He still couldn't stand the idea of my mom dating again, even though he'd dumped her years earlier, and he'd been with many women since then. I guess technically he didn't dump her. He dumped me. The two of us just happened to be a package deal at the time.

So, as the sun died and the sky started turning dark, he stood there, sipping a Pepsi, thinking about what he would have done if he'd caught his wife with another man while they were married. He thought about it a little too long, which is one of the dangers of living by yourself in a remote area with poor television reception. He thought about Ken Chamberlain's wife having sex with the next-door neighbor and about unfaithful wives in general, which naturally turned his thoughts to the unfaithful wife with whom he was most familiar, Loraine Phillips. And the more he thought about Loraine Phillips, the more he wondered why a man with a history of violence, like John Phillips, hadn't come after him. Sure, Andy was quite a bit bigger than he was, but that hadn't stopped John years earlier when he beat up a guy bad enough to earn himself three years in the state pen.

Andy took a long, last drink of the Pepsi in his hand and turned to his standard answer. *John took out his anger on his* son, he mused. *That was the best way he had to get back at Loraine for what she'd done to him. Besides, Gabe wasn't even his son.* He paused as the last thought ran through his head. *Or was he?* Loraine had told him he wasn't, but something didn't seem quite right about that. *Gabe sure looked a lot like John. Same eyes. Same smile. Same build. John had to be his father. But if Loraine lied to me about that...?* A chorus of tree frogs serenaded him as he stood, lost in thought, on his deck. *Why, then, would he hurt his own son rather than coming after me?* He turned the Pepsi can up for another drink, but nothing came out. Shaking the can, he walked into his kitchen and grabbed another out of the refrigerator. Popping the top, he turned his thoughts back to Ken Chamberlain sitting in a jail cell. *Chamberlain's actions made a lot more sense. You wouldn't kill your kid to get back at your wife for screwing around on you. You'd go after her or the bastard who was nailing her.*

He walked back out onto his deck, with its chorus of tree frogs, and thought about jealous husbands and revenge. *Why the hell didn't he come after me?* Andy asked himself. *That's what I would have done.* He's kind of a strange man, my biological father. Once his mind locks onto something, he can't let it go, sort of like a mental snapping turtle. He might have asked the guy directly, but you can't just pick up a phone and call someone on death row, and driving five hours for a question this small didn't make a lot of sense. So Andy walked back into his cabin, fished out a piece of paper and a pen from a drawer in the kitchen, and sat down at his table and began writing. His letter was short and to the point. "Dear John," he wrote, "If you knew your wife was sleeping around, why didn't you do anything about it? Most men would have gone after whoever was having sex with their wife. Why didn't you? Why did you take your anger out on your son instead?" He signed his name to the bottom, shoved it in an envelope, addressed it, stuck a stamp on it, and put it in the mail the next day on his way to work.

Andy had pretty much forgotten about writing John, when, a few weeks later, he pulled up to the mailbox next to his driveway. A padded manila envelope with a lump in the middle was mixed in with the usual assortment of bills and circulars. Up at the top of the envelope was John's name, his inmate number, and a return address that ended with Michigan City, IN. "Well, I'll be a son of a bitch," Andy said. "He wrote back. I wonder what else he crammed in there." He tossed the envelope, along with the rest of the mail, onto the car seat and drove on up to his cabin. When he got out of his car, he purposefully left the mail where he'd laid it. It was still there the next morning when he went to work and the next evening when he returned home. He piled on a few more days' worth of mail before finally carrying it into his house. Inside, he let it collect dust on his kitchen table for nearly a week before he finally pulled John's letter out of the stack to open it. He shoved a pocketknife blade into the space at the top of the envelope, and started to rip it open, when he stopped himself. For some reason he couldn't do it. He sat there like that for at least two or three minutes before pulling the knife away from the letter, closing the blade, and dropping the letter back onto his kitchen table. A week later he moved the envelope from his table to his mantel, where it remained, unopened, for at least a year, maybe more.

Even though he couldn't bring himself to open the enve-lope to read John's response to his question, the damage was done. I think it would have been easier on Andy if he'd read the letter and whatever else John stuck in the envelope, then tossed it into the trash. But, by allowing it to come into his house as a permanent resident, Andy now had a constant reminder of his past in his living room. Every time he walked from his kitchen to his bedroom, or vice versa, he had to go past it. And he always noticed it. The name John Phillips might as well have been written in that big type the newspapers used when the space shuttle blew up, which made this reminder even worse than those he would see in Trask every day. Instead of reminding him of a little boy who died needlessly and tragically, this letter reminded Andy of a man Andy helped put on death row, a man Andy could not figure out. A man who should have come after him, but didn't.

And that unnerved him.

You would think Andy would have just thrown the letter away, but he couldn't without reading it first, but he couldn't bring himself to read it because he was afraid John's answer might plant some seeds of doubt in his mind. And Andy didn't need any doubts about John Phillips. "I wish they would just fry the bastard and get this over with," he said early one Saturday morning as he stumbled from his bedroom toward the kitchen for a cup of coffee. By this point the letter had collected at least a year's worth of dust. "How long is it supposed to take to execute a convicted child killer? Whatever it is, this is too damn long."

A couple of weeks later another letter arrived. Instead of preprinted postage, this one came with a green "certified" sticker on the front and a return receipt card on the back. The return address read: "State Appeals Court,

Indianapolis." Andy had a pretty good idea what the letter was even before he opened it. He cursed under his breath as he tore the envelope open. The letter, written on official letterhead, requested he appear before the court as a witness exactly one month from the day he opened the letter. And, of course, the case was none other than John Phillips's appeal. "Dammit," he said as he read the first paragraph. "Damn it to hell." According to the letter, Rachel Maris would argue the case for the state. That made Andy feel a little better. Although it had been a few years since he'd seen her, he remembered feeling a little chemistry between them. She, like Andy, no longer lived in Harris County. After Reginald Chambliss, Esquire, changed his title from county district attorney to governor, she picked up a new position in the state attorney general's office. It was a pretty good gig for a woman under thirty. Andy wondered if her new position was in recognition of a job well done or a reward for a little something else. Yeah, his attitudes toward women needed a lot of work. He didn't recognize the name of the attorney representing John. Old Donald Edmonds was long gone, apparently. Andy guessed that one of the anti-capital-punishment groups who'd been protesting John's case for forever must have ponied up the money for this lawyer.

For the next week Andy did his best to forget he had to go up to Indianapolis to testify about a man he wished would go ahead and die already. Just like he always did, he poured himself into his job, and when he wasn't working, he ran like he was training for a marathon.

One evening after returning home from work, thoughts of John and Gabe started closing in on him. They pushed so hard that he walked over to the locked drawer in the bottom of his gun cabinet and started to put the key into the keyhole. "What am I doing?" He stopped himself and said aloud, "I'm not blowing three years for this guy. Hell no!" Instead, he walked into his bedroom, stripped off his uniform, and pulled on an old Indiana University T-shirt and running shorts. The night of Gabe's death still played in his head as he put on his new Nike running shoes, which made him start off running down his quarter-mile-long driveway without warming up or stretching first. Once he cleared the driveway, he turned right and ran down the road that leads toward the big city of Gnaw Bone (I wish I'd made up the name of that town, but I didn't). He pushed through Gnaw Bone, and turned left onto Highway 46 and continued running down the very narrow strip of asphalt that passes for a shoulder on the right-hand side of the yellow line toward Nashville. The shadows had already grown dark by the time Andy hit Highway 46, but he didn't notice. The sound of his feet on the asphalt and the hum of cars buzzing by couldn't drown out the sound of John Phillips's voice ringing in his ears. He could hear him on the night of Gabe's death: *"It all happened so fast...I heard him screaming, but I thought I was the one having the bad dream."*

"Why did you kill your son, you son of a bitch?!" Andy yelled as he kicked up his pace. By this point he'd already put a couple of miles between himself and Gnaw Bone. The shadows had taken over and the road was becoming harder and harder for Andy to see. *"By the time I got to him, it was too late. I could feel his spirit slipping out of him,"* John's voice in Andy's head said. *"I only had time to kiss him good-bye and promise I would see him soon."*

"It will be sooner than you think, you bastard," Andy

said. Then he yelled, "Why did you let Gabe die!!!!" Without realizing it, Andy was now running in a full sprint down the shoulder of a highway he could barely see. His legs and chest ached, but he kept pushing himself down the road, harder and harder and harder.

Andy didn't even know he'd been hit until he landed headfirst in the ditch that ran next to Highway 46. His legs whipped up and over his body. A small tree came up to meet his side, and Andy swears to this day he can remember hearing his ribs crack. He ricocheted off the tree, his body twisting counterclockwise. Rolling twice more, he came to rest on his back in a small pool of stagnant water surrounded by tall weeds. Pain radiated through his body as he pushed down with his right arm, trying to lift himself out of the water. His collarbone was broken on the right side, but he wouldn't know that for sure for a couple of days.

Andy's splash landing in the water stirred up a swarm of mosquitoes, which began feasting on his face, neck, and arms. He swatted them away as best he could with his left arm as he pushed hard with his legs to try to get out of the water. Pain shot up through his left leg, while his right foot slipped in the mud. He let out a long string of profanity and yelled for help. Lying back, he listened. Nothing. The car that clipped him never stopped. All he could hear was the buzzing of the mosquitoes around him and the high-pitched squeal of tires on asphalt on the road somewhere up above him. The greasy water soaked into his shorts and T-shirt. He shouted again for help. Only then did he realize how long he'd been running, and how dark the night had become. *You gotta get out of the cesspool, Andy,* he thought. He tried lifting himself up with his left arm, with only a little success. He once again tried pushing with his legs, but the pain shooting through his left leg almost made him pass out. "Crap, it's probably busted," he said to himself.

He lay back for a moment and tried to figure out what to do. "Can anyone hear me?!" he screamed as he lay back in the water. Again, his cry for help was greeted with silence. "All right, all right, you're okay. You just gotta get up out of this ditch and go flag down some help on the road. Concentrate. You can do this." He rolled over onto his stomach in the water and pushed himself up on his knees. Cradling his right arm to his stomach, he managed to crawl up out of the water, then collapsed in the weeds. Headlights from a passing car shone into the tops of the small trees and bushes around him. That's when he realized he'd crawled up on the wrong side of the water in the ditch. To get to the road, he'd have to go back through the water. "Oh, crap," he said. He let out a long sigh and rolled over onto his back in the weeds and lay down. "Oh, God," he said under his breath. "Oh, God, oh, God, oh, God." The pain made his head spin. Stars burst in front of his eyes as he lay back in the weeds and passed out.

Water splashing in his face woke Andy up, that and his body shivering. He had no idea how long he'd been lying in the weeds. The water turned out to be rain, but at least it made the mosquitoes stop biting. "Oh, God, I'm cold," he said as his teeth chattered. Late-September nights in Indiana usually feel pretty comfortable, unless you're lying next to a ditch wearing nothing but running shorts and a soaking wet T-shirt. The sharp pain from the car's impact had given way to a dull ache that covered every inch of his body. He wasn't sure he could move even if he'd wanted to. At this point, even as cold as he was, he didn't want to move. He couldn't move. The rain stopped, and Andy drifted in and out of consciousness.

He was back in Trask, driving his patrol car down Jackson Street. He stopped in front of 230 East Jackson, the house where he and my mother lived before they split up. "What the hell?" he said as he walked up toward the door and noticed the strange car parked at the side of the house. The front door stood open, and he walked inside. "Carol," he called out. "Carol, I'm home. Is someone here? I didn't recognize the car outside."

Then he saw my mom come running out of a back bedroom, pulling on her clothes. He said it was my mom, even though she didn't exactly look like my mom. She looked more like Loraine Phillips, but Andy swears it was my mother. "What are you doing home already?" she said in that same tone of voice you hear in a math classroom when someone says, "What do you mean we have a test today? No one told me we had a test today."

"Nothing much was going on in town, so I thought I'd knock off early. Is everything okay?" Andy asked. My mom didn't answer. She just glanced back at the bedroom with a panicked look on her face. "What?" Andy asked. "What the hell is going on here?" He stormed back toward the bedroom, while my mom pleaded with him to walk away.

Throwing open the door, he saw John Phillips lying in Andy's bed, puffing on a cigarette, a smile on his face. "Thanks for the use of your wife, Officer Myers. I could get used to this," he said.

"What are you talking about? What are you doing here?" Andy screamed.

"What do you think I'm doing here?" John asked. "I'm doing your wife, of course."

"Like hell you are!" Andy screamed. He whipped out his service revolver and pumped three rounds into John's chest.

John didn't flinch and the bullets seemed to pass right through him without doing any harm. He just lay there, puffing on his cigarette, the same smile on his face. "Yep, I could get used to this," John said with a little laugh.

The pain in Andy's ribs and shoulders brought him back to the high weeds next to the ditch full of stagnant water along Highway 46, about three miles outside of Gnaw Bone. When he looked up, the sky was lighter. Andy let out a long moan. He tried raising up, but fell back again into Trask. The scene had changed. He was back at the Madison Park Apartments, slowly climbing the stairs of building three. With each step he told himself to stop, but his legs wouldn't listen. He kept climbing and climbing and climbing. Finally he reached the top of the stairs and began walking down the corridor. A door stood open, and he turned and walked through it. Gabe Phillips sat on a couch just inside the door, his eyes red as if he'd been crying. "They're in there," Gabe said as he motioned Andy down the hall. Andy tried to walk over to Gabe, but his legs wouldn't obey. They moved him down the hallway instead, to a small bedroom with a floor that appeared to be painted red. A small, crumpled body lay on the floor. Loraine stood over it. She looked up at Andy as he walked into the room, her eyes cold and flat. "What have we done?" she said as he moved closer. Andy rushed over to the body, but Loraine said, "It won't do any good. You're too late."

Ignoring her, Andy instinctively pushed the two forefingers

of his right hand onto the body's neck, looking for a pulse. "When did this happen?" he asked, his heart racing.

"Does it matter?" Loraine said.

"Of course, it matters! Maybe I can save him," he shouted. He squared himself around to start CPR, and only then did he take a close look at the body's face. "John?" Andy said.

"You knew my husband?" Loraine asked. "How?"

"I'm a friend of his son," Andy said but didn't elaborate. He cleared his throat and tried to speak, but the words wouldn't come. "How...how did...?"

"How did this happen?" Loraine said, finishing Andy's sentence for him. "You already know the answer to that, don't you?" She pushed past Andy to leave the room. As she reached the door, she looked back at him. Only then did Andy notice the blood that covered her nightgown. "What have we done?" She shook her head and said in an almost playful tone, "Oh, yes, what have we done?" She walked out the door and into the night.

"What?! We?! What do you mean *we*?!" Andy shouted. He yelled it so loud that he woke himself. When he opened his eyes, he found himself staring up at a blue sky surrounded by high weeds. His face and every exposed inch of skin itched, but he could hardly move his left arm to scratch. "Oh, God," he said, but this time the words came out different than they did when he first landed in the ditch. It was the first time he'd prayed since he could remember when. Maybe it was his first time ever. "O God, help me," he prayed. He closed his eyes and drifted back out of consciousness, repeating the same phrase over and over again, "O God, help me."

The next thing Andy remembered was waking up in the Columbus hospital. Apparently, some retired guy out looking for discarded pop bottles and aluminum cans stumbled upon Andy around noon the day after he was hit. The old guy nearly had a heart attack when he found him. He thought Andy was dead. Then he heard Andy moan, and that almost scared him more than finding what he thought was a body. They kept Andy in the hospital for over a week. He'd messed up his leg pretty bad. They had to put a couple of screws in it to hold it together. His doctor told him he'd never go through another metal detector without setting it off. They were shocked that Andy hadn't suffered more internal injuries. At first, they were afraid they would have to do surgery on his shoulder, as well as his leg, but they didn't. They loaded him down with casts and slings and painkillers and sent him home. Since he lived by himself out in the middle of nowhere, Andy had to pay a local woman to come out to his house for a few hours a day to do some basic housecleaning and cooking. It was, I believe, the first time he really missed being married, at least the domestic side of marriage.

For a week and a half, Andy did nothing but sit in a chair, watch the NBC affiliate station out of Indianapolis (which was the only station he could pick up and even then it was fuzzy) and get hooked on *Days of Our Lives*. Given his background of trouble with alcohol, his painkiller prescriptions only lasted a week. That left his head clear to do a lot of thinking the second week he was laid up, which also happened to be the week leading up to his testimony at John's appeal hearing. "I'd rather get hit by another damned car," he said every time he thought about testifying. The more he thought about it, the more nervous energy built up inside him. Normally, he would have worn out the floors pacing, or shot out the door jogging, but since that's what put him in his current physical predicament, he couldn't do anything but sit, think, and contemplate how like sands through an hourglass, so are the days of our lives.

I'm not sure what made him so nervous about testifying at that hearing. After all, he testified in court cases two or three times a month. There was something very different about this one, and I've always suspected there was more than meets the eye. This was the last of John's appeals on a state level, and that could have had Andy worked up. Maybe it was the dreams he had while lying in the ditch. Andy said he passed those off as nothing more than the random firing of neurons in his brain and the effects of shock on his body. Who am I to say different? Maybe he was nervous because of what he knew he had to say. I guess I should go ahead and answer the questions you've probably been thinking for a while now: Did Andy coach his witnesses and convince them to tell outright lies on the witness stand against John? Is that what had him so worked up over appearing in front of the appeals court? I will tell you the same thing he told me when I asked him that.

# CHAPTER

## 19

ANDY LOOKED REALLY BAD when the day of the hearing rolled around. The bruises on his face had pretty much cleared up, but the scrapes remained. He also had to wear a shoulder sling that kept his collarbone in place. Even though he wore it under his shirt, it pulled his shoulders back like some guy trying to impress a girl walking by on the beach. His ribs remained tender, which made him move very slowly. That wasn't much of a problem, since he could barely walk anyway with his busted-up leg. They suggested he use a wheelchair, but my old man is pretty stubborn. He thought by pushing himself he could make the bones heal faster. The crutches made his shoulder hurt so bad he would nearly pass out, but he used them anyway. To me, being a tough guy sounds a lot like being really stupid.

One of the guys he worked with in Columbus drove him up to Indy for the hearing. The guy had work to do at the capitol building, which meant Andy would have some time to kill after he testified. Andy and his coworker didn't talk much on the way up, since they didn't really know one another outside of work. My old man had become a bit of a hermit after moving down to Brown County. He kept all social connections to a minimum. He wore his uniform to court; it had changed from a lowly Trask police officer to a state trooper since he testified against John the first time. He had to ruin a pair of his uniform trousers by cutting out one of the seams to get it over his cast. Part of him thought the defense attorney and the judges might go easy on him because of his injuries. After all, an injured state trooper is a pretty sympathetic figure. Or, at least, Andy hoped it would be. The hearing was scheduled to begin at nine in the morning, which meant Andy had to sit around and wait in a holding room. It was torture. He could never get comfortable with the bad ribs and collarbone, and the institutional chairs in the holding room only made matters worse. Finally a bailiff stuck his head in the door, pointed at Andy, and said, "You're on."

The appeals courtroom wasn't set up like the traffic courts and district courts he was used to. There was no jury box, nor were there seats for a gallery. Instead, a large table sat at the front of the room, with three large chairs behind it, one for each of the appeals judges. Across from the judges' table sat another shorter table, where those testifying would sit. On either side were other tables for the attorneys for both the state and the one making the appeal. I think there's some fancy name for the one appealing his case. It's not defendant, I don't think. But then again, I guess it doesn't really matter what anyone was called. The point was, Andy had to go up in front of these appeals judges and answer their questions under oath.

He didn't so much walk into the courtroom as hobble. If

I had to guess, I would say he limped and winced and acted all in pain just a little more than normal, just to make sure everyone in the room understood how difficult it was for him to come in and testify. Unfortunately, I have no idea whether his tactic worked. No matter how much I badgered him, he never told me what he was asked or what he said. He said it didn't matter. He told me, "When the appellate court issued its ruling, John was still on death row and one step closer to being strapped into a chair and having two thousand volts shot through him. That was all that mattered to me at the time." Sure, I wanted details, but, hey, you can't make someone talk when they don't want to. Me, that's never been much of a problem. Once you get me talking, I can hardly shut up.

What made Andy's trip to the appeals court very interesting wasn't the testimony he gave inside, but what was waiting for him as he left the building. Going down the stone stairs on crutches with a bum shoulder wasn't easy. Every step made him cringe with pain and curse under his breath. With all his cringing and cursing and slowly moving down the stairs, he did not notice the very large man moving up the stairs toward him until he slid his broken foot right on top of the man's shoe.

"I'm sorry, excuse me," Andy said, his eyes still more focused on where his foot should land than on anyone around him.

"God heard your prayer in that ditch," the man connected to the foot said. Andy's head snapped up, which made him sick with pain from his broken collarbone. The first thing he noticed about the source of the voice was the scar right below his Adam's apple. His eyes fixated on the scar and could not move higher until the man said again, "God heard your prayer in that ditch, and He will if you let Him."

"What?" Andy asked as his eyes moved on up to the man's face. He recognized him as the man who sat behind John during his sentencing hearing. Standing close up, the man appeared much larger than he had in the courtroom. Although he and Andy were about the same height, this man had at least fifty pounds on Andy, and all of it solid muscle. "He w-will...?" Andy stammered. "He will what?"

"Help," the man said, then turned and walked down the stairs.

Andy tried to follow him, but he couldn't at the "step, cringe, and curse" pace he had to use to go down the stairs. By the time Andy made it down two steps, the man with the message had disappeared. Andy looked right and left, trying to spot where the man might have gone, or at least the car he'd climbed into, but he didn't see a thing. It was almost as though the man had vanished. "Dammit," he growled.

"I see you have the same eloquent vocabulary you've always had," Ted Jackson said as he came down the stairs behind Andy. "You always were the smooth talker."

Andy smiled at the sound of Ted's voice. He tried turning around quickly, which made him curse again from the pain.

"It's good to see you, too," Ted said.

"Sorry, Ted," Andy said. "Didn't mean to cuss you. I'm a little busted-up right now."

"Yeah, you look like crap. What happened? Some jealous husband finally catch you in the act."

"Yeah, yeah, very funny," Andy said, although he felt a little uneasy about how close Ted had come to the truth. "Long story. Basically, I was out running too late in the evening and a car clipped me."

"Running? You?"

"Yep. It's what keeps me sober. Haven't had a drink since I left Trask."

"Good for you. Good for you. Man, I was worried about you there for a while. It looked like you were trying to commit slow suicide. Glad you stopped. I don't like funerals any better than you do." Then, suddenly changing gears, Ted said, "So what were you talking to Eli Williams about?"

"Who?"

"Eli Williams, the guy you were just talking to. I didn't realize you knew him," Ted said.

"I don't. Who is he?" Andy asked.

"You're kidding me? I thought you knew everything there was to know about John Phillips. Eli Williams was the guy John nearly killed in Pendleton, but ended up saving his life."

"That guy?!" Andy said. "You're telling me that John Phillips took *that guy*? How? And what's he doing here now?"

"Hey, I don't explain 'em, I just report 'em. All I know is that is the guy who tried to mess up Phillips in prison, but Phillips turned the tables on him and nearly killed the guy. But then again, Eli wouldn't be alive right now if it weren't for John. He stays pretty close to any courtroom where Phillips's case is being discussed. I don't know why," Ted said.

"I saw him at the sentencing hearing," Andy said. "To me, looked like he was praying through the whole thing."

"Yeah, that fits what I've heard about him. So what were you talking to him about?" Andy didn't answer with words, but the look on his face must have given something away because Ted said, "Did he threaten you? I know the guy is really upset about Phillips being on death row."

"No…" Andy dragged out his answer. "No, it was nothing like that."

"What then?" Ted asked.

"I don't really know." Andy looked around as if he expected the guy to return. "He…uh…" Andy couldn't find the right words. Finally he said, "You know, it's nothing. The guy must be a friend of Phillips because the two are both pretty strange." I think Andy was trying to convince himself more than Ted with his answer.

Ted took a close look at Andy. "You have time to go somewhere where we can sit down and talk. You don't look like you're going to be able to stand up much longer."

"Ya think," Andy said. Ted helped him down the steps and down the street to a small diner a block or so from the courthouse complex. The place was pretty much empty. The two walked inside and found a spot in a back booth. They spent the next half hour drinking bad coffee and getting caught up on the three years since Andy had moved away. Eventually Andy asked, "So, did they bring you in for the appeal hearing as well?"

"What appeal hearing?" Ted asked.

"You know damn good and well what appeal hearing, and don't tell me you don't," Andy said.

"You mean Phillips? Yeah. I had to answer a bunch of procedural questions, how we gathered our evidence, how we found our witnesses, that sort of thing. You?"

"Yep."

"So, did you ever get over your obsession with getting a confession?" Ted asked.

"I wrote him a letter a little over a year ago," Andy said.

"You what?"

"Yeah. I wrote him a letter basically asking the same thing I always ask him." That wasn't entirely true, but Andy didn't want anyone else to know what he'd really written.

"Why?" Ted asked. "Aren't you ever going to let this thing go?"

"I thought I had, but something made me start thinking about it again. So I wrote. I figured it was better than driving all the way up to Michigan City. I really don't ever want to see that guy's face again."

"So, did you get your confession?"

"Nah," Andy said. "It's like you always say, they don't call these guys cons for nothing." Andy didn't see much point in telling Ted how he couldn't bring himself to read John's response. He did not want to admit to Ted, or to himself, that he wasn't nearly as certain about John as he once had been.

Ted leaned back in the booth, took a drink of his coffee, and said, "Did you really think he would?"

"Yeah," Andy said with a laugh, "I did. I know, I'm naïve. I spent too many hours, growing up, watching *Perry Mason*. By the way, that's not a problem anymore. I can't get but one station at my place down in Brown County." He paused for a moment, then said, "So what do you think motivates a guy to keep claiming he's innocent even when he's about to fry? I mean, this has to be his last appeal, right? And I know the governor's not going to lift a finger to save the guy's sorry ass. Chambliss has to be salivating at signing the death order, since this is the case that got him elected."

"I don't know, Andy. Honestly, I don't ever think about it.

We proved he was guilty beyond a reasonable doubt. Case closed. Life goes on. I mean, look at you. You've moved on." Then another thought hit Ted, one it appeared he'd rather not entertain, because he stopped talking and looked down at his cup of coffee.

"What?" Andy asked.

"You probably don't take the Adamsburg paper anymore, do you?"

"Hell no. I didn't take it when I lived in Trask. Why?" Andy asked.

"You probably haven't heard then," Ted said.

"Heard what?"

"About Loraine Phillips. She, uh…" Ted stumbled over his words. "Hell, I don't know how to put it, so I might as well just say it. About three months ago we got called out to her place. The man she was apparently living with walked in and found her body lying on the floor. She h-had," Ted stammered, "she had…uh…blown her brains out. Suicide. A snub-nosed .38 was in her hand, and the powder burns left no doubt. She killed herself. Left a note with only four words on it. She wrote, 'What have we done?' Didn't make any sense to any of us. The tox screen on her came back like a science fair exhibit, so it must have been the chemicals in her system doing the talking. I don't know. Anyway, I thought you might want to know about her. You were pretty close to her at one time," Ted said.

Andy couldn't say anything for several minutes. His mind raced back to the day he'd given her that gun. She wanted something for protection. He'd planned to show her how to use it, but their relationship fell apart before he could. "Wow," he finally said. He had trouble catching his breath.

"Wow," he said again. Inside his head the words "what have we done?" replayed over and over. She'd said it to Andy the night Gabe died and again in his dream in the ditch. Andy took a deep breath, then said, "Man. I had no idea. Why uh... why... didn't you call me when... uh?"

"Are you okay, man?" Ted said. "You look like you're about to pass out."

Andy did. Pass out, that is. He blamed it on his injuries from getting hit by the car. His little trip to Indy was, he claimed, the most activity he'd tried since he got out of the hospital. "I just overdid it," he said when he came to a few moments after passing out. Ted didn't buy his excuse, although he didn't press the issue. He waited a few minutes for Andy to get his bearings, then found his ride back to Brown County. As Ted loaded Andy into the trooper's car, he told him, "Take care of yourself" and "Keep in touch." Andy slept most of the trip back down south. At least he pretended to be asleep. It had been a very long day.

Once he was finally home, Andy tried to get comfortable on the couch in his cabin, but he couldn't. His shoulder hurt. His ribs ached. And his leg screamed with pain. He welcomed the pain from all three because they helped distract him, just a little, from the thoughts that closed in around him. "What have we done?" he said to himself, repeating the words of Loraine's suicide note. "H-how...," he stammered, then swallowed hard. "How... I mean, she only said it that once. How in the hell...?" Nervous energy welled up inside him. He wanted to get up and walk around, but he couldn't. He could barely move. He wasn't lying when he told Ted that he'd overdone it with the trip to Indy. Now he didn't have the energy to do much more than sit on the couch and wish he had turned on the television before he sat down.

Andy leaned his head back and tried to go to sleep. As soon as he closed his eyes, he found himself in Trask, back at apartment 323 of the Madison Park Apartments, back in a small bedroom. He could see John standing in the doorway, and Gabe on the floor. *"You knew my son? How?"* he could hear John say. "I wish I'd never known him," Andy said aloud. "I wish I'd run away from that crazy lady the minute I met her and I wish I'd never talked with that kid of hers and I wish I could forget about the lot of them and never think about them again as long as I live." *"God will, if you let him"* flashed in his mind. "Good God, that's all I need, more voices in my head." Andy picked up the throw pillow closest to him and did just that. He threw it across the room, where it knocked the rabbit ears off the top of his television. "God will help? Help what? Is he going to help me like he helped Gabe? Is he going to help me like he helped John Phillips?! God gave him a screwball of a wife who emptied his house while he was out doing God's work and left him with nothing. Hell, if I'd been married to her, I might have been driven to kill as well. But I sure as hell wouldn't have killed my son if I had a son…"

And then he remembered me. *"If I had a son…"* That phrase stuck in his head. For the first time ever, he thought of me as an actual flesh-and-blood human being. Until then all I had been was a name attached to a child support payment some judge ordered him to make every month. Nothing more. Then he heard John Phillips say, *"The truth is I loved my son more than you can understand."*

"Then how could you have hurt him?!" Andy yelled. Loraine's voice answered his question. Andy could hear her say, *"You have a son. Is a father's love so strong that he would never do anything to harm his precious child?"*

"But I never hurt my son...," Andy protested. The foolishness of his words hit him even before they fell from his lips. "Oh, God," he said. *"He will, if you let him,"* he could hear the guy on the courthouse steps say. Andy let out a long groan. He forced himself up from his couch. The pain was excruciating, but it didn't matter. He stumbled across his cabin over to his gun cabinet. His hand shook as he forced the key into the keyhole. Opening the drawer, he pulled out the bottle he'd stashed there long ago. If ever there was a time to pull out the emergency bender kit, he thought this was it. Shoving the bottle under his arm, he made his way back to the sofa, opened the bottle, and did his best to silence the voices from his past.

When he awoke, he found himself on his bed. His service revolver lay next to his right hand, a box of shells spilled out over the comforter. Andy tried to rise up with only limited success. "Oooohhhhhh," he groaned. He reached up to rub his head with his left hand, only to find it clutched tightly to something. Pulling his hand up in front of his face ever so carefully, he tried to focus. "A Bible? When did I get a Bible?" It wasn't like it was a whole Bible. This was a small, thin New Testament. The cover had what looked to Andy to be a pot of some sort printed on it, with the words "A gift from the Gideons" printed right above it. "I don't know anyone named Gideon. Where did this come from?"

As he stared at the small Bible in his hand, he noticed his thumb held a page open. "What the hell?" he said. His eyes scanned over the page when a weird-looking name jumped out at him, Zacchaeus. Then his eyes hit a verse in the story of Zacchaeus that seemed to leap off the page, "…and if I have taken any thing from any man by false accusation, I restore *him* fourfold.*" Andy stared at the verse for several minutes. He couldn't seem to pull his eyes off it. Finally he managed to toss the Bible out of his hand. He raised himself up on the bed, .38 shells sticking to his side, where his shirt had pulled up revealing bare skin. Brushing them off, he said, "What is all this?" Then he saw the bullet holes in the wall on the left side of his bed. "What the…," he said. He let out a long groan. "Now I remember," he said.

Slowly Andy pushed himself from his bed. He limped into the living room. His two table lamps were both smashed on the floor and he noticed that he'd apparently given his television the Elvis treatment. (In case you don't remember, Elvis once shot his television. So did Andy.) Shuffling slowly into the room, his right foot nearly slipped on some torn-up pieces of paper lying on his hardwood floor next to the mantel. He looked down and saw the padded envelope from John there, ripped open. "Ouch, dammit!" he growled as he lowered himself to the floor. "Man, I am a world-class idiot," he said as he gathered each of the small pieces of paper. He wadded them in his hand and reached over to toss them into the fireplace, but stopped himself. Instead, he moved over to the couch and spread the papers out on the coffee table.

Now, I've heard this part of the story many, many times, but I never cease to be amazed at how calm Andy was through all this. Think about it. His house is wrecked. There are gunshot holes in his television and in the wall near his bedroom. The way the ammunition was spread out on his bed, you

*Luke 19:8, King James Version.

would think he had been under attack the night before, and from the looks of his living room, that would be a pretty good guess. But Andy didn't react to any of it. He couldn't remember much after he took his first drink, he downed that bottle so fast, but somehow he could recall that all the damage to his house was self-inflicted. He'd never been a violent drunk before, so something had to set him off, and that something was probably in pieces on top of his coffee table. Yet he sat down and started putting the letter back together like he was working on a jigsaw puzzle. Go figure.

It took him about five minutes to put the letter back together, which is pretty good considering how hungover he was. He sat back and stared at it. "Huh," he said. "Well, no wonder…" He then gathered the pieces of paper together and threw them in the trash. I don't know what the letter said, but I do know that, whatever it was, it put Andy in his car the minute his doctor cleared him to drive and he headed north to Michigan City. Yep, you guessed it. He drove up for what he hoped would be his last face-to-face with John.

# CHAPTER

## 20

THE DRIVE NORTH went faster than Andy had anticipated. The state of Indiana allows troopers to drive their cars anywhere within the state, and he took advantage of that little provision for this trip. Although he didn't want to be one of those troopers who make other drivers mad by blowing past the speed limit, he couldn't help himself. The drive was so long and boring that he couldn't bring himself to drag it out any longer than he had to. Unlike the last time he had a face-to-face conversation with John Phillips, Andy didn't play this one out in his mind ahead of time. He just drove. He emptied his head by cranking up Jackson Browne on the car stereo, and pointed his patrol car north. He didn't stop until he arrived at Michigan City. Several times along the way he had to pull over, get out of the car, and stretch. Fall was about to give way to winter, although this particular early December day was warmer than usual. Nevertheless, it was still cool enough to make his bones ache, even though his breaks had technically healed.

Andy pulled into the parking lot of Indiana's primary

maximum-security prison nearly an hour before his scheduled time with John Phillips. But then again, he was always
early for appointments. He parked in the law enforcement
parking section, and climbed out of his car. The old stone
walls topped with razor wire grabbed his attention and he
felt a cold chill run up his back. This would be his first time
to actually walk inside prison gates. He'd helped send his
fair share of people there, but he'd never been there himself.
Cops usually aren't huge fans of going to prisons. The odds
are too high of running into someone who would be less
than happy to see you, if you catch my drift.

Although Andy had arranged to meet with John in one of
the prison holding rooms (and, no, that's hardly standard
procedure—being a state cop has its privileges), he wanted to
walk onto death row himself prior to his meeting. Not many
people are allowed onto death row. The state never meant
for it to be a tourist stop for people driving from Chicago
to Kalamazoo. But for state troopers, that's another thing
completely. Andy knew the prison would roll out the red carpet for him, and let him see anything he wanted. That was
part of the reason why he arrived so early, that and the fact
that he hardly slept the night before. He was pretty anxious
to have this meeting.

A guard greeted him as he stepped into the visitor's center
through which every outside person who arrives at the
prison must pass. Andy wasn't in uniform, but he must have
still looked like a cop because the guard smiled and asked
him, "May I have your name please, Officer?"

"Myers. Andy Myers."

The guard glanced down at his clipboard. "Ah, you're a
little earlier than we expected, Officer Myers."

"Thanks. Yeah, I know I'm early. It's a curse my mother inflicted on me. She had an allergic reaction to lateness. Since I'm early, do you think I could take a look around? I would especially like to see where the baby-killing son of a bitch I helped put in here is kept," Andy said.

"I think we can arrange that, sir." The guard pushed a button, which allowed Andy to go through the first of a series of steel doors. He still walked with a pronounced limp.

On the other side of the door, a female guard greeted him. "I just need you to sign your name here," she said as she pointed down to a page on a clipboard with a series of lines on it. After Andy had signed in, she handed him a visitor's badge. "Are you carrying your sidearm this morning? If so, we will need to lock it up in here for you."

"No," Andy said.

"Any pocketknives or any other kind of weapon, sir?" she asked.

"Nope," Andy replied.

"All right then, please empty your pockets in this dish and go ahead and step through the metal detector for me." And then she added, almost apologetically, "We have to do this for everyone, no matter who they are."

"Don't worry about it. I understand," Andy said as he walked through the small arch of the machine. He had barely stepped into it when the alarm went off. Andy laughed. "The doctors told me when they screwed my leg back together that I would give these things fits. I guess they knew what they were talking about."

"That's not the first time this has happened," the guard said, "but we have to make sure." She walked over to Andy with a hand wand. "Which leg is it?" she asked.

"Left. Below the knee. Got hit by a car while I was out jogging."

The female guard let out a gasp as she passed the wand over his leg. It beeped loudly as it passed the site of the screws. "You're kidding!" she said.

"Nope. And the car didn't even stop. We never did catch the guy who did it."

"Oh, that's terrible," she said. "How long ago was that?"

"September," he said.

"I am so sorry," she said. She stepped back. "Okay, you're good to go," she said.

"So where to now?" Andy asked.

"I'm afraid nowhere for a while. The population is locked down for count, and we can't let you go back until it clears." Once or twice or three times a day, I'm not sure how many, all the prisoners are pulled in off the exercise yard and work details and locked back in their cells for a head count. That's what was going on when Andy arrived.

"When will that be?" Andy asked.

The guard sighed. "It should have finished ten minutes ago. Unfortunately, we occasionally run into problems, which make it run longer. Today seems to be one of those days. We will take you back just as soon as we can," she said.

"Thanks," Andy grumbled. He looked around the narrow security corridor and imagined that this must be how it feels to be in the limbo of purgatory. *If there was such a thing as purgatory,* he thought. A line of four hard-plastic chairs were shoved up against the eastern wall. "I guess I will wait here."

"I appreciate your patience. It shouldn't be too much longer," the guard said.

Andy glanced at his watch. His appointment was now

less than twenty-five minutes away. If they let him through the gate right now, that would give him enough time to tour death row, but not to talk to those taking care of the inmates. And that was his true intent for going back there. He didn't give two hoots to a holler, as we say back home, about seeing where John spent his days. The guy could spend them in hell for all Andy cared.

Clearing count took much longer than anyone expected, and with each passing minute, the plastic chair became a little harder, and Andy's butt became a little more numb. He shuffled from side to side, trying to get comfortable. The only reading material he could find was a two-year-old copy of *Outdoor Life* with half the cover torn off. The pages felt a little funky, so Andy dropped it back onto one of the chairs and continued to wait. By the time the all-clear whistle sounded, Andy barely had enough time to get back to the holding area in which he would meet with John.

"An officer will be up here in just a moment and he will take you back," the guard said.

"Thanks," Andy said.

A few minutes later a guard arrived, who, to Andy, looked like he should be a little farther down the road in South Bend playing middle linebacker for the "Fighting Irish." Andy was no shrimp, but he felt like Richard Simmons compared to this man. "Good to meet you," the guard said in a voice that was far too high a pitch for his tremendous size. From the way Andy described it, the guy sounded a little like he'd swallowed Richard Simmons. A big man with such an effeminate voice struck Andy as an odd combination, and he could barely keep from laughing. The guard stuck out his hand and said, "Steve Jacobs."

"Andy Myers," Andy said as he shook Jacobs's hand.

"I understand you're a state trooper down south. What brings you up to our neck of the woods?"

"Three years ago I put a guy away for murder. There are still a couple of loose ends I need to tie up in my own mind with the case. I figure he's been in here long enough to be ready to cooperate," Andy said.

"Interesting," Jacobs said. "Follow me and we will get you set up." Andy did as he was instructed and fell in step behind Steve Jacobs. They passed through a heavy steel door, and passed into a wide corridor that stretched up to the roofline. The polished concrete floor beneath their feet reflected the harsh cathode lights overhead. On either side the walls were made of concrete block. The place smelled like the basement of a very old house. About ten yards down the main corridor, Jacobs led Andy to another locked steel door on their right. A thick window sat off to the side, and Andy could see another officer inside, who pressed a button. A buzzer buzzed. Jacobs pushed the door open and led Andy down another, much narrower and shorter corridor. Actually, it was a normal-sized hallway, but coming out from the giant main corridor, one felt almost claustrophobic. This hallway led to another door, with another buzzer, which led into a suite of rooms. A short, stocky, balding man, waited in the main lobby of the suites.

"Trooper Myers, nice to meet you. I'm Charles Wells, one of the assistant wardens." He stuck out his hand.

"Good to meet you," Andy said. "I appreciate your setting this up for me."

"Our privilege," the warden said. "Go ahead and make yourself comfortable in this room right over here"—and he motioned toward one of the holding rooms—"and we will have your Mr.

Phillips brought right in to you." Again, this was hardly standard operating procedure for visiting a death row inmate.

Andy sat down behind a table and waited. Apart from its location, the room felt very much like the last room in which he'd talked with John. It had the same fluorescent lights overhead, the same institutional smell, the same type of wooden table, and the same uncomfortable wooden chairs. Unlike during their last meeting, Andy stood as John entered the room. He immediately noticed the toll the years behind bars had taken on John. The man was always thin, but now his face appeared gaunt. His clothes hung on him like a hanger, which made him appear much smaller than he actually was. In a way, John now reminded Andy of Gabriel Phillips more than he ever had before. Also, unlike during their last meeting, Andy noticed John didn't walk with the distinctive jingling slump of handcuffs and leg irons. That struck him as a bit odd. He'd heard stories of death row inmates who had to be put into straightjackets before they were even let out to take a shower. *Someone must be slipping,* he thought.

"Officer Myers," John said with a smile. "It's good to see you again. I had a feeling you might come to see me eventually."

"Glad I didn't disappoint you," Andy replied. He didn't return the smile. "Have a seat." He motioned toward the chair across from his own and sat down.

"I appreciated the letter you sent and your coming up to see me now," John said.

"Yeah," Andy replied with a flat tone of voice. "This isn't a social call."

"No. I didn't expect that it was," John said. "Did you get my reply and the—"

Andy cut him off. "Yeah, I got it. All of it. *Thanks.*" He said that last word with a tone that said anything *but* thank you. "Let me get right to it, John. You're out of appeals."

"Yes."

"The state will set an execution date soon, and you can bet your ass that the governor will not step in to save you at the last minute."

"I realize that."

"You almost sound anxious to get it over with," Andy said.

"You know, honestly, it doesn't matter. I find there's something liberating about living in death's shadow," John said. "We're all going to die eventually, which, when you think about it, means we all live under a death sentence."

Andy sighed. "Okay, John. Whatever. You're missing the point. And the point is, you really are about to fry. They're going to take you into a room, strap you in a chair, and send a few thousand volts through your system. You're a dead man, and nothing will change that."

John gave a little laugh. "I know that may sound really earth-shattering to you, Officer, but I live on a place known as death row. We're all dead men back there."

Andy shook his head in frustration. "This isn't a laughing matter. Look, John, would you come clean with me once and for all? I've listened to your religious bull crap since the night you killed your son. You gave me a little sermon in my squad car, and I've heard several variations on that same theme so many times since, that it makes me want to puke. Just once, quit hiding behind the God talk and be honest with me and yourself."

"You want to know why I killed my son," John said.

"That's a step in the right direction. At least you now admit that you killed him." A sense of relief swept over Andy. It was short-lived.

"I didn't say that," John said. "But you believe I killed him, and you want to know why I would do such a thing. Why is this so important to you, Officer Myers? Do you do this in every murder case you investigate?"

"Usually," Andy said. His statement was more than a little disingenuous. Thus far in his illustrious law enforcement career, Andy had investigated exactly one murder. And unless he moved up the ranks of the state police, it would probably stay that way. He might come across another dead body; he might even come upon one with a real, live murder weapon still sticking out of its forehead, but he wouldn't be able to stay on the case past his initial report. "You want to know why this is so important to me?" Andy said. "I'll tell you. I knew your son. I found him to be unlike any other child I've ever been around. And no matter how hard I try to understand it, I cannot comprehend how you could take his life as you did. I don't know how any father could do such a thing to his own flesh and blood."

"You once said you didn't believe Gabriel was my flesh and blood. Have you changed your mind about that?" John asked.

"I'm the one asking the questions," Andy shot back.

"That's fine," John said. "In the trial they said I did it as an act of jealousy to get back at my wife for leaving me for another man. Do you believe that would be enough to push a man to kill?" John asked.

Andy paused before answering. Finally he said, "I'm not sure. You tell me."

"My wife told me I had to choose, her or Jesus. She told me that right before I left to go on a mission trip to Guatemala. I knew it was coming, I'd known it for a long time. But you are never really prepared when something like that comes. I was packing my bags the night before the trip and she asked me not to go. I told her that I wasn't going to be gone that long. But she said, no, please don't go. Then she asked me why we couldn't go back to the way things used to be, before I went to prison the first time. She said she missed the old me. This conversation went on for a while, until finally she said, 'I'm sick and tired of your Jesus crap. You need to choose, him or me.'"

"What did you say?" Andy asked. He could hear Loraine making a request like that. It sounded exactly like the woman he once knew.

"I told her the choice had already been made. I told her I loved her, but I loved Jesus more. If I had to choose, I chose Him. But then I told her I wished she would make the same choice. I pleaded with her to love Jesus more than me or Gabe or anything else in the world. We talked a little longer, but when she drove me to the airport the next morning, I knew it was over. I knew she would be gone when I returned. And she was—cleaned everything out of our house and moved away.

"That's also when she started sleeping with another man. She wanted to make sure I knew she'd gone out and found someone else." John paused and looked Andy in the eye. "Officer Myers, I know you were that man." If you had been sitting in that room, I think you would have heard the "ooph" coming out of my old man's mouth just like someone had kicked him in the screws of his busted leg. "My son told me about how he met you. He was too young to think anything of finding you in his mother's house the first thing in the morning. After all, he'd grown accustomed to finding strangers in the house before his mother and I split. Jesus said that we're supposed to show hospitality toward strangers, and I was just crazy enough to believe He meant it. But when Gabriel told me about meeting you in the kitchen early one Saturday morning, I knew what was going on. She wanted to make sure I knew."

Andy couldn't say anything in response. He just sat there, wondering why on earth he'd felt so compelled to have this conversation. He opened his mouth once or twice, but he couldn't force any words out. John finally bailed him out. "So I have to ask you, Officer. Do you think I would kill my only son because of you?" The words may have been the same as those Andy heard many, many months before in his dream, but the tone was completely different. John didn't say this accusingly. Instead, he spoke very softly, almost like a father telling his son he still loves him, even though the boy had broken a garage window with a baseball.

Andy swallowed hard. He felt tears well up in his eyes. In a whisper, just like in his dream, he said, "Yes."

"Why?" John asked with an almost pleading tone in his voice.

The tears gave way to anger. "Why the hell do you think? Isn't it obvious?"

"It's not to me," John said.

Andy sighed. He could feel himself start to lose control, and that's the last thing he wanted to happen. He closed his eyes, and took a deep breath. "I don't want to split hairs here, but if you killed him to get back at your wife for sleeping with another man, and that other man happened to be me, and I'm not saying it was, then in a way you did do it because of me."

Silence filled the room for several minutes. John folded his hands in front of him, put his index fingers together, and raised them up to his forehead, his eyes closed. Finally he said, "And that's why Gabriel's death haunts you. You blame yourself for his death, and that's what drives you to avenge him."

"That's a load of crap," Andy said, although his voice cracked as he said it.

"Officer Myers, believe me when I tell you, I do not hold anything you did against you. I forgave my wife for leaving me, and I forgave her for finding someone else, and I forgave you a long time ago for sleeping with her."

"Stop it," Andy said. "Stop the act."

"That's why my son's death haunts you," John said, completely ignoring what Andy had just said. "You don't just blame me. You blame yourself. But you don't have to. I forgave you a long time ago, and nothing can ever change that. You do not need to feel guilty about him any longer. His death doesn't have to haunt you. You were not responsible in any way, I swear to you," John said.

Andy fought back tears. "I don't need your forgiveness," he said as he stood up to leave.

"Don't you?"

"NO!" Andy yelled. "I don't need the forgiveness of a man who kills defenseless little boys."

"Do you really believe I killed him? You asked me to get honest with you. Okay. I have. But now I want you to get honest with me. Deep down, right now this moment, do you really believe I killed Gabriel?" John said.

"I proved you did it," Andy said as he turned and leaned

across the table like a prosecuting attorney. "I proved it beyond a doubt. Chambliss got all the credit, but I did the work. I found the witnesses. I found the evidence. I pushed the county to keep investigating when they didn't think anything was there and I made sure the D.A. prosecuted. I did it. I proved you killed him."

"You didn't answer my question," John said.

"It's the same damn thing!" Andy said.

"Is it?" John asked very softly.

"If you were so damned innocent, why didn't you defend yourself? You just sat there and took everything that was said about you in the trial without lifting a finger to help yourself. Hell, you won't defend yourself even now. You wouldn't cooperate with the people who were trying to save your life with appeals, and now the clock's run out. Everything you've done since the moment I walked into your apartment and found your dead son lying there screams, 'I did it. Lock me up and throw away the key.' Innocent men fight to prove their innocence. You..." Andy couldn't finish his thought. He turned away with disgust.

"Jesus didn't defend Himself, and He was innocent," was all John said in response.

"Well, bub, you ain't Jesus," Andy said. He pushed back from the table and started to get up, but stopped himself. "You know Loraine killed herself, don't you?" he said.

John didn't flinch. He sat back in his chair and took a deep breath. "Guilt," he said.

"What?"

"Guilt destroys the soul," John said. "It eats and eats at it until there's nothing left." He let out a long sigh, then looked up at Andy. He didn't say anything, but his look made Andy want to crawl under the table and hide. No, he didn't give him the stink eye or anything like that. Instead, John looked across the table at Andy with a look you would never think a condemned man could give the man responsible for putting him there. I didn't see either, but I've got to think that it was like the look Jesus gave Peter after Peter denied him three times. And it had the same effect.

"I've gotta go," Andy said as he stood. He walked over toward the door, then turned around and asked, "You ever hear of a guy named Zacchaeus?"

"Yes," John said.

"What did he mean when he said, 'and if I have taken any thing from any man by false accusation, I restore *him* fourfold'?"

"Zacchaeus was a tax collector who stole money from people. After he met Jesus, he vowed to make things right with everyone he'd wronged. Why?"

"No reason," Andy said. He reached down and grabbed the doorknob. He tried to tell John he would be back to watch him fry, but he couldn't force the words out of his mouth. Instead, he gathered himself and walked out the door.

The assistant warden walked over to Andy. "Is everything all right, Officer?" Wells asked.

"Uh…yeah, everything is fine. Thank you. And thanks for letting me sit down with Mr. Phillips like this. I appreciate it very much."

"Anytime. I'm just glad we could help. Oh, by the way, you had asked about visiting death row. I'm sorry we couldn't work that out when you first arrived, but I can take you there now, if you like," Wells said.

"Yes, I would like that very much," Andy said. The warden led Andy through the rat maze of hallways back to the main corridor, which eventually wound down to the far northern end of the prison. Wells asked some basic questions like, "where are you from?" and "how long have you been a state trooper?" Andy gave short, curt answers. He wasn't really in a mood to talk. They turned right and passed through two large classic prison bar gates, which took them to a guard's station in front of a large sign that read: RESTRICTED AREA.

"I'm going to hand you off to Sergeant Dale Nelson here. He takes care of this little corner of our facility for us. Dale," Wells said, turning to a guard who stepped out of the guard station, "this is Andy Myers, one of our fine state troopers. He helped make one of your guests' reservations, and he wanted to see the place for himself. Can you help him out for me?"

"Sure. Love to do it," Nelson replied. Nelson had that classic Hollywood movie prison guard look, complete with military buzz haircut. Turning to Andy, he said, "There's really not that much to see back here. We try to keep our part of the facility as quiet and uneventful as we can. Just knowing why they are here is enough stress for most of these men."

"You're in good hands," the assistant warden said as he turned and walked away.

"So which of our guys did you put here?" Nelson asked.

"John Phillips," Andy said.

"Oh." Nelson's entire demeanor changed.

"Has Phillips been a problem?" Andy asked.

"Uh, no," Nelson said. "Anything but. In fact, those of us who work back here find it almost unbelievable that he's here. He's not like the other inmates. Not at all."

"How so?" Andy said.

"We've had a lot of men find God back here. Hell, if you were about to meet your Maker, you'd want to make your peace with Him yourself. John obviously isn't a jailhouse conversion. He's…" Nelson's voice trailed off without finishing his sentence. He thought for a moment, then continued, "Okay, here's an example. One of my guys back here, young guy named Chuck Brosius, who started working here about the same time that John moved in, he got married a couple of months ago. While Chuck's on his honeymoon, his wife doubles over in pain, starts coughing up blood, and goes downhill from there. They bring her back here and put her in a hospital over in Chicago, but the doctors don't know what's going on. They can't figure it out. So Chuck had already used up the little vacation time he had, so he has to leave the hospital, drive over here, and report for work. You can imagine how this all affects the guy. So John notices. He asks Chuck what's going on. Chuck tells him, because he's so upset, he's not really thinking straight. We don't normally share our personal problems with the cons. But Chuck does and John says, 'Let me pray for her.' By this point Chuck is open to anything, so he says okay. John prays with Chuck right then." Nelson stops.

"Okay, he likes to pray for people. Lots of people do that," Andy says.

"Two days later, Chuck's wife walks out of the hospital. Doctors never did figure out what was wrong with her. All of her symptoms just went away, and it started when John started praying."

*This guy's been in the bowels of this prison a little too long,* Andy thought. Nelson could probably read the skepticism on his face because he said, "Don't believe me if you want, but I'm telling you that it happened."

"I'm not saying it didn't," Andy said.

"You didn't have to. I know, it sounds pretty *Twilight Zone*. But that's not the only thing that makes this guy stand out. He doesn't hate the world for putting him here, and he doesn't hate us for making sure he stays. Just to look at the guy, you would think he was hanging out in the bleachers at Wrigley Field, instead of living on death row waiting to die. He's always got a smile on his face, and when he asks how you are doing, he actually wants to know. At first, we all thought he was a nut job, but he's not. Don't tell my boss this, but he may be the most well-adjusted person in this entire place, and that includes the staff," Nelson said.

"But that doesn't change the fact he killed his son," Andy said.

"Yeah. I know," Nelson said. "It's just hard to figure that a guy like this could do something like that. But then again, stranger things have happened. Anyway, you wanted to take a little look around."

"You know, I don't think that will be necessary. I think I've seen enough already," Andy said.

"All right. Suit yourself." Nelson walked back into his station and called for an escort to lead Andy back to the main entrance.

# CHAPTER

## 21

Andy made the drive home from the prison on autopilot. His brain felt numb, and he didn't dare think too much because he knew what his mind would immediately lock onto. Instead, he sat behind the wheel of his car, his foot on the gas, and drove in a daze. All he wanted to do was get home and get back to work. He had a physical scheduled the following week, which, he hoped, would clear him to go back on patrol. He hated working behind a desk, which he'd had to do during his rehab. The daze lifted when he pulled up in his driveway. "How did I get here?" he said aloud.

The man who'd bought Andy's house was up on a ladder putting up Christmas lights. He jumped down off the ladder and walked over to Andy's patrol car. "Officer Myers, good to see you. What brings you back to town?"

Andy had to think fast. "Oh, nothing really. I was passing through the area and just thought I would see how the old hometown was doing."

"Nothing's changed," the man said with a laugh. "But then again, has it ever?"

"No," Andy said with a forced smile and a fake laugh. "I lived in Trask nearly all my life, and it was always pretty much the same, all the time."

"Do you still have family in town?" the man asked. By this point Andy had reached his absolute limit on small talk.

"No. Just some friends. Well, anyway, I probably need to go. Good seeing you again," Andy said without calling the guy by name (since he couldn't remember it). He started the car and backed out of the driveway without ever getting out. The man had a puzzled look on his face as Andy drove away, not that Andy cared. As he drove down Elm Street, he thought about pulling into the police station to visit with his old boss. He turned on his left blinker, and slowed down to make the turn into the station parking lot, but sped up and kept going before he could turn. "Why would I want to see Spence?" Andy said to the empty car. "It's not like I've heard from him since I left this dump."

When he reached the intersection of Elm and Main, he stopped at the light and turned on his left turn signal. "I don't know how I ended up here, but I'm ready to get out of here and get home." The light turned green, and he turned right. Instead of heading toward the interstate and home, he drove down Main to Pine, hung a left on Pine, then took a right on Madison. A couple of minutes later he pulled into the parking lot of the Madison Park Apartments. The parking lot had a few more potholes than he remembered, and someone had repainted the sign, but other than that, it looked just as depressing as he remembered it. Andy climbed out of his car and headed toward building three. The sun sunk low in the southwestern sky, and the air had a more pronounced chill. Andy's left leg ached and his shoulder felt very stiff. "Same old Madison Park, just as cheery and inviting as ever." He stopped at the base of the stairs that led up to apartment 323 and stared up at the doors in the hallway above. All of his previous trips up those stairs, both real and imagined, flashed in his head. Finally after I don't know how long, he turned and went back to his car. No one saw him, or if they did, no one talked to him or asked him what he wanted.

Andy was determined to get back on the interstate and go home to Brown County the moment he left the apartment parking lot. But, of course, he didn't quite make it. Instead, he drove twenty minutes from Trask to Adamsburg and went straight to the cemetery. Although it had been a long time since his last visit, he knew where to go. The sun had dropped below the horizon as he walked over to Gabriel Phillips's grave. Looking around, he was a little surprised Loraine's grave wasn't nearby, surprised but not disappointed. "Oh, yeah," he said, "they only bury babies and little children in this section. That explains it."

Gabe's grave had been there long enough that the grass over the top looked like it had never been disturbed. Unlike during his last visit, it now had a headstone. "'Gabriel Keith Phillips,'" Andy read. "'November 2, 1969, to June 13, 1978. Safe in the angels' arms.'" No flowers adorned the headstone. Andy reached out and traced his fingers along Gabriel's name. The granite still felt warm from the sun.

"Safe in the angels' arms," Andy said. "That sure doesn't say much about who you were, does it, Gabe?" He paused and stared at the words for a while longer. "But I guess they can't really put all that on a tombstone." He sighed. "I don't know if I ever really told you how much you meant to me, how special you were. Maybe it's just as well things turned out this way. I'm afraid you wouldn't like me very much if you were still here. I'm really not a very good man. Not like..." He stopped himself.

"Well...anyway...I thought..." He swallowed hard. "I thought I was doing you a favor, spending time with you...I thought you needed me. Truth is...I needed you." Andy paused and glanced up toward the darkening sky. "I wish I could have protected you, but I guess I didn't do a very good job of that. Seeing you lying there, well, I...uh...I wanted to save you. God, how I wanted to save you. Then I just wanted to get justice for you. I thought if I could do that, then some-how that would make things all right. I always said I was doing it for you. But...uh"—a lump grew in his throat and he had trouble seeing because of the tears welling up in his eyes—"but now I'm not so sure." Tears flowed freely now. "I'm sorry, Gabe. I'm sorry I didn't walk away from your mother at the very beginning. I'm sorry I let myself fall into that game she wanted to play. I knew better, but I didn't care. I wasn't thinking about you. Or her. Or anyone. I was just thinking about myself. I should have known..." He let out a long sigh. "I just made things worse for you. I thought I could make that up to you, but...I...uh..." The words stalled on his tongue.

"Yeah, well, I just wanted to tell you that I'm sorry. I know that's not nearly good enough, but...but it's all I can do." Andy leaned down and gently kissed the top of the head-stone. Then he turned and walked back to his car. Two hours later he finally made it back to his cabin.

# CHAPTER

## 22

"EXECUTION DATE SET FOR CONVICTED CHILD KILLER," the headline of the *Indianapolis Star* said in big, bold print. Andy pulled out a quarter and slid it into the vending machine. "Well, that's a heck of a Christmas present," Andy said to himself.

"You've got that right," said a fifty-something man walking by. From the way he was dressed, Andy figured him to be a farmer or a factory worker, or both. That combination was pretty common back then in Indiana. "They should have put him to death a long time ago, if you ask me. I don't know what takes so long. The courts give scum like that way too many appeals. They should have taken him straight from the courtroom to the electric chair. That's what I think."

Andy just smiled and nodded in response. That must have made the guy feel a little self-conscious because he immediately said, "Oh, I'm sorry to go off like that, Officer."

"That's all right, sir," Andy said as he stuck the paper under his arm. "I figure everyone's probably talking about this case right now. Think nothing of it."

"Are you coming inside? Let me buy you a cup of coffee."
The man walked over toward the door of Denny's.

"No, I was just leaving," Andy lied. "Thank you anyway."

"You guys do a great job out there," the man said. "Yep,
that's what I always say, even when one of you gives me a
ticket." He let out a loud nervous laugh.

"I appreciate that," Andy said with a fake smile. "Well, if
you'll excuse me, I have to get back on patrol."

"Nail some more speeders," the man said.

"Yep," Andy said as he turned to walk away. "Gotta keep
the highways safe."

"Well, you do a hell of a job." Since this man seemed determined to have the last word, Andy just smiled and walked
back to his patrol car. His stomach growled, but he decided it
would be better to put off lunch for a little while than to have
to keep that conversation going. He climbed into his car and
cranked the heater. Winter had arrived right on schedule.
The moment the calendar hit December 21, the temperature
took a nosedive. Rather than drive off immediately, Andy
unfolded the paper and read the lead story. It said, in part:

> The governor's office announced today that John Phil-
> lips's final appeal had been denied, and an execution
> date has now been set. Phillips, convicted of the June
> 1978 killing of his son, Gabriel, will be put to death by
> electric chair on March 8 of next year. "We are pleased
> that justice will finally be served for the family of little
> Gabriel Phillips," a spokesman for Governor Chamb-
> liss said. It should be noted that it was the governor's
> prosecution of the Phillips case while district attor-
> ney in Harris County that propelled Chambliss into

statewide politics and the governor's mansion. Because of his connection to the case, and because this will be Indiana's first execution since the death penalty was reinstated in 1977, the governor himself will be present when the sentence is carried out.

"Yeah, I bet he's pleased," Andy said. "I'm just not too sure who the family is that he's talking about. The mom's dead and the dad is the one in prison. Maybe there's still a grandmother alive out there, somewhere, dying for some justice, but I haven't heard anything about her." He read the rest of the story, then folded the paper and tossed it into the passenger seat. "Justice," he said. "That's all I ever wanted. Plain old-fashioned justice." He put the car in gear and drove south to the next exit off Interstate 65. The truck stop's food didn't compare to Denny's, but at least Andy would be able to eat in peace.

After his shift ended, Andy called the state attorney general's office in Indianapolis. "Rachel Maris, please," he said to the operator who answered the call.

"Please hold." One minute later another woman's voice said, "Rachel Maris, may I help you?"

"Hi, Rachel. This is Officer Andrew Myers. I'm not sure if you remember me, but I was one of the investigators on the John Phillips case. At the time I was a patrolman with the Trask Police Department. I discovered the boy's body."

"Of course, I remember you, Andy. I'm sorry I missed you when you testified at the appeal hearing earlier this fall. How are you? I heard you were in some kind of an accident."

"Yeah, got hit by a car while I was out jogging. It was my

own stupid fault. I should have known better than to have gone out running down a narrow road after dark."

"Are you better now?"

"Pretty much. The cold weather affects me more than it used to, but, hey, that's life. How's the new job in the attorney general's office?"

"It isn't exactly new anymore, but I'm enjoying it. It's quite the change from Harris County, I can tell you that. I understand that you've changed jobs."

"Yeah, I'm with the state police now. Have been for a couple of years."

"Well, good for you. You were too good a policeman to be stuck on such a small force. A place like Trask would never bring out your full potential." As she said this, Andy wondered if she was flirting a little with him. *Probably just my imagination,* he thought.

"That's very kind of you to say. Hey, listen, the reason I called was I read today that you've set a date for John Phillips's execution."

"Yes. March eighth."

"Good, good. I was wondering if I could somehow be allowed in the prison to witness the actual execution. You know, I've been a part of this case since the beginning. I would really like to see it through to completion."

"Sure, I can understand that. I really can. You know, I'm not sure how many spots we have available…" Andy thought she sounded like she was talking about tickets to an IU basketball game. "Let me see what I can do. The governor wants to keep this from turning into a circus, which means not many people will be allowed into the execution room galley, but you never know. I know back when we prosecuted this case, Reg said he wouldn't have been able to get a conviction without you. I'll call him and get back with you. What's your number?"

Andy gave her his phone number, then added, "I really appreciate this. You know, back on the night that this happened, I made a promise to Gabriel's mother and to myself that I would make sure if John had anything to do with this, he would get what he deserves."

"That's so sweet. Do you think the mother might also want to be there? Sometimes they do, you know."

"No. I doubt if she would," Andy said.

One week later, Andy's phone rang. "Hello," he said.

"Please hold for the governor," an operator said. A couple of moments later, Andy heard a familiar voice. "Hello, Officer Myers, how are you?"

"Very well, Governor, very well. And may I say congratulations on your election, sir."

"Thank you, Officer, that's very kind of you. You know, we've already had to start making plans for the reelection campaign."

"I'm sure you won't have any problem winning a second term, sir," Andy said. *Same old Reginald Chambliss, Esquire,* he thought. *The guy is so full of baloney, I can smell him through the phone lines.*

"Thank you. Let's hope you're right. But, listen, the reason I called was because Rachel Maris told me you would like to be there when John Phillips is executed."

"Yes, sir."

"I tell you, Andy, I've never forgotten the help you gave us on this case. Getting a conviction would have been much more difficult without your hard work."

"I appreciate that, sir."

"You already know how near and dear this case is to my own heart. That's why I'm going to be there. And I would like for you to be there with me."

"Excuse me, sir."

"Yes, Andy. I would like for you to sit next to me at the execution. My office will make all the arrangements. I understand that you are now a state trooper, is that correct?"

"Yes, sir." *Yeah, you wrote a letter of recommendation for me, don't you remember?* Andy thought that, but didn't dare say it.

"Excellent. Excellent. Be sure to wear your uniform then. I would also like for you to stand on the platform with me during my news conferences both before and after the actual execution."

"Really, sir? That's very kind of you. It will be an honor."

"The pleasure is all mine. You're out there on the front line in my campaign to make Indiana safe. You deserve all the credit you can get." Yeah, old Reginald Chambliss could sure lay it on thick. "As I said, my office will be in touch with you to make all the arrangements. I think the date is pretty firm. The state appeals court turned him down for the last time, and barring intervention by the supreme court, the eighth of March should be a go."

"I'll be there," Andy said. Shortly after he hung up, his phone rang again. The governor's office didn't waste any time. An assistant had called to confirm Andy's address, phone number, and the station out of which he worked. He was told that a package would arrive the following week with his hotel information and everything else he needed for the trip to John's execution. "Good. Thank you. I appreciate it," Andy said in response.

Back when John was first convicted, Andy had told him he would be there to see him fry. Now he had a front-row seat. Not only would Andy be able to see John, John should be able to see him. It was exactly what Andy had always hoped for. He hadn't been able to see his face when the jury handed down its guilty plea, but he would be able to see it when it mattered most. Andy circled the date on his calendar and let out a sigh of relief. "Finally," he said, "the end is in sight. Thank God."

The woman in charge of shuffling schedules at the Columbus state police headquarters gave Andy a look that said *you're kidding* when he turned in his vacation request. "Didn't you just take a bunch of time off?" she asked. Andy didn't know her name. Or should I say, he never made the effort to remember it. Everyone called her the "Vacation Nazi." This was his first time to have to deal with her.

"I wouldn't exactly call lying in the hospital a vacation," Andy said.

"Well, of course, I know you were off because of your accident, but still...," she said. This woman had the well-earned reputation of being a pain in the rear. Any request for time off she treated as an insult to the state police and the state of Indiana. In her mind the act of wearing the badge was such an honor that no one would ever voluntarily take time off. Of course, that didn't stop her from using every vacation and sick day she had every year. But then again, the Vacation Nazi didn't wear the badge. She just worked there.

"If you'll check your records, you'll notice that I haven't taken one vacation day since I joined the force. And the sick days I used right after the operation on my leg are the only ones I've ever used, and even then I badgered the doctor to let me come back to work a month earlier than he wanted."

"I guess that's true. So how much time do you want to take off?"

"All of it."

"What?"

"All of it that I've accrued so far."

The Vacation Nazi sputtered. "I—I…well, I'll have to make sure we can do that. How much time do you think you have coming?"

"By my calculations, a month."

"A month! Heavens no. There's no way you can take a full month off."

"Okay, three weeks," Andy said. Before she could say a word, he said, "I'll be back at the end of my shift to sign the request form. Make sure it's ready. Besides, the first part of it can hardly be called a vacation, since I'm going to have to spend it in uniform next to the governor."

"What?! You know the governor?"

Andy gave her a wink, smiled, and said, "Three weeks. I'll save the other week for Memorial Day. Who knows? I may want to go to the race and will need the time off."

During his lunch break Andy went by a travel agency in downtown Columbus. "I want to go on a trip, but I'm not sure about exactly when I can leave. It may fluctuate by a day or two, and I may have to change it at the last minute. Oh, and I need to fly out of Chicago. I'll be up there anyway, and it will be much more convenient for me," he told the clerk.

"Where do you want to go?" she asked.

"I don't know. Where would you suggest?"

"When, approximately, are you planning on leaving?"

"Around the eighth of March. It may be that day or the day after, I'm not sure exactly when I can get away."

"Why don't you play it safe and schedule your trip for the ninth. That will save you money and we can lock in the fare."

"No, I really want to be able to leave as soon as I can. If it costs me a little extra for some flexibility, that's okay. I might as well spend it on something fun, right?"

The clerk smiled. "I guess so. So where do you want to go?"

"Where do you suggest?"

The clerk laughed. "Oh, I guess we already had that conversation, didn't we? Well, if I were planning a trip for early March, I would go somewhere south, where it's warm. Most people are sick and tired of winter by March and want to go someplace nice and sunny."

"I'm sick of it, and it's still January."

"Me too. So, like I was saying, I would go south. A lot of people enjoy Florida that time of year, especially southern Florida or one of the keys. I personally have heard Key West is a wonderful place to go."

"That sounds like a possibility. What else do you have?"

"Well, the Gulf Coast is nice, but it can be a little nippy still in March, unless you go down to South Texas. There's a place called South Padre Island that is a very nice place to go."

"Okay. That might work. What else do you have?"

"There's always Arizona, unless you want beach, and I personally don't think it's a vacation without time on the beach," the clerk said with a laugh.

"I can go either way. I've never been that much of a beach person. But then again, I live in Indiana. The only beach I've ever been to is alongside Brookville Lake."

"If you've never been to the beach, you ought to go. California has a lot of beaches, but the water is cold. If you don't want to swim, you might consider going there."

"All right, I will. What else do you suggest?"

The clerk slumped in her chair and thought for a moment.

"What about outside the States?" Andy asked.

"Well, that can be quite expensive. And you will have to have a passport."

"I've been saving for something like this for a long time, and the passport desk in the back of the post office is my next stop."

"How far out of the country do you want to go?"

"Not too far. I was reading in the *National Geographic* the other day about Belize. It said they speak English down there."

"I'm not sure about that," the woman said.

"You know, the more I think about it, the more I want to be adventurous. Let's do Belize. Can you set everything up?"

"Of course, but it will take a few days." She looked at Andy like he'd lost his mind.

"And remember, I want the tickets to be flexible, just in case my schedule changes. I have something important happening on the eighth of March, but it may get bumped back by a day or two, so I don't want to miss it."

"I can set your trip up that way. When do you want to return?"

"Can I leave that open as well? I may get down there and

figure out I hate the place. I've watched *National Geographic* specials my whole life, and I always wanted to try my hand at exploring. But if I find out I stink at it, I don't want to get stuck in a strange country for too long, even if they do speak English there."

"I understand completely," she said with a smile. "But that will make this very expensive."

"Don't worry about it. I've lived way below my means for as long as I can remember, and I've saved more money than I really know what to do with. I think it's time to live a little."

"If you say so, sir," the clerk said as Andy got up to leave.

The next week, when he went in to pick up his plane tickets and finalize his hotel reservations, the same woman waited on him. "You piqued my curiosity, Officer," she said. "I went to the library and did a little research into the country of Belize. They say that it has some of the best scuba diving in Central America. Do you scuba dive?"

"No," Andy said, "but who knows, maybe I will give it a try."

"It also has miles and miles of pristine rain forest. It sounds like a wonderful place to try your hand as an explorer, and you won't even have to learn a different language."

"That's what I intend to do," Andy said. He glanced over his tickets. "So these are completely flexible as to when I leave and when I come back?"

"Yes, sir. You will need to double-check with the airlines and make sure of their flight schedule. But, yes, they are open-ended and fully refundable and transferable."

"What does that mean?" Andy asked.

"If for some reason you couldn't use them, you could give them away to someone else or, I suppose, sell them. Again, just let the airline know ahead of time, and everything will be fine," she said. Now, you have to keep in mind that this was long before 9/11 and all the changes that brought to traveling by plane. Back then, everyone seemed pretty laid-back about all of that.

"Hmm, that's interesting. I can't imagine that I would ever need to do that, but it's good to know just in case. Who knows? Maybe I'll get down to the rain forest and decide I want to live there. It's good to know I can sell my ticket home for a little extra spending money." He laughed and the clerk joined in.

The next few weeks flew by without a hitch. Andy stayed busy making arrangements for his time away. He applied for a passport and visa, both of which arrived about a week before he was scheduled to leave. The Vacation Nazi turned loose his time off, and even had the nerve to ask if he would like his fourth week. Andy didn't take it. He told her that three weeks where he was going would probably be more than enough, if he could last that long. Packing for such a lengthy trip didn't take him as long as you might expect. He didn't plan on taking much with him. He figured he could pick up most of what he needed after he arrived. That's not the way I pack for a trip. My wife makes sure I have at least one set of clothes for every day, along with two alternates. Andy, he wasn't married, so I guess he figured on traveling light.

Although he didn't have any pets, he wanted to make sure his cabin didn't fall apart while he was gone. A young married couple he'd met in Nashville, Indiana, the previous summer agreed to house-sit for him. Their names were, or are, Doug and Dana. They're still married all these years later.

I've talked to them a few times. Nice people. They welcomed the invitation to stay in Andy's little cabin. It beat staying with Doug's parents, which is where they were living at the time. And, yeah, it surprised me, too, to hear that Andy had actually made some friends. I thought after moving down south he'd become a complete and total hermit except for the time he spent at work. Even then, he rode around all by himself in a squad car. That made him a mobile hermit, but a hermit nonetheless. I'm not sure how the hermit actually found it within himself to connect with another human being, especially two human beings. I guess my dad didn't tell me everything he did with his time.

# CHAPTER

## 23

THE BANK TELLER did not want to take no for an answer. "Sir, haven't you seen the Karl Malden commercials? You should never carry cash while traveling. You should always use traveler's checks," she said.

"But I don't like checks," Andy said over and over.

"You don't understand. These are just like cash, except, if they are lost or stolen, you can get your money back."

"But I don't like checks. Besides, I don't plan on losing my money, and if someone steals it from me, what kind of cop am I?"

"I don't know about that. But I do know that almost all of our customers who travel out of the country use traveler's checks, especially those who plan on carrying as much money as you withdrew."

"But I don't like checks. Listen, I appreciate your concern. I really do. But believe me. I'll be fine. Just give me the cash. I'm willing to live a little dangerous."

"Okay. If you insist." She crinkled her brow and made it very clear that she believed Andy was making a huge mistake. However, she dutifully counted out twenty-four one-hundred-dollar bills, and five twenties. "Enjoy your trip," she said as Andy gathered up his money.

He smiled and said, "I plan on it. I've needed to do something like this for a very long time." He placed the twenties in his wallet, and put the Benjamins in one of those bank envelopes and shoved it in his pocket. "I'll see you when I get back," he said with a wave.

Because his flight left out of Chicago, Andy drove his old Impala rather than his squad car up to Michigan City. He could drive his state police car anywhere in the state of Indiana, but he didn't want to take it across the state line. Doug followed him into Columbus that morning so Andy could park his police car at the station rather than leave it at his house. I guess he figured it would be safer there, not that there's a big crime problem just north of Gnaw Bone, Indiana. On his way out of Columbus, Andy swung by the post office and mailed a few letters. One of them was to me. It was the first real letter he'd ever written me. Since he'd never flown before, he wanted to make sure he covered all his bases just in case the plane crashed in the jungle or something. At least that's why he told me he wrote. He also mailed an updated copy of his will to his attorney and another letter to Ted Jackson. Like I said, he'd never flown before. I guess people who have never been on a plane figure the odds of the plane crashing at around fifty-fifty. Me, I would rather fly than drive, but that's just me.

Andy was on the road, heading north, by ten-thirty on the morning of March 7. He didn't pay much attention to his speed, even though he was in his own car and was wearing a pair of jeans and an old Indiana Pacers T-shirt. The state trooper uniform hanging in the back pretty much insured that he could go as fast as he wanted without worrying about any tickets. He stopped in Indianapolis for lunch, if you can call a bag of sliders lunch. His leg and shoulder stiffened up a few times during the rest of the drive, which meant he had to stop and stretch frequently. But that was why he drove up a day early. He didn't want to stumble around like Herman Munster when he accompanied the governor into the prison. The extra day would give his body a chance to get back to normal after such a long drive.

The area around the state prison wasn't exactly the tourist center of Indiana. Most of the hotels catered to the families of inmates who come up for visitation on the weekends. All of that means that finding a decent place to stay can be tough. Andy decided to stay at the Holiday Inn in Merrillville, just off Interstate 65 and just south of Gary. He definitely didn't want to stay in Gary. I think it was because of a bad reaction to *The Music Man* back when he was a kid. Once he settled into his room, he called the state attorney general's office and asked for Rachel Maris. She planned to drive up in the governor's motorcade early on the morning of the eighth. John's execution wouldn't take place until just before midnight on that day, which gave them plenty of time to arrive. Like I said, Andy drove up early to give his stiff bones a chance to loosen up after the long drive.

Rachel answered on the first ring. "Hello. Rachel Maris speaking."

"Hey, Rachel, it's Andy Myers checking in."

"Andy! It's good to hear your voice." Andy still couldn't figure out if she was just as good a politician as her boss, or if she was interested in him. He never quite got the chance to find out. "I trust you had a good trip."

"I can't complain. I'm staying at the Holiday Inn in Merrillville, room 104."

"Good. Now, do you want a driver to swing by and pick you up tomorrow night?"

"No, I'd rather drive myself. I'm going to leave from the prison for a much needed vacation right after this is all over."

"In the middle of the night?"

"I'm going to catch a red-eye out of O'Hare. I figure I might as well do something productive, because I doubt if I will be able to go to sleep after this one."

"No, probably not."

"Are you going to be in the observation room when it happens?"

"No, no. Not me. I don't have any interest in watching something like this. I believe in the death penalty, but that doesn't mean I want to see it carried out." Andy wasn't surprised by her answer. Although Maris came across as very tough, very self-assured, he knew she had a soft streak in her that she did her best to keep at bay. Watching a man die in a chair might melt away her tough exterior and make it impossible for her to do her job.

"But I will see you at the news conference before, right?"

"You can count on it. And if you need anything between now and then, be sure to call." She gave Andy the number of the hotel where the governor's entourage would stay. It had been a long time since a woman had given Andy her number. "I gotta get out more," he said to himself after he hung up the phone.

*     *     *

His wake-up call came at six the next morning, but Andy was already awake. After grabbing a doughnut and a cup of coffee at a nearby diner, he drove over here, actually. Yeah, he came right here to Indiana Dunes State Park. No one else was on the beach when he went for a walk down the sand, probably right around the same area where we are now. The wind whipped off the lake and the sun stayed behind the clouds. Needless to say, he pretty much had the beach to himself. He told me he just wanted to spend some time in a quiet place, where he could sit back and soak in the beauty of creation before he had to go into the prison and be confronted with the ugliness of man. Living alone for so long had made him quite the philosopher. On his way back to his hotel, he stopped and gassed up the Impala. Premium gas, that is. It wouldn't run on regular unleaded, and the government had outlawed leaded gas by this time.

Although he didn't plan on sleeping in his hotel room after the execution, he had paid for an extra night, just in case. If nothing else, it gave him a place to stay while he waited for the big event to roll around. An envelope lay on the floor just inside his hotel room door when he walked back into his room. The envelope smelled of perfume, although it wasn't scented. Andy just had an extrasensitive smeller. Inside was a brief note from Rachel Maris, along with a schedule of the day's events leading up to John's execution. "Good ole Chambliss is working this thing like a campaign rally," Andy said. He had a meeting scheduled with the leaders of the local law enforcement community at four-thirty in the afternoon, followed by an appearance at the Hammond VFW at six. Dinner with the mayors of Gary, Hammond, East Chicago, and Michigan City would be at 7:00 p.m. The governor was scheduled to arrive at the prison by eight-thirty in the evening, with his preexecution news conference from the prison visitor's center slated for one hour later. "Giving plenty of time for all the members of the press corps to go through security," Andy said with a laugh. "Chambliss and his people think of everything." The actual execution would take place at eleven-fifteen, or right in the middle of the nightly eleven o'clock news. "After all, this is the story of the year," Andy said as he folded the schedule and laid it on top of the television.

He picked up the phone and called the local number Rachel Maris had given him. No answer. Glancing down at his watch, he said, "Three-oh-nine, they must already be going full steam ahead." He grabbed the schedule and glanced over it again, then read Rachel's note. "Andy," it read, "Feel free to join us for any of the day's events or to spend the time relaxing before your trip. Either way, please be at the prison by eight. One of our staff will meet you at the main entrance and brief you on the governor's plans for his press conference. I think you'll be pleasantly surprised." She signed it, "Rachel." Andy looked back at his watch. "Looks like I've got a few hours to kill." He spent the next hour or so flipping back and forth between *I Love Lucy* reruns, *Phil Donahue,* and *Jeopardy!* When he got bored with that, he wrote a couple more letters and repacked his bags. Around the same time the governor was pressing the flesh with some local veterans, Andy put on his state trooper's uniform, threw his bags in his Impala, and went out to find a place to eat. The wild man ended up at Denny's. He told me nothing tastes better at five-thirty in the evening than the original Grand Slam. Go figure.

The prison parking lot was over three-quarters full when Andy pulled in at 7:30 p.m. He didn't go to the law enforcement section, since he was driving his old Impala. Instead, he pulled into a spot under a light pole and next to a Volkswagen minibus with Illinois plates and an EXECUTE THE DEATH PENALTY bumper sticker plastered next to another that said SAVE THE WHALES. Over farther to the south sat two old-school yellow school buses, but the names of the school district had been sanded off. Just to the side of the buses, a group of protesters looked to be organizing their efforts. Andy saw plenty of bullhorns and protest signs stacked up on one of the buses. They didn't notice him as he walked to the front gate. A guard waved him through. As he walked into the security area, a familiar face greeted him.

"Andy, it's good to see you again," Rachel Maris said.

He smiled and shook his head. "I thought some staffer would be here. I never expected it would be you."

"Yeah, well, I can only take so much politics in any one day. Reg didn't need me, so I thought I would head on over. Looks like we're in for quite a show, doesn't it?"

"Bringing 'em by the busload, aren't they?"

"We expected it. We did our homework and found from other states that executions bring out a wide variety of protesters, everyone from radical hippy types, who can't believe the sixties actually ended, to church groups. They rarely, if ever, get violent. Usually, they yell their slogans and protest while the dignitaries arrive. Then they switch to a quiet candlelight vigil. We're going to keep the police presence pretty low-key, but we will have the resources we need close by, just in case."

"Sounds like a good plan." Andy tried to sound interested. "So, is that why the governor wanted me in uniform?"

Rachel laughed. "No, he has something much bigger in mind for you; that is, if you don't mind. Reg and I talked a lot about you since you called asking if you could attend Phillips's execution. The governor never forgot all the work you put in on this case. He's not just blowing smoke when he says that he wouldn't have had a case without you. He really means it. Now here's what he would like to do. During his press conference he would like to introduce you and tell how instrumental you were in this case. Then, and this is the part that we want to make sure you are up to, he would like for you to answer a few questions. Now don't panic. We've hand-selected the reporters who will ask you these questions, and we also prepared the questions ahead of time. I'll give them to you in a minute, if you want to do this. If you don't, he'll just introduce you, then let you step back into the background."

"Wow. That's quite an honor. I never expected anything like this."

Rachel smiled. "I thought you'd be thrilled with it. And that's not the best of it. Reg is the kind of man who likes to reward those who help him along the way. We checked into your service record since you joined the state police. I've got to say, Andy, it's really impressive."

"Yeah, well, I don't know about that."

"Don't sell yourself short. Anyway, the governor would like for you to consider being reassigned to Indianapolis as part of his personal security detail. Basically, that means you would be one of the troopers who travels with the governor wherever he goes." She let out a huge smile. "You'd have to move to Indy, but it would be a big boost in your career."

"I don't know what to say. Wow. I'm shocked. Wow."

"I thought you would be. I know you said you were going on a trip right after this, so you can think about this while you're gone and give us an answer when you get back."

"Okay, I will. Thanks." Rachel leaned over and gave Andy a hug, which, again, he wasn't really sure what it meant. He found it very interesting how she always referred to Reginald Chambliss, Esquire, as "Reg," and to the two of them as "we."

"So what do we do now?" he asked.

"We'll wait here for the governor and the rest of his party. Then we will all go through security together and head back for the news conference."

"With cameras rolling the whole time, of course," Andy said.

"Of course."

*   *   *

THE GOVERNOR'S MOTORCADE pulled into the prison compound that night at precisely eight-thirty on the nose. State police cars led the way, their lights flashing and sirens blowing. As if on cue, the protestors, who now numbered in the hundreds, sprang into action. They started chanting in their bullhorns and waving their signs around. Local police confined them to a specified protest area, but that didn't stop them from coming into physical contact with Reginald Chambliss himself. That, however, was his doing. He climbed out of his limo and walked straight over to the crowd. The consummate politician, he couldn't let an opportunity like this pass him by. With a covey of reporters in tow, Chambliss addressed the crowd, which, surprisingly enough, quieted down and listened. Chambliss told them how he shared their concerns about escalating violence, and that he agreed with them, violence would never be a cure for violence. If you didn't know better, you would have almost thought that he was there to join in the protest himself. But then he turned the whole thing around and started talking about justice and the plight of the victims of crime. "Someone has to stand up for those who cannot stand up for themselves," he told the crowd. He went on from there. It was all quite moving, if hearing how a politician feels your pain moves you.

By 8:40 p.m., the governor walked into the security screening area, along with the rest of his staff and the reporters covering the event for every media outlet in Indiana, Chicago, and southern Michigan. Andy stayed as out of sight as was humanly possible in a confined space filled with an attention-hugging governor and hordes of cameras. The governor made a few remarks, then walked over to the security station. Andy noticed the same guard who'd worked the metal detector the day he last visited John was working the same station on this evening. She was, however, much more excited, and was wearing more makeup than she had that day.

"Good evening, Governor Chambliss," she said with a giddy smile. "Would you please empty your pockets in this tray and step through the metal detector for me?"

"My pleasure," Chambliss said as flashbulbs popped all around him.

The rest of the governor's staff followed. When it was Andy's turn, he said, "Good evening, Officer. It's good to see you again." The guard acted surprised, and did not immediately recognize him. "I was here a couple of months ago visiting Phillips." When his face still didn't register with her, he said, "I set off your machine with all the screws in my leg."

"Oh, yeah, I remember. You were hit by a car while jogging." A smile broke out on her face. "How's that leg doing? You were still limping pretty good when you were here the last time."

"Cold weather doesn't do it any good, but it's better than it was. Still sets off metal detectors, though," he said with a laugh. He stepped through the arch of the machine, which made a siren go off. "Told you."

"I guess you know the drill then," the guard said as she stepped out with the wand in her hand. "Which leg is it, again?" she asked.

"Left."

She passed the wand over his left leg, which made it howl. "Go on through," she said without bothering to wand any other part of his body. "Next." A very junior staff member started dumping out his pockets as Andy stepped up his pace to catch up with the governor's entourage.

"Governor, you remember Officer Myers," Rachel said as she led Andy over to the makeshift platform the prison had set up for the news conference.

"Of course," he said as he smiled and extended his hand. "Good to see you again, Andy. Glad you could make it."

"My pleasure, sir."

"Rachel here says you're fine with answering a few questions from the press."

"I'm a little nervous, but, yeah, I think I can do it."

Chambliss slapped Andy on the back. "You'll do great,"

he said. "There's nothing to it. I think you'll enjoy the experience. She also told me you're ready to come join my staff. That's great. Can't wait to have you."

"Thank you, sir. Just being asked is a huge honor." Andy didn't bother correcting him by telling him that he hadn't agreed to anything yet. Men like Chambliss don't listen to much of what anyone says. Their entire lives are scripted to get them where they want to go as quickly as possible. Andy knew he was nothing more than a political prop, but he could live with that. This would all be over soon enough. He could put up with being a prop for a little while.

When the lights came on, Chambliss really shone. He opened his press conference by talking about justice and defending the rights of the victims of crime. He said something like, "I started this fight a long time ago, long before I ever even dreamed of running for statewide office. In spite of what the protestors would lead you to believe, this case is not about John Phillips and his rights. It is about a little boy whose life was taken away in a brutal, calculated act of cold-blooded murder. And it is about that child's mother who, to this day, is still heartbroken over the loss of her child." Apparently, no one in the governor's office bothered to find out anything about Loraine's current status. She, like Andy, was nothing more than a minor player in this grand theater.

Chambliss went on for a while longer, before turning to Andy and saying, "I would like to introduce to you the police officer who was instrumental in securing justice for poor little Gabriel Phillips. Officer Andrew Myers is now a proud member of the Indiana State Police. However, in June of 1978, he was a patrolman in the small town of Trask. He responded to a call of a domestic disturbance, and discovered the ghastly scene of Gabriel Phillips lying in a pool of his own blood. Officer Myers worked diligently, chasing down leads and interviewing witnesses, all in his tireless efforts to help us discover the truth of what happened in that home that night." He motioned for Andy to step forward. "Officer Myers, on behalf of the entire state of Indiana, and on behalf of the victims of violent crime everywhere, I would like to say thank you." Chambliss started the applause, and the members of the press joined in. Once the applause died down, the governor said, "I'll now take a few questions…"

And that was it. Andy didn't answer any questions. He didn't share the press conference in any way. Not that he minded. Far from it. Andy stepped back into his place while Reginald Chambliss, Esquire, did what he did best. I guess the guy just couldn't bring himself to share the spotlight. After answering questions for an hour, the governor thanked the members of the press for coming, then excused himself to take care of what he called "a very sad but necessary task."

# CHAPTER

## 24

THE OBSERVATION ROOM for the execution chamber wasn't built for the number of people who tried to squeeze into it. Andy was right. John Phillips's date with the electric chair was *the* story of the year. Although no cameras were allowed in this part of the prison, television reporters with press passes lined up alongside print reporters and a couple of members of the national media. Listening to some of the conversation in the room, Andy discovered that most of those there were surprised it had taken this long for Indiana to carry out a death sentence. After all, it is one of those conservative heartland states that doesn't mess around when it comes to crime.

Because of the overflow crowd, prison officials moved the governor, and the one member of his staff in attendance, from the glassed-off main gallery to a section just to the side of the actual area where the sentence would be carried out. The staff member was a slight little man who worked in the attorney general's office. The attorney general refused to attend, out of his opposition to capital punishment. However, he never said anything publicly. To do so would embarrass the governor, and put his own job in jeopardy.

When they moved the governor out of the gallery, Andy started to stay behind with the press. Chambliss motioned for him. "Come on in here, Andy. You've earned it. This is the culmination of all you've done." Andy fell in step behind him. Then in a rare moment of honesty, Chambliss said, "I guess if I'm going to support these things, I need to see it up close and personal, instead of getting the sanitized version."

"I guess so, sir," Andy said.

Andy found himself standing directly next to the governor, with the other staff member on the opposite side. The place where they stood felt secluded, at least as secluded as a place could be with so many people around. A large window allowed those in the gallery to see the electric chair, but Andy and the governor were far enough to the side that they were out of view of everyone except the prison officials who would carry out the death sentence. There were no chairs in this part of the room, which neither Andy nor the governor seemed to mind. The warden stood on the opposite side of the room, near where the guards carrying out the sentence would be. Andy figured it was so he could issue the final order to carry out the sentence.

At 11:05 p. m., a door opened, and two guards came walking in with John Phillips between them. One guard had his hand on John's shoulders. Both guards' faces were streaked red, their eyes bloodshot. One wiped away tears as he entered. John...well, John didn't look nearly as upset as the guards. He wasn't upset at all. He walked in with a smile on his face. Most of those watching must have thought he was crazy, but then again, a guy would have to be pretty much nuts to kill his own child. When one of the guards seemed to stumble as if his knees had gone weak, John patted him on the back and said, "It's okay. You can do this."

Chambliss glanced over at Andy with a smirk. "What the hell was that?" the governor whispered.

"I'm not real sure, sir," Andy whispered back. "It looks like the guards are having a hard time doing their jobs."

"Remind me to fire them later," Chambliss joked.

The guards led John to the electric chair itself. He plopped down into it like an old man settling into his favorite chair to watch *Gunsmoke*. This caused the guard on his left to break down emotionally. As he started weeping, he looked up and noticed the governor. Andy described the look the guard shot Chambliss as more lethal than anything they would do to John. The other guard whispered something to his partner, and both straightened up. A prison chaplain entered the execution room and put his arm around John. "Let's pray," he said to both John and everyone in attendance. A speaker system allowed the gallery to hear him. Andy watched as the two guards lowered their heads, as did the warden. Even Reginald Chambliss, Esquire, dropped his head like a kid in a Sunday school class.

And that's when Andy did it.

As the chaplain said, "Our Father in heaven," Andy stepped back and behind the governor, then reached below his shirt with his right hand and pulled out his service revolver. With his left hand he took hold of Chambliss's arm, just above his elbow, and pulled him back toward himself as he pushed the gun into his back. "Shhhhhh," Andy whispered in the governor's ear, "don't make a sound and you won't get hurt.

Just do exactly what I say and you will walk out of here alive. Otherwise, I can't make any promises."

"By your rich mercy and grace we beseech thee, O Lord," the chaplain prayed.

"Now this is how this is all going to go down," Andy whispered. "There's been a change of plans, new evidence if you will." He released the governor's arm for just a moment and reached back to pull out two envelopes he had stuffed into his belt inside his shirt, just above his back. He placed them in the governor's hand. "The small one, that's for the warden. Make sure he reads every word out loud."

"How can I give it to him if you're holding me here?" Chambliss said ever so softly.

"O Giver of Life, who creates all men in his image," the chaplain continued.

"Give it to your assistant and have him take it over. The other one, the thick manila envelope, that's for Phillips. Got it?" Andy said.

"We ask that you will have pity on the soul of John Phillips," the chaplain went on.

"You'll never get away with this," Chambliss growled.

"That's all right," Andy said with a smile, "I don't plan to."

"This is a prison, filled with armed guards. They'll drop you with one shot as soon as they realize what you are doing."

"You're probably right. But then again, you'll be dead a half second before me."

"Why are you doing this?" Chambliss's voice was a mixture of shock, fear, and anger.

"Let's just call it my own little witness protection program," Andy said.

"We ask all of this in the name of your precious Son, Jesus Christ. Amen."

The chaplain patted John on the shoulder and leaned down to whisper something in his ear. As he did, Andy pressed the gun a little harder into the governor's back. Chambliss then spoke up like a puppet on a ventriloquist's lap. "Simon"—his assistant's name was Simon—"would you have the warden read this for me." Simon looked a little surprised, but he did what he was told. Apparently, Reginald Chambliss rarely if ever did anything that hadn't been carefully choreographed first.

Simon walked across the room, passing directly in front of John and the guards, as well as the glass window separating this room from the observation gallery. "The governor asked if you would read this for him."

The warden looked over at Chambliss with a shocked look on his face. "Now?" Chambliss nodded. The warden glanced down at the words on the page, then looked up quickly. "Really?!" Chambliss nodded again. "Out loud?!"

"Yes. Out loud. Now," Chambliss said, very much annoyed.

The warden cleared his throat, then said to the two guards who were about to soak the sponge that would go between John's head and the electrodes, "There's been a change of plans here today." The moment he said this, both guards looked visibly relieved. Very, very relieved. "Governor Chambliss has just handed me a statement he has prepared. He asked that I read it to you." Now, I can't quote the whole statement word for word, but I can give you the gist of what it said. Basically, "the governor's" statement said that new evidence had just come to light that exonerated John Phillips. He went on to say that he was only now revealing this new evidence to draw attention to the injustices and inequities of the criminal justice system. That system, along with the appeals courts, had failed John. He was—and this was why Andy had the warden read it rather than Reginald Chambliss himself, because ole Chambliss would have choked on these words—the victim of a rush to judgment by a cynical investigative team more interested in proving a point than uncovering the truth, and an overeager prosecutor who viewed this case as an opportunity for political advancement. The statement didn't mention that Chambliss himself was that overeager prosecutor, but Andy figured everyone would make that connection themselves. Therefore, the statement said, "I am granting John Phillips a full pardon. Even that is a misnomer, for a pardon implies guilt, but Mr. Phillips has done nothing wrong. I hereby order his immediate release and, on behalf of the state of Indiana, extend to him our deepest apologies." That last part I can quote. Written below the public statement was a set of instructions the warden was to give to the guards. He communicated those to them directly, but no one else could hear what he said.

I wish I could have seen for myself the scene that unfolded as the warden read the statement Andy had written for the governor. The two guards began weeping with joy as they listened to it. When the warden got down to the part about the pardon, they walked over and embraced John. After spending over three years with John, they knew better than anyone else that he didn't deserve the sentence he'd been given—well, almost anyone else. I even think the warden himself was a little relieved. Outside of Reginald Chambliss, Esquire, there wasn't a person in the room that truly believed John was guilty. John, he didn't cry. A little grin broke out on his face as his eyes looked up toward heaven. Andy could read his lips saying, "Thank you" to God. None of them had any idea what was really happening. No one did, or Andy would have never gotten away with it.

From the other side of the glass, Andy could hear both cheers and anger from those watching all this unfold. Everyone seemed to accept what was happening without question. At least it seemed that way to Andy. Of course, he couldn't see any of them, and they couldn't see him.

While this was all going on, Chambliss turned about eight shades of red. Apparently, Chambliss believed Andy would pull the trigger because he never said or did anything to tip off those in the room that something was amiss. As for Andy, he didn't move. He stood behind the governor, his .38 pressed up tight into Chambliss's back, and showed no expression whatsoever.

Once the warden finished reading the "governor's" statement, Chambliss handed the other envelope to his assistant and told him to give it to John. Simon did exactly as he was told. John opened it and pulled out the note inside. Then he stood up from the electric chair and walked out of the room with the two guards, both hugging him on the way out. Per their instructions, they took him immediately to the front gate. The last they or anyone else saw of him, he was walking out into the parking lot. No one else left the room until the two guards returned. This created a rather awkward situation. When the warden tried to walk over to Chambliss, the governor told him to stay where he was. The warden looked at him like he was nuts, which would have been a pretty good assessment if Chambliss had actually written the prepared statement that set John free. Finally the two guards walked back into the execution chamber. "He's gone," one of them said.

As soon as they said that, Andy stepped out from behind the governor and dropped his gun to the floor. "What the...?" the warden said. The guards looked at one another with shock. "Hey, no one is supposed to have any firearms in here."

"Seize him, you fools!" Chambliss yelled. "Don't you realize what he just did!?" Of course, none of them did. No one had a clue as to what had just happened, except that the governor had committed political suicide. There wouldn't be any second terms for Reginald Chambliss, Esquire. After this, there probably wouldn't even be a sign on the city limits of Silver City announcing it as the home of Reginald Chambliss, the governor of the great state of Indiana. When no one rushed Andy, Chambliss pushed past him, grabbed his gun, and pointed it at Andy. But he didn't just point it at him. He grabbed the grip with both hands and shoved the gun out in front of him, with his legs spread wide, like a scene out of a bad cop movie.

Andy laughed. "It won't do you much good," he said. "There aren't any bullets in it."

Now this really set Chambliss off. He was so mad, he seemed to completely lose sight of who he was and where he was standing. His arms started shaking, and his eyes bulged out, and before he realized what he had done, he pulled the trigger. Nothing happened. He pulled it again and again and again, until he finally flung it away from himself. If he'd been paying a little more attention, he probably would have thrown it to his right or just dropped it on the ground. Instead, he ended up throwing the gun right through the window that separated the execution chamber from the observation gallery. He didn't know what he had done until he heard the crashing of the glass. Most of the reporters were still sitting there, waiting for the governor to come out and give them a full statement. I guess, technically, they weren't actually sitting down. They all jumped when they saw the governor point a gun at a state trooper. Most knew that John Phillips had just been replaced as the biggest story of the year, although they didn't know exactly what that story was just yet.

"ARREST THIS MAN!" Chambliss screamed. "He just set a murderer free." Still, no one moved. The warden and the guards and Simon and everyone else just stared at the governor like he'd lost his mind.

Finally Andy spoke up. "He's right. But you don't need to arrest me. I give myself up." With that, he dropped down on his knees and placed his hands behind his head, his fingers interlocked. He'd asked his share of people to assume that position when he arrested them, so he knew what to do. The warden grabbed a phone, and within a few seconds a team of guards came rushing in.

"Why?" Chambliss yelled at Andy. "Why would you do this?"

"Justice," Andy said. "Plain old simple justice. Well, justice and forgiveness."

"What!? I don't understand. How was this justice!?"

"John Phillips didn't kill his son. Gabriel Phillips hit his head and died when he fell out of his bunk bed. I never could believe this myself until just a few weeks ago. Of course, by then it was too late. I so badly wanted to believe John was guilty, that I couldn't see the evidence any other way. By the time the truth hit me, it was too late. His appeals had all run out, and I knew you wouldn't believe me."

Chambliss stood there, his jaw hanging open, a look of total disgust on his face. "You're crazy. You could have come to me."

"No. No, I couldn't."

"But why this?"

"Luke 19:8?" Andy said.

"Who?" Chambliss asked.

"It's not a who. It's a verse in the Bible about a guy named Zacchaeus. He wasn't a nice man, but when Jesus forgave him, it changed him. He went out and set things right with the people he'd harmed. Well, I've found the same forgiveness Zacchaeus experienced, and it feels pretty good. But that's not enough. I did more harm to the Phillips family than I could ever make up for in one lifetime. Setting John free like this was the least I could do."

"You're nuts."

Andy just smiled. "Yeah. I guess I am. But for the first time in my life, I feel completely free." The irony of that statement wasn't lost on him. He knew he wouldn't walk out on the streets as a free man for a very long time. Twenty-six years, three months, and nineteen days, as of tomorrow, to be exact. He said it was a small price to pay. Justice never tasted so sweet, he said. And after all, that's all he ever really wanted for Gabriel Phillips. Justice.

# CHAPTER

## 25

IF YOU HAVEN'T figured it out already, all of this is why I am here right now. My dad gets out of prison tomorrow. He served all of his time not far from here in the same prison where John served his time on death row. Of course, Andy spent his years in a different part of the prison. As much as Chambliss might have wanted, he couldn't get a court to give Andy death. As it turns out, Andy spent a lot more time in prison than John did. I never heard him complain about it, but I know he's anxious to get out. He gets to meet his grandson for the very first time tomorrow. My wife and I named him after my dad. It was her idea, but I thought it was a pretty good one.

I'm not sure what ever happened to John. In the letter he wrote to him, Andy explained everything he was doing and why. The plane tickets were in the envelope, along with the keys to the Impala. The money and some clothes were in the car waiting for him. In all the confusion, it took a while for a real manhunt to get under way. Police officers surrounded O'Hare Airport in Chicago and they stopped every flight out of there for over a day. Not that it did any good. John didn't turn up there. Chambliss also put up blockades around the Indianapolis airport, but all that did was make a lot of travelers mad. Andy had anticipated both airports would be targeted, which is why he bought fully transferable tickets. I think John might have flown out of Detroit. It could have been Cleveland, for that matter. He might have flown to Belize. No one really knows, and my dad would never say. That's part of the reason my dad never made parole until now. All Andy would ever say was that John was now on an extended mission trip and probably wouldn't be back.

The manhunt for John lost its steam after Chambliss left office. He didn't get a second term. It wasn't so much the way this case turned out, although that certainly didn't help, as it was the image of him pulling the trigger on an unarmed man. Voters never really got over that one. The new attorney general's office opened a full-scale investigation into the whole affair, going back to the original investigation of Gabe's death. They found "gross errors" had been made in the case, but they stopped short of exonerating John. They did, however, remove him from the wanted criminals list. The report ended Chambliss's political career, however. Last I heard, he was living somewhere in Florida. Or Arizona. Or someplace warm.

But I guess I ought to answer the biggest question you probably have right now. Why did Andy do what he did, and how did that bring me to where I am right now? After all, nothing I've told you so far would lead you to believe that I should have any kind of relationship with my biological father. It's a long story, but I'll spare you. One long story is enough.

The long and the short of it is this. After Andy's trip to see John after his last appeal was denied, and after his trip to visit Gabe's grave in Adamsburg, Andy started thinking about everything John had told him, especially the part about guilt and forgiveness. Andy knew guilt would kill him. It nearly did. The bullet holes in the walls of his cabin were meant for his head. I don't know if he was so drunk that he missed, or if God pushed his hand up at just the right moment. Either way, his suicide attempt failed. That's when he tore open the package from John and discovered both a letter and a small Gideons Bible. John's letter answered Andy's question by saying that he forgave the man who was sleeping with his wife the moment he found out about it. Then he went on to explain how such an act was impossible on a human level. John could forgive others because God had forgiven him. The little New Testament had several verses underlined for Andy to read, verses that explained both the hows and whys behind the forgiveness God offers through His Son, Jesus. By the way, the story of Zacchaeus was *not* one of the verses John had marked.

Andy started reading through what John had marked for him. The more he read, the more sense it made. Pretty soon, he discovered he believed what he was reading, which led to him making a life-altering decision. No, not the decision to pull a gun on the governor. That came later. No, this decision had to do with the direction of his life, and handing control of it over to Jesus. I know this sounds a little preachy, but, hey, it is what it is. Most people who don't think much about God think anything that talks about Him is preachy. So there you have it. Guilty as charged.

Andy's decision to follow Jesus ultimately led to his decision to make things right with John in the only way he knew how. It wasn't just John. Andy carried a load of guilt about Loraine, and her suicide only made it worse. He had given her the gun she ultimately used to kill herself. She said she needed it for protection. Andy never would have guessed she needed to be protected from herself. God gave him a peace about all of this, but he still felt compelled to, in the words of Zacchaeus, pay back those he'd wronged. That led to setting John free, and it also led to him contacting me.

When the first letter arrived, my mother threw it away. And the second. And the third. And I don't know how many. Pretty soon the letters arrived so frequently that she finally decided she ought to let me read one. I think I was around thirteen at the time. I didn't even know I had a father. Well, I knew I had to have some sort of biological father. I had no illusions about being born of a virgin. But I never knew I had a father out there that was still alive. I'd built up this little fantasy about my dad as this heroic guy who was shot down in a blaze of glory after shooting down about fifty Nazi warplanes. So I wasn't too good at history and I watched way too many John Wayne movies when I was a little kid. What can I say?

Actually, that isn't entirely true. I knew my father had abandoned me, and I hated him for it. But until the letters arrived, he was just an invisible someone out there I despised. My fantasy dad would have hunted him down and killed him, if the Nazis hadn't gotten to him first.

The letters from my dad started off with an apology for how he had wronged me. He also apologized for repeating himself, because he was going to say the same thing in every letter until he received word that I'd read one of them. After the way he treated my mother, he must have assumed she would throw them away. For the brief time they were married, he knew her pretty well. When I wrote him back the first time, I told him I'd received his letter and please don't write back again. He ignored my request. The letters kept coming. When Andy Myers puts his mind to something, he gets it done. And he had put his mind to building a relationship with me. As you can see, it worked.

I read his letters. All of them. And I kept them. I still have them today. About the time I finished high school, I drove up from Saint Louis and visited him in prison. I was still skeptical, but eventually I came around. I prayed to receive Christ with my dad in that same prison visitation room several years later. That day changed my life, just like it changed his. Once I was forgiven, I realized that the one person I'd wronged above all others was my father. I wouldn't forgive him for the longest time, even after I could tell he wanted my forgiveness more than anything else in this world. That's all changed now. Like I said, my wife and I named our little boy after him. At least his first name. His middle name is Gabriel.

So that's it. That's my story. That's why I'm here.

# DISCUSSION GROUP QUESTIONS

1. Gabriel Phillips is gone when the story begins, but his presence is powerful throughout. What about this little boy was so special that he would have such an impact on so many lives so long after his death?

2. John Phillips had a peace about his son's death that was inconceivable to Andy Myers and most of the authorities. What about his demeanor and his speech do you think made him look so suspicious? Why do you think it was so easy to believe he was guilty?

3. Andy Myers threw himself into the investigation of Gabriel's death and made it his personal campaign to get justice for the boy. What do you think was really behind this obsession?

4. Loraine Phillips asked Andy in his dreams and face to face a question that haunted him: What have we done? Why do you think this question was so troublesome for Andy? What do you think was the source of the guilt he felt?

5. John Phillips seemed to have experienced a dramatic transformation in prison and was embraced by his religious community. Do you think the change was

real? Do you think even violent criminals can receive redemption?

6. Loraine Phillips could not recover from the death of her child or cope with the role she played and eventually took her own life. What do you think was the primary responsibility she had in these events? Why do you think her guilt consumed her? What could she have done to save herself?

7. Eli Williams was the prisoner nearly killed by John, yet he stood by John throughout his trial and appeals. Do you think you could forgive someone something that big and even befriend them? What do you think gave Eli the strength to be so forgiving?

8. Andy eventually came to comprehend something of what was behind John's faith and peace. What do you believe was the turning point for him? What finally helped him to understand and accept the Christian message John had been trying to share with him?

9. Andy's son serves as the narrator for the story and only learned about Andy through their correspondence while Andy was in prison. Do you think Andy's determination to restore their relationship had a positive impact on his son's life?

10. Many of the characters in this story deal with feelings of guilt and struggle with forgiveness. Which of these characters address these issues the right way and which handle them poorly? What do you think made the difference in how each of them did so?

11. John refused to defend himself in court and resigned himself to accepting whatever was in God's will for his life. What do you think enabled him to have that

resolve? Do you think you could be as open to God's plan for your life, even if it meant taking punishment for a crime you didn't commit?

12. John disappeared after Andy's rescue at the planned execution and was never heard from again. Do you think running and hiding was out of character for him? If so, why do you think he did something so uncharacteristic? Do you think he saw this as another part of God's plan for his life?

13. Andy provided John with the means to go anywhere and do anything. What do you think John did? What do you think he did with his newfound freedom?

14. There are a number of themes in this story that deal with interpersonal relationships and relationship with God. What do you think is the prevailing message of this story?

15. The title of this book is *The Death and Life of Gabriel Phillips*. Why do you think it was phrased in this way? What message is in the arrangement of the words "Life" and "Death"?

# ABOUT THE AUTHORS

Stephen Baldwin, actor, family man, born-again Christian. Through an impressive body of work, Stephen continues to be a popular and sought-after talent in the film and television industry. Stephen makes his home in upstate New York with his wife and two young daughters.

Mark Tabb has authored and co-authored over twenty books. His March, 2008 release, *Mistaken Identity*, debuted at number one on the *New York Times* bestseller list. He also worked with Alec Baldwin on *A Promise to Ourselves*. Mark's solo titles include the 2006 release, *Living with Less, The Upside of Downsizing Your Life*, and the 2004 ECPA Gold Medallion finalist, *Out of the Whirlwind* along with many other titles. Mark and his family live in Indiana.

## READ STEPHEN BALDWIN'S
### EXTRAORDINARY MEMOIR

In THE UNUSUAL SUSPECT
Stephen Baldwin reveals
his unbelievable change
from a hardcore party boy
to a hardcore follower of
Jesus Christ. To Stephen,
"hardcore faith" is the
willingness to put your life
and future completely in the
hands of the invisible God,
obeying His direction to
the death. Stephen's offers
brazen observations about
the culture at large and the work of the Church in it.
The core of his message: "You must be willing to try
faith God's way, not yours, and when you do you will find
a life beyond anything you could have dreamed."

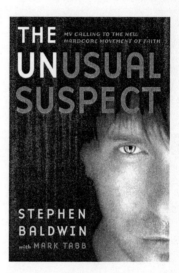

Available in trade paperback wherever books are sold.

Contact Stephen Baldwin:

The Breakthrough Ministry
P.O. Box 936
Nyack, NY 10960

**General info:**
info@stephenbaldwin.com

**Media/PR:**
agent5@globalbtm.com

\*\*\*

You can visit his Web site

www.stephenbaldwin.com

for information on Stephen, his activities, and the ministries he supports.

\*\*\*